# Carl Weber's Kingpins:

# Queens

## Part 1

### Carl Weber Presents

# Carl Weber's Kingpins:

# Queens

## Part 1

### Carl Weber Presents

Erick S. Gray

www.urbanbooks.net

Urban Books, LLC
300 Farmingdale Road, N.Y.-Route 109
Farmingdale, NY 11735

Carl Weber's Kingpins: Queens; Part 1; Carl Weber
Presents Copyright © 2022 Erick S. Gray

ISBN 13: 978-1-64556-369-3
ISBN 10: 1-64556-369-3

First Trade Paperback Printing October 2022
Printed in the United States of America

10 9 8 7 6 5 4 3 2 1

*This is a work of fiction. Any references or similarities
to actual events, real people, living or dead, or to real
locales are intended to give the novel a sense of reality.
Any similarity in other names, characters, places, and
incidents is entirely coincidental.*

Distributed by Kensington Publishing Corp.
Submit orders to:
Customer Service
400 Hahn Road
Westminster, MD 21157-4627
Phone: 1-800-733-3000
Fax: 1-800-659-2436

# Prologue

The inner city of Queens was a spectacle of lower-income homes, drugs, and criminal activity—along with torrential prostitution. Dusk had settled over the city. The late-night hour brought about the lows and undesirables in the town in a specific seedy area. South Road and the adjacent blocks surrounding it were a hotbed for hookers, young and old, their male tricks, and drug users and sellers. The hookers walked around the minor industrial part of the city littered with a few dilapidated structures, old warehouses, storage units, and garages, some abandoned and some active. The blocks were dimly lit and sparse of traffic, making it the perfect place for the girls to sell pussy to lone, passing cars.

Nearly a dozen streetwalkers walked the shifty and squalid streets in their most provocative outfits—some leaving nothing to the imagination. They waved and signaled at passing cars, trying to catch a trick's attention. They smiled, and some daringly flashed their tits and private parts to the male drivers, leaving some in absolute awe. Then they hopped in and out of cars during the late-night hours. The area was a breeding ground for sex, as the girls turned out their tricks in parked cars scattered in hidden and darkened pockets of the site.

Diamond, clad in a short skirt that revealed her meaty, thick thighs, strutted up and down the poorly lit street in her stilettos. On one side of the road, a sprawling brick wall was covered with gang graffiti, and on the opposite of that, a run-down yard with an aging fence, and inside it, trucks and dump trucks were parked. The block had little to no traffic, only a smidgen of passing traffic. And each car that passed, Diamond smiled and waved at them, but to no avail. No business came her way . . . not until a black-colored Chevy Malibu slowly turned the corner onto the street she walked and approached her. Diamond noticed the car the second it turned on the block and traveled into her area. Her eyes became fixed on the slow-moving vehicle. She put a little pep into her walk and smiled.

The Malibu came to a slow stop near the curb, and the passenger window came rolling down. Diamond stepped closer to the vehicle, hunched toward the window, and looked inside. The male stranger stared her way deadpan.

"Ooh, you're a cutie," she continued to smile. "You lookin' to have some fun tonight?"

"How much?" asked the driver.

"For half and half, one hundred," she replied.

"Are you worth it?"

She stood upright to give the driver a glance at her thick, curvy figure and, for good measure, quickly pulled up her short skirt to reveal that she wasn't wearing any panties. It was an enticing sight. She curved toward the passenger window again, knowing she had this date confirmed.

"So, you ready to have some fun tonight?"

"Get in," he responded mechanically.

Diamond opened the door and slid into the front seat of the Malibu. Her long legs were a treat to see. She smiled and was ready to show him a good time for the right price. The man drove off.

She couldn't take her eyes off the man, who was extremely handsome and well dressed in a black suit and long tie that fitted his frame perfectly. She figured him to be some kind of businessman, maybe married, and assumed he had a penchant for prostitutes. She had never seen him before, and he was far more alluring than her regulars.

He stood six feet tall. His skin was Hershey's milk chocolate color and looked like the smoothest of satin covering rippling, bulging muscles. His facial features were soft, distinct, refined, and corresponded with his trimmed goatee. And he had beautiful black eyes, thick brows, and snow-white teeth.

"So, you wanna do this in the car or get a room?" she asked him. "Because I know of a cheap motel nearby, and I can make it worth your time in a room."

"No room," he uttered right away.

She shrugged. "Cool."

He drove to a dead-end street close by, where several unhitched tractor-trailers were taking up space in the area. The Malibu parked discreetly between two trailers giving the two the needed privacy for some debauchery. Unfortunately, the night was growing late, and traffic, either foot or vehicular, was nonexistent.

He gave her a folded hundred-dollar bill, indicating he wanted the half and half, a blowjob followed by sex. She beamed. She placed the C-note into her clutch bag and got ready to handle her business.

"I'm 'bout to make you come so nice . . . like a geyser," she joked.

He didn't smile or laugh. Instead, he carried the same deadpan expression as Diamond curved into his lap, undoing his pants. She was ready to open wide and swallow him whole. He was big, and she was impressed. And his balls were hairy and full and hung heavy and low. Instead, she took his erection into her hand and effortlessly shoved his dick down her throat. The feel of her wet, full lips sliding up and down against his skin finally elicited a reaction from him as he moaned and groaned. His erection suffocated her as it stretched inside her mouth. She sucked, licked, and stroked him. While doing so, she could feel his masculine fingers part her moistened pussy lips, exposing her hardened clit.

He inhaled her scent, and he was intoxicated by it— craving her, her essence. She thought she heard him growl for a moment as she desperately tried to deep throat him.

Stopping her oral pleasing, she looked at him and asked, "You wanna fuck me now?"

He eyed her momentarily with his intense dark eyes.

"We don't have all night, baby," she added.

Weirdly, he proclaimed out of the blue, "I will not look with approval on anything vile. I hate what faithless people do. I will have no part in it."

She became confused by the bizarre statement. "Huh? Nigga, you tryin'a hit this pussy or what? You already paid for it."

His hunger was intense, and he couldn't resist.

They fucked doggie style in the back seat. He gripped her hips and squeezed her tits. He continued to become intoxicated by her sultry scent. And she felt every inch of him inside of her as she huffed and puffed. It felt as if they'd become one.

Once again, he spewed another bizarre verse. "Do not lust in your heart after her beauty or let her beauty captivate you with her eyes."

He didn't make sense to her. She just wanted him to come. The dick was stimulating and powerful, but Diamond became uneasy around him. Something about him was off, and she picked up on it too late. She was already vulnerable and exposed to him, as he was deep inside her and caressing her body. The back seat of his Malibu started to feel cramped and strange, and his hold around her began to feel more threatening and controlling than pleasing.

"C'mon, daddy, just come for me already," she said hastily.

His hold around the back of her neck was tightening. His fingers felt crushing, and he was becoming more volatile and rough.

"This is sin . . . This is death," he announced loudly.

The remarks were creeping her out, and what she wanted to do was quickly reach for the handle of the back door, leap from the car, and run away from him half-naked. But it would be impossible. His muscular frame continued to crowd her in the back seat, both inside of her and externally. He was a strong and imposing man, and if she needed to escape, it would be fruitless. He wasn't going to make it easy.

Finally, she felt him coming. She wanted him to finish quickly and pull out of her so she could collect herself and end the date with him. But instead, after ejaculating, he lingered inside of her and looked pensive about something.

"Hon, did you have a good time?" she asked nervously. "Okay, your time is up."

He remained silent. Diamond tried to free herself from him—from their sexual position. Upon doing so, he reacted, instantly grabbing the back of Diamond's neck and her right arm with a compelling force that surrendered her to pain. He pushed her face down into the seat.

"No!" he shouted. "No."

"Please . . ." she whimpered. "Let me go."

"See no evil, speak no evil," he uttered sneeringly. "The sin! The sin!"

A slight struggle ensued as Diamond tried to fight him, kicking, punching, and screaming, but it quickly ended. He punched her in the back of her head with brute force, nearly knocking her unconscious, and then he wrapped the garrote wire around her neck and tugged viciously on it. The wire sharply cut into her throat. Diamond tried to fight but to no avail. She gasped and struggled to breathe—and thrashed about to live. Her eyes bulged as she felt her life cruelly ending. She couldn't even scream for help, though it would have been ineffective because of the secluded area.

Her arteries became obstructed, cutting off oxygen to the brain. Things were becoming painful. Her attacker then strengthened his hold and gave the garrote wire one final and forceful tug, and he felt her neck snap in his grasp like a twig. Diamond's fight ended as her body suddenly went limp in his grip. He removed the wire from around her neck, and she fell face down and slumped in the back seat of the car. Her eyes were still open even after her death.

He inhaled and exhaled. It needed doing. But he still had more to do. The smell of death was refreshing for him. It was almost better than sex. He gazed at the body for a lingering moment and seemed fascinated by his actions. There wasn't an ounce of apprehension inside of him. Instead, he was calm and collected. He climbed out of the vehicle, fixed his slightly disheveled attire, removed the body from the back seat, and placed it into the trunk. Fleetingly, he observed his surroundings. No one was around, just him and the night—him and death. He inhaled the scent of death once more and slowly exhaled, subsequently climbing back into the driver's seat and leaving the area, driving to a different location.

The scene he created was his ritual. It was secluded and quiet. Diamond's naked body had been placed on a clear plastic tarp. Her hands were folded over her chest, emulating as if she were inside a casket. Beside the body were the tools he needed to mutilate her body—sharp knives and razors.

He called himself the Wolf. He stripped naked and crouched near the body as if he were inspecting it. He was in perfect health. His abs were rippling, his chest slightly protruding, and his arms well defined. He picked up a K1 round aluminum handle knife, which was handy for precision cutting, trimming, and stripping paper, plastic, wood, cloth, etc. He put it toward her right eye. Then he jabbed at it with precision and gradually gouged it out. He repeated the same action with her left eye, and then with a different blade, he cut out her tongue and used a pair of shears to cut off her fingertips. When completed, he shrouded the body inside the plastic tarp, carried it over his shoulder outside to the Malibu, and tossed his work back into the trunk.

The Wolf dumped the body in a wooded and secluded area near a hikers' trail in Forest Park. He wanted her to be found, like his other victims. He wanted to cleanse his soul and wash away his sins with purity. And now it was phase two of his redemption—finding his wholesomeness and young purity to consume. He couldn't help himself.

# Chapter One

Jamaica, Queens, 1999

The blacktop streets absorbed the spring sunshine, with a nice breeze being a sweet, fragranced petal wrapped around the urban neighborhood. It was a bright day, and a yellow taxicab came to a stop in front of the rundown row house on an underprivileged block in one of the worst neighborhoods in the city—Jamaica, Queens. It was early morning, and the activity on the block was minimal. The drug dealers, the knuckleheads, and residents were still asleep, and everything seemed still for the moment. But that would change in a few hours. It was Sunday morning, and the only movement happening was the people going to church.

Sincere stared at the row house from the back seat of the cab. He looked like he didn't want to be there. He looked reluctant to get out.

"This the right place, right?" the driver asked.

"Yeah, it is," Sincere replied.

Sincere sighed. He paid the fare and climbed out of the cab in his army fatigues, carrying a military-issued duffle bag. He stood tall on the block clad in camouflage and tan-colored boots. The cab drove off, leaving Sincere alone. He looked around, and everything looked the same, including the dilapidated blacktop basketball court on the corner. He had been gone for four years, and his memories of the place were ambivalent.

Sincere approached the row house. It was one of many crowded homes in poor conditions on the street. It was the ghetto. He knew it was still violent, poor, and plagued with drug use. During his time in the army, he traveled and was able to see the world. For two years, he was stationed in Japan—at Camp Zama. To him, it was a beautiful country. It was amazing to him that he was living across the world from where he'd grown up. At first, the language barrier was pretty hard for him, but he'd learned a few phrases.

Now that he was back in South Jamaica, Queens, he would have to readjust again—to the hood. Sincere slung the duffle bag over his shoulder and walked the steps to the row house. He knocked on the door and waited. It was eight a.m., and he doubted his family would be up. He tried the doorknob, and it was locked. Sincere continued to knock until his sister, Denise, answered the door. When she saw her older brother, her eyes lit up with glory, and she screamed in joy.

"Sincere, you're home," Denise hollered.

She leaped into his arms, and they hugged each other. They both were happy to see each other.

"Why didn't you tell us you were coming home?" Denise asked.

"I wanted to surprise y'all," he replied.

She finally released her embrace of him and beamed. Denise was 16 years old. Sincere took a step back and stared at her. "Little sis, you're growing up."

Denise smiled. She had rich, ebony skin and an angelic face with high cheekbones and curves.

"Am I going to have to grill and intimidate a boyfriend?"

"I don't have a boyfriend, not yet, anyway," she said.

Sincere grinned. "Good. Because you're still my little sister, no matter how much you're filling out."

"And I can take care of myself, Sincere. I don't need a babysitter or a bodyguard."

Sincere laughed. "Okay. Where's Ma and Maurice?"

"Ma is sleeping upstairs, and Maurice isn't here," she said.

"What you mean Maurice isn't here?"

"He comes and goes, Sincere. Sometimes he's gone for days," Denise let it be known.

Sincere looked troubled by the news. Maurice was his 19-year-old little brother. Before Sincere shipped out, Maurice had a penchant for getting into trouble. Growing up, Sincere had always been his little brother's guardian angel. Before Sincere was a soldier for the United States Army, he was a soldier for the "Gotti Boys." They were a gang out of Queens known for drug dealing, violence, prostitution, murders, racketeering, and extortion. The gang was run by Dominique and Trey-Trey, brothers with a penchant for violence. They were feared and respected.

Eventually, Trey-Trey was murdered by rivals, and Dominique was indicted under the Kingpin and RICO Act. He received a life sentence. Fortunately for Sincere, he was low on the totem pole when the Feds came crashing down on the gang, and he escaped indictment. He'd joined the military and cleaned up his entire act.

Sincere entered the house and, to his shock, saw that things had changed a bit. An upgrade had taken place. A big-screen TV was in the living room. Their furniture wasn't secondhand. Leather couches and stylish coffee tables decorated the living room. There was even an elegant dining room set.

"Whoa," Sincere uttered. "Where did all of this come from?"

"Maurice has been helping out lately," said Denise.

"Helping out, huh?"

When Sincere left, things were poor. Now, his home looked like a scene out of *New Jack City*. Sincere knew what Maurice was into. He wasn't stupid. Unfortunately, his little brother had followed in his footsteps.

"We were drowning, Sincere," said Denise. "You weren't here."

Sincere sighed. He set down his duffle bag and continued to look around.

"Are you hungry? I can make you some breakfast," Denise said.

Sincere grinned. "You cooking now?"

"Yup. Ma ain't doin' it, so someone had to step up."

"Cool."

"You want me to wake up Ma?"

"Nah, let her sleep," he replied.

He followed her into the kitchen. There was a small TV on the counter, and the fridge was filled with food. Sincere took a seat at the table. Denise started the preparations for breakfast.

"I'm gonna make you some French toast, cheese eggs, grits, and bacon," she said.

"Damn, I get the royal treatment, huh?"

"Of course." Denise smiled.

As Denise cooked, the two talked and did some catching up.

"Tell me about Japan," Denise asked.

"It's far," he joked. "But I liked it. The people are nice."

The aroma from Denise's cooking permeated the entire home. Soon, their mother entered the kitchen, tying together her silk robe.

"Denise, what you in here cooking?" Janet asked.

Right away, she saw her son, Sincere, seated at the table. She froze, shocked by his sudden presence. Sincere smiled. "Hey, Ma."

"Sincere, is that you?"

Sincere rose from the table, and his mother greeted him with open arms. It was a happy reunion. She hugged her son so tight it almost felt like she was about to crush him.

"You should have told me you were arriving today," said Janet.

"I wanted to surprise everyone."

"Well, I'm surprised."

Janet looked her son up and down. The glee in her eyes was so bright that the kitchen temperature went up. Sincere looked exceptionally handsome in his uniform. He stood six foot one with a muscular build and shaved head. Growing up, he had always been fit, but the military made him stronger. And he had cut off his braids.

Janet hugged her son again. And then she asked, "Are you home for good?"

Sincere nodded. "Yeah, honorable discharge," he said.

Janet smiled. "Well, we need to celebrate. My baby is back home. Let me go upstairs and put on some clothes."

Janet pivoted and left the kitchen. Denise set a hot, steaming plate of breakfast on the table for her brother. Sincere looked at her and asked, "How's she been doing? She looks good."

"She's been doing okay. Been clean for the past year now," said Denise.

Sincere was pleased to hear that. He smiled. It was hard to be the oldest sibling and deal with his mother's drug use in the past. Crack was her drug of choice, and Janet had put her family through hell. So, to see her clean was a relief for Sincere. When he'd left for the army, Denise was 12, and Maurice was 15. It was a hard choice for him to make because they were young, but it had to be done. He would have been dead or locked up if he had stayed in Queens.

"Sit down and eat, big bro."

Sincere sat at the table. "Let me see if you got skills in the kitchen. But keep 911 on speed dial just in case," he joked.

"Oh, I got skills. My cooking will taste like sex in your mouth," Denise quipped.

Sincere chuckled at the comment. "I didn't need to know all that."

"When I graduate, I want to go to culinary school," Denise said.

Sincere was surprised. "Oh, word? That's what's up, sis. I'm proud of you."

He took a few mouthfuls of his sister's cooking, and his face lit up. "Damn, girl, you weren't lying. What the hell you put in these eggs?"

Denise beamed. "If I tell you, then I will have to kill you," she joked.

Sincere continued to devour her cooking. Finally, he was home, and he was happy to see his family doing good. He thought he would come home to dysfunction and chaos, maybe with his siblings in foster care and his mother still on crack. He felt guilty that he'd lost contact with them, becoming a different person on the other side of the world. He underestimated them. Now, his only concern was Maurice.

Sincere continued to enjoy his sister's cooking with Maurice heavy on his mind.

# Chapter Two

Maurice took a few deep pulls from the blunt, inhaling the potent marijuana, readying himself for tonight's event. He sat in the passenger seat of the Dodge Intrepid, clad in all black, as it traveled east on the Belt Parkway. Rap music blared inside the car. Voltron was driving the vehicle. Sitting in the back seat was a man named Drip-Drip.

It was nearing midnight, making traffic on the parkway sparse. The large green sign above read: "*Southern State Parkway, Eastern L.I.*" It's where they were going. Voltron steered the Intrepid onto the Southern State Parkway, heading into the suburbs of Long Island. They continued to smoke and listen to rap music. Maurice looked calm. He gazed out the window in silence. The scenery transformed from urban Queens to sprawling, green suburbs within ten minutes.

The trio inside the car was on a mission. They were determined to get rich and make money by any means necessary. They were young, hungry, and reckless. They traveled deeper into Long Island and arrived at a community called Valley Stream. Maurice read off the navigational instructions to an address written on paper.

"It says turn right," said Maurice.

Voltron turned right. Valley Stream, Long Island, was a diverse and middle-class town along with the Nassau and Queens border in Long Island. They drove through the neighborhood for ten minutes and soon arrived at a Cape Cod-style home. It was a tidy little rectangle of a house with its long side facing the street. Shutters adorned the windows.

"This is it," Maurice pointed out.

The men stared at the residence. It was dark and quiet with a manicured lawn. There wasn't any movement inside. On both sides of the property were neatly trimmed, high shrubberies, and in the driveway was a Lexus Coupe. Voltron looked at Maurice and Drip-Drip and said, "Y'all niggas ready to get this money?"

Both men nodded.

"No doubt," Maurice replied.

What looked like a quiet, family home in the suburbs was the opposite. It was a stash house for one of the most notorious drug dealers in Queens, a man named Zulu. The house was meant to look family-oriented and unassuming. Only a handful of people knew about the location. Voltron and Drip-Drip had gotten the location from a source and information that the stash house held 9 percent of Zulu's fortune. They brought along Maurice, knowing he was a rider like them.

Drip-Drip and Maurice masked up and armed themselves with semiautomatic pistols. They climbed out of the vehicle, stealthily moved toward the home, hid behind the trimmed shrubberies, and waited. Voltron kept a lookout inside the nondescript Intrepid. The only thing they needed to do was be patient and see if their source was correct.

A silver BMW 528i pulled into the driveway behind the Lexus twenty minutes later. Two men, Frank and Heat, climbed out of the Beamer and opened the trunk. They removed a small, black duffle bag and approached the front entrance to the house. The two men notified the occupants of the house that they were there. The moment the front door opened, Drip-Drip and Maurice sprang from the bushes and charged at them with their guns drawn.

Voltron leaped from the car and hurried toward the action with his pistol in hand. Drip-Drip and Maurice forced the men inside at gunpoint.

"Get the fuck down! Get the fuck down," Drip-Drip shouted at everyone, waving his pistol wildly.

The two occupants of the house, a man and a woman, were shocked and hesitant to comply.

"Y'all niggas really doin' this?" the woman uttered with contempt. "Y'all must be fuckin' suicidal."

Maurice thrust his gun into her face and growled, "Bitch, if you don't shut the fuck up, I'ma blow ya fuckin' brains out."

She frowned, relenting. Drip-Drip relieved the men of their weapons. Everyone was lying face down on the ground, handcuffed and held at gunpoint. Voltron snatched the bag from the men and unzipped it. Bundles of cash inside filled it up. Voltron smiled and uttered, "Bingo."

"Fuck all of you niggas. I guarantee we gonna find out who you are, then come after you and your fuckin' families," Frank growled from the floor.

Drip-Drip spun his way, scowling. "What you say, nigga?"

Drip-Drip didn't give Frank a chance to repeat himself. Instead, he stood over Frank and started to pistol-whip him while he was handcuffed. It was brutal. The occupants could only look on in horror.

"Talk that shit now, nigga. Huh, nigga?" Drip-Drip shouted as the butt of his pistol repeatedly smashed against Frank's face.

"Yo, he said no bodies," Maurice reminded them.

"Fuck that," Drip-Drip said, and suddenly, his gun went off. Frank's face exploded, splattering his brain across the floor with his blood quickly pooling.

Voltron and Maurice stared at Drip-Drip in shock. But then, that fast, things went south.

"Nigga, what the fuck did you do?" Maurice screamed.

"He shouldn't have been talkin' that shit," Drip-Drip countered with apathy.

The occupants were horrified. They knew they were going to die soon. Voltron and Drip-Drip exchanged knowing looks, and then Voltron fired a bullet into the back of Heat's head. Drip-Drip killed the third man. Then only the woman was left. Both men stared at Maurice.

"What you waiting for, nigga?" asked Drip-Drip. "Do that bitch."

Maurice was hesitant. He'd never killed anyone before. He thought it would be a simple robbery, but now it was bloodshed.

"You down or not?" asked Voltron.

"Please, don't kill me! I'll do whatever y'all want," she begged.

Drip-Drip smirked. "First, this bitch hard core. Now, she ready to suck dick to survive," he mocked.

"Please . . ."

Drip-Drip crouched to her and uttered, "You cute. You wanna suck my dick?"

She whimpered. She was bound and at their mercy. But deep inside, she knew there would be no mercy for her. Evil lurked in their eyes.

Drip-Drip stood up and remarked, "Fuck this bitch." He looked at Maurice and said, "Do this bitch now, nigga." He wasn't taking no for an answer.

Maurice pointed the pistol at her as she continued to cry out for mercy, but her words fell on deaf ears. Finally, reluctantly, he squeezed the trigger.

*Bak bak bak!*

He pumped several rounds into the back of her head and back. Her cries were now still. Voltron and Drip-Drip gawked at Maurice, and they were satisfied.

"You did good, my nigga," said Drip-Drip.

Maurice stood there with the smoking gun in his hand, stunned by his actions. Voltron lifted his mask to reveal his identity. "Let's be out," he said.

Drip-Drip picked up the duffle bag filled with cash and started toward the door. Maurice and Voltron were right behind him. However, unbeknownst to the three men, when Voltron had lifted his mask, his reflection had hit a mirror situated on a nearby wall. Someone hiding in a hallway closet recognized him.

When the three men left, the survivor, a soldier named Keys, emerged from his hiding spot in the closet, thankful to be alive. However, he was appalled by the grizzly scene. They were all executed. He frowned and right away made the needed phone call.

# Chapter Three

The early-morning sun surged through the bedroom window. It was another bright spring day and Sincere's second day home. He glanced at the time. It was six a.m. Sincere had slept in his little brother's bedroom. When he woke up to see Maurice didn't come home, he sighed. He didn't want to worry. Denise mentioned that he had a girlfriend and sometimes stayed at her place. However, Sincere wanted to see his little brother again. It had been four years, and he missed him.

Sincere did a few morning calisthenics in the bedroom, push-ups and sit-ups. It was routine for him. He then walked into the hallway to find Denise getting ready for school and his mother getting ready for work.

"Good morning, everyone." Sincere smiled.

They replied, "Good morning," and Denise disappeared into the bathroom.

It was a happy home for once. Janet was working as a cashier at a retail store. She'd been there for five months, and Denise was a straight-A student at Jamaica High School. Sincere was proud of them.

While Denise and Janet went to school and work, Sincere decided to jog around the neighborhood. He felt it would allow him to catch up on things and see what had changed and what didn't. So, wearing basketball shorts and a white tank top, with his physique showing, Sincere started his early-morning jog. In Japan, every morning, he ran three miles.

He headed toward Guy R. Brewer Blvd., a busy two-way street inundated with storefronts, homes, and traffic. Everyone was going to work or school. Next, he decided to jog south, down the boulevard. He raced to Linden Blvd. and decided to turn back around and head back to the location from where he started. While jogging, Sincere took in the neighborhood. Much hadn't changed. Certain areas and locations triggered memories of his earlier life when he was with the Gotti Boys. Thirty minutes later, he jogged by the notorious housing projects, South Jamaica Housing, a.k.a. 40 Projects. It was still morning, and the activity was picking up. Now that the kids were in school and residents were at work, the morning hustlers and drug dealers emerged. The crackheads were roaming about, searching for their daily high.

Sincere jogged parallel to the sprawling projects. He was in great shape. When he was about to cross the small intersection, he noticed a green Honda Accord making a left turn near him. It was blaring rap music. It came to a stop, and the horn blew. Sincere eyed the vehicle, being cautious. If an attack was to happen, though he was unarmed, he was trained to defend himself. The driver's door opened, and Sincere was ready to react. Friend or foe? he wondered.

"Sincere, nigga, is that you?" someone called out.

Sincere eyed the driver climbing out, and he breathed a sigh of relief. It was his day one homie, Nasir. Nasir was all smiles.

"Nasir?" Sincere called out.

He approached Nasir, and they embraced, giving each other a brotherly hug.

"Damn, my nigga, you lookin' all swollen and shit. The army got you lookin' like the Terminator," Nasir joked. "When did you get back?"

"Yesterday."

"That's what up. So, what, you were over there fighting terrorists, making our country safe?"

Sincere chuckled. "Nah. Just doing my job."

"No doubt."

"That's your ride?" Sincere asked him.

"Yup. That's my baby."

It was a '95 midsized Honda Accord with tinted windows and chromed rims. It was showy like Nasir. A large, gold chain with a diamond-encrusted Jesus pendant dangled around Nasir's neck. He also wore fresh, beige Tims. In addition, he sported a throwback Chicago Bulls Jersey and a diamond pinky ring shined on his left hand. Sincere already knew what his friend was into.

Sincere and Nasir met during their freshmen year in high school in 1989. They both were pretty boys with catchy names. Nasir even joked, "Sincere and Nasir; nigga, we sound like a duo." Sincere had laughed. They both were on the high school basketball team, and they dated pretty girls. And they both had dropped out of high school to run the streets and sell dope. But it was Sincere who decided to get his GED a year later.

While conversing, Nasir's sky pager beeped. He checked it. It seemed necessary.

"It's good to see you, Sincere. We definitely need to catch up," Nasir said.

"Yeah, we need to."

They dapped each other once again, and Nasir pivoted to leave. But Sincere had an afterthought. Before Nasir climbed into his car, Sincere asked him, "Yo, have you seen Maurice around?"

Nasir stared at his friend for a moment. There was something he wasn't saying. Finally, he replied, "Maurice on a different playing field, Sincere."

"What do you mean by that?"

"You remember Voltron and Drip-Drip?"

"Yeah, two young and stupid knuckleheads always got into some dumb shit back in the day. Isn't Drip-Drip Rafe's little brother?"

"Yeah. Rafe came up. He on some kingpin status on these streets right now; got shit on lock," said Nasir.

Sincere wasn't surprised by the news. He barely knew Rafe, but his reputation preceded him. Some say that he was the Nino Brown of Queens. He was smart, calculating, and wasn't afraid to kill any man himself.

Sincere watched his friend drive away. He took in what Nasir had told him about Maurice. It troubled him that his little brother was hanging out with those two lunatics. They had been bad news since they were playing in the sandbox. And whatever they were into, Sincere knew he had to pull his brother away from them. The last thing he wanted to see was Maurice caught up in some bullshit.

He exhaled, and then he started his run again. He ran for a few more blocks, and then he came to a complete stop in front of a friendly-looking, two-story home on Union Hall Street. It appeared to be vacant. Nostalgia showed on Sincere's face because it used to be the home of his ex-girlfriend, Monica. He hadn't seen or heard from her a month before he left for basic training. They had gotten into an argument. She was pregnant with his baby, and she wanted to keep it. Sincere was adamant that she have an abortion. His reason was that he was leaving soon, and he wouldn't be around to see his child born. But rumors were spreading about Monica having an affair with a hustler named Mighty. Sincere didn't know what to believe.

It was 1994, and the streets were ablaze with murders, drugs, and violent crimes. There were 2,000 murders that year in the city, and Queens felt like a hotbed for homicides. Sincere was beefing with Mighty and his crew over corners and pussy. Some believed it was over pussy rather than money. Monica was a beautiful woman. She was brown-skinned, petite, and well-toned, and she ran track in high school. She had a promising future. The two supposedly were madly in love; Sincere would have done anything for her and vice versa with Monica. But then Mighty came into the picture, and things changed.

Sincere stared at the vacant home for a moment. He then left and headed back home.

The moment Sincere turned the corner to 164th Street, he noticed Maurice climbing out of the back seat of a dark green Jeep Cherokee. Sincere was excited to see Maurice was home. The Cherokee pulled away from the curb, and it was coming his way. While it passed him, Sincere caught a glimpse of Voltron and Drip-Drip in the front seat. The two men glanced his way, but they probably didn't recognize him.

Sincere frowned at them, knowing they were trouble for his little brother. He watched the Jeep turn the corner, and then he shifted his attention back to Maurice climbing the steps to the row house.

He called out, "Maurice!"

Maurice stopped and looked and saw Sincere approaching him. He gazed at his older brother deadpan and uttered, "Sincere, what the fuck you doin' back?"

It wasn't the reaction Sincere expected from his little brother. Maurice didn't rush to embrace him as their mother and sister had. Instead, he stood on the concrete steps and seemed upset.

"Damn, that's the reaction I get from you after four years?" Sincere replied.

"What you want from me? You want me to jump in your arms and kiss your ass?" Maurice uttered.

Wow. Sincere was taken aback by the response. He felt offended that his little brother wasn't happy to see him.

"I missed you, Maurice," he said.

"Missed me? Nigga, you left us to join the white man's army and didn't give a fuck about home," Maurice griped. "While you were gone, it was hell, Sincere. Do you know that?"

"And I'm sorry, but I had my reasons, Maurice."

Maurice scoffed at his brother. "Fuck your reasons. We should have been your reason to stay home."

The tension with Maurice threw Sincere for a loop. Sincere walked closer to his brother with a look that said, "*Please forgive me.*"

"Let's go inside and talk," said Sincere.

"Fuck you, man. I don't wanna be around you. I'm sure you already went inside and saw what I've done to the place. I took care of ma-dukes and sis. I made sure we had everything we needed while you went off to become a GI Joe," Maurice proclaimed.

Sincere huffed. He had no idea his brother hated him.

"And I respect that," Sincere replied. "But listen—"

"Nigga, I ain't gotta listen to you," Maurice exclaimed. "I'm out. I'm not tryin'a be in the same place as you."

Maurice removed himself from the steps and marched away, going the opposite way from Sincere. Sincere wanted to chase after him, but he didn't. He wanted to give Maurice some space. He stood there and watched his brother storm off. He huffed and muttered, "Fuck."

Sincere was determined to reach out to his brother and make things right with him.

# Chapter Four

Detective Michael Acosta and his partner, Chris Emerson, climbed out of the dark blue Ford Crown Victoria on Myrtle Avenue. Both men were clad in dark suits and ties. They were police veterans, with a combined thirty-five years between them. Acosta was a Black man who stood six foot one with a five o'clock shadow and hard eyes. He had seen it all—the good, the bad, and the ugly. Emerson was a white male who matched his partner's height and outlook. They were two peas in a pod with a keen nose for solving cases.

It was a hot spring day, and they were there to investigate a body found at a park. Forest Park spanned 538 acres, and it was the third-largest park in Queens. Detective Emerson scanned the park and uttered, "I hate parks."

Police activity was heavy throughout the park. Finally, a police sergeant approached the detectives. Acosta asked him, "Who found her?"

"Two joggers early this morning," the sergeant replied.

The two detectives followed the bread crumbs that led to the body. Acosta carried a crime scene kit and a legal-sized portfolio. The sergeant led them deeper into the park, which felt like they were in the woods.

"You know this park used to be called Brooklyn Forest Park," Emerson uttered. "Brooklyn technically owned it."

"Didn't know that," Acosta replied.

They soon walked into an impromptu encampment. It was an open area with a discarded tent and trash spewed on the ground. Finally, an officer raised the yellow police tape so they could go underneath. Immediately, their eyes became fixed on a naked, young girl lying on her back. Her body had been mutilated. It was a grizzly scene. Emerson sighed. He had seen far too many young victims like this during his stint as a homicide detective. Acosta stared at the body deadpan. Both detectives went from hard-looking veterans to having soft eyes on the crime scene. Right away, they took in everything. They understood everything mattered, no matter how small or big it looked—never undervalue its importance.

"Any ID on her?" Emerson asked the sergeant.

"Nothing."

The detectives put on a pair of latex gloves and approached the body. Emerson was the first to comment. "She was young . . . pretty too."

Acosta crouched closer to the victim. "The killer cut off her fingers and removed her eyes." He inspected the victim sharper and added, "Jesus, he cut out her tongue too."

"You ever seen anything like this?" Emerson asked.

Acosta shook his head. "No."

"What kind of monster are we dealing with?" Emerson uttered.

"Satanic. Maybe . . . a ritual," said Acosta.

"The last thing we need is a sadistic serial killer in Queens," said Emerson.

"There are no ligature marks at her wrists or ankles. She wasn't tied up. Most likely, she was killed and then mutilated." Acosta stood upright. He skimmed the crime scene carefully. "And she was dumped here too," he uttered.

"The killer may be familiar with this park and this area," Emerson said. "It's a big park with lots of secluded places to do some nasty things to people."

Acosta walked toward the sergeant, and he instructed, "We need more of a grid search. I need your men to set up a wide perimeter around every road and trail into this park. One of your officers posts up. Take license plates of anything that passes too."

The sergeant nodded and walked away to tell his men. Acosta and Emerson continued their investigation.

"What are you thinking?" Emerson asked.

"Our worst nightmare . . . He's just getting started," Acosta replied.

# Chapter Five

It was a warm morning when the corrections officer walked the tier with his radio crackling. He stopped at a particular cell and stared at one of the two inmates inside. One inmate was still asleep while the other was doing push-ups in the enclosed compartment.

"Mob Allah, let's go," said the guard.

Mob Allah, tall, dark, and his body shrouded with tattoos, stopped doing his regular push-ups and stood to his feet. He was shirtless and muscular. He stared at the guard who uttered, "It's that time."

Mob Allah nodded. He threw on his shirt and collected a few things from his cell. His cell mate had woken up and grinned at him.

"I'm gonna miss you, my nigga," said the cell mate. "Be safe out there."

"And you the same in here," replied Allah. His cell mate still had seven years to go on a twenty-year bid.

The two said their goodbyes, and Mob Allah followed the guard across the tier. Several other inmates made it a point to be up early to see Mob Allah leave and say their goodbyes.

"Hold it down, Mob Allah," one shouted.

"Supreme Nation, my nigga. One up," another inmate shouted.

He was well known and highly respected inside Attica State Prison. Mob Allah had done eight years inside, and he was about to become a free man again.

He walked across the compound with the few things he'd decided meant enough to carry out. He stopped in an office where he was given some street clothes and turned in his prison garb. He changed into khakis, a black T-shirt, and a pair of brown boots. It wasn't the best clothing, but it indicated life and independence again.

Mob Allah was escorted through an endless series of locked doors and gates. Finally, he signed for an envelope with an ATM card and a little cash in it. It was what remained from his commissary account. There was also a bus ticket to the city, but Mob Allah did not need it. To him, it felt weird to touch money again after not seeing it for eight years.

A massive corrections officer walked him to the front gate. He stood six-six and towered over Mob Allah, who was already a tall and imposing figure. The guard was humorless. Mob Allah managed to smile as the gates opened for his departure from state lockup. He was a few feet away from freedom.

Idling outside the gates of Attica was a burgundy Land Rover. Zulu and Big Will were seated inside the Land Rover. The moment they spotted Mob Allah exiting the prison, they climbed out of the vehicle and went to greet him.

"There he goes, king of all kings," Zulu shouted proudly. "My nigga is finally out."

Mob Allah smiled. Zulu greeted him with an elaborate hand gesture, indicating their gang sign and affiliation to the Supreme Nation, a remembrance to the Supreme Team. Big Will greeted Mob Allah with the same elaborate hand gesture.

"Welcome home, Mob Allah," uttered Big Will.

Mob Allah stared at the Land Rover sitting on 22-inch chromed rims. Then he uttered, "Damn, that shit nice right there."

"Nigga, you know you coming home in style . . . Ain't no other fuckin' way," said Zulu.

Mob Allah nodded in respect. He climbed into the passenger seat, riding shotgun, while Big Will climbed into the back seat. They drove away with Mob Allah not looking back. He wanted to leave Attica a distant memory.

While Zulu steered the vehicle through the rural, small, upstate town, he said to Mob Allah, "The first thing we gonna get you tonight is some pussy. I know you need it."

"No doubt," Mob Allah replied. "But business first. Run things down to me, Zulu. I wanna be informed before we touch down in the city."

"We had a few hiccups the past few weeks," said Zulu.

"Like what? You know me, Zulu. I want it unequivocal."

"One of our stash houses got hit a few days ago. Four dead . . . culprits got away with a hundred and twenty thousand."

"But we on it," Big Will chimed in.

"I'm talking to Zulu, not you, Big Will. So, shut the fuck up," Mob Allah chastised.

Big Will sat back and knew to keep his mouth shut.

"We know who hit us?"

"Yeah, Keys was in hiding. Saw one of their faces," Zulu went on.

"Who face he saw?"

"Voltron."

"Who the fuck is Voltron?" Mob Allah exclaimed.

"A soldier from Rafe's organization."

"Rafe," Mob Allah chuckled. "Why the fuck is that clown still alive?"

"It's been peace for a while in the hood. We gettin' money, Mob. Ain't tryin'a rock the boat. We got our blocks, and they got theirs."

"What the fuck? Y'all niggas the UN now? The United Nations? I'm gone eight years, and we are holding hands with muthafuckas. That's why y'all niggas got hit the other night. Muthafuckas think we're weak," Mob Allah exclaimed.

"We ain't weak out here, Mob," Zulu defended. "I make sure of that."

"You feel that way? When was the last time anything of ours got robbed?" Mob Allah asked him.

Zulu remained quiet, pondering.

"Listen, Zulu, what I always tell you . . . always remind muthafuckas on these streets what they should be afraid of. Niggas forget. They get ambitious and bold. And we can't have that. I'm home now, and I'm 'bout to jog these fools' memories," Mob Allah proclaimed wholeheartedly.

Zulu and Big Will nodded their heads. Mob Allah was a force to be reckoned with. He came up under the Supreme Team in the '80s and knew Supreme and Prince personally. His father used to be a hitter in Harlem for Nicky Barnes in the early '70s, and his mother was a number's runner. Mob Allah was born into a life of crime. He was molded to become a drug kingpin. Of the many crimes he committed, including murder and extortion, he was sentenced to eight years for selling and transporting assault weapons, a Class C felony. The DA wanted Mob Allah with a hard-on. They couldn't indict him on any other charges, so they indicted him on someone else's fuckup.

A soldier of theirs had left the weapons in the trunk of the car Mob Allah was driving, and they were under investigation. An unmarked unit pulled over the car he was driving, searched it, found the weapons in the trunk, and arrested Mob Allah. The charges were bullshit, but the DA was able to indict and prosecute Mob Allah on the charges, and he was found guilty in the court of law. It also didn't help him that he already had a criminal record. Unfortunately, the soldier who made the mistake was dealt with, and Mob Allah did his time.

"What other hiccups y'all been having?" Mob Allah asked Zulu.

"One of Coffee's bitches went missing a few nights ago," said Zulu. "This bitch named Diamond. Cops found her body in Forest Park."

"So, a stash house got hit, four of ours died, and a bitch is killed. Also, we got the police in our business," Mob Allah uttered. "It's been a great fuckin' week, I see. Coffee is under our protection, so we need to look into that."

"I got my people on it," Zulu replied.

Coffee was a Queens' pimp paying taxes to the Supreme Nation for territory and protection. Mob Allah believed in maximizing profits. His mother taught things like up-sell, cross-sell, resell, assessing and reducing operating costs, reviewing your product portfolio, pricing, and lowering your overhead. Mob Allah was smart enough to run a Fortune 500 company; unfortunately, he felt his calling was to the streets.

A few hours later, as they crossed over the George Washington Bridge heading into the vibrant city, the towering skyline caught Mob Allah's attention and hit him with nostalgia. It had been eight years too long for him.

"It's good to be home," he uttered.

# Chapter Six

Sincere entered the classroom and took a seat at a desk. He looked around. Over two dozen people, men and women, many young and some old, in the same classroom, ready to take the same test. He wanted to become an NYPD officer because he felt it fitted him. He didn't want to work an office job or a dead-end job. Being a cop was the next step in his life.

The police entrance exam was comprised of several sections; there was a written exam, an oral interview, a physical agility test, a medical and psychological check, and a background review. The written test was a crucial step. Sincere wore a dark blue suit to take the test, and he was nervous. Transitioning from the military to civilian life had been somewhat turbulent. The entrance exam was approximately eighty-five questions covering nine cognitive abilities topics. And Sincere had two and half hours to complete it.

"Focus," Sincere said to himself.

Wanting to become a police officer wasn't a popular choice where he comes from, but Sincere always wanted to help people. So he joined the army to get away from the negativity in the streets. And it didn't hurt that he'd gotten to travel and see the world—also learn a new skill. He wanted to become a cop because being in the army ignited something inside him. He wanted to keep that fire burning.

He completed the exam under the time limit and stepped out of the building to take a breather. Sincere had a lot on his mind, including his little brother, Maurice. Since his return home, Maurice made it clear that he didn't want anything to do with him. Somehow, they'd become estranged. Maurice was upset and jealous that Sincere had abandoned them for the United States government. Sincere wanted to make things right, but he knew that once his little brother found out he wanted to become a cop, it would only make things worse.

A cab arrived at his location, and he climbed into the back seat. He huffed and said to the driver, "Take me to Jamaica, Queens."

The driver nodded. While en route to Queens, Sincere stared out the window looking transfixed by something. Being back in the States, he left something special in Japan. He'd met a woman while he was stationed at Camp Zama. Her name was Asuka Nakamura. She was beautiful, intelligent, and funny. They'd fallen in love. She'd gotten pregnant and gave birth to a baby girl, his daughter. He wanted to see his daughter, but she was across the world.

Sincere had reached out to the US Embassy in Japan to report his daughter's birth. Because military bases outside of the US are not considered part of the United States regarding birthright citizenship, the only way that a child abroad can acquire citizenship at birth is through their parents. But Asuka wasn't a US citizen. Sincere spoke to a counselor about his case. He didn't want to become an absentee father to his daughter. He didn't see his daughter as a mistake. Her name was Akari, and the moment Sincere saw her, he fell in love with her.

Sincere did his best to keep in contact with Asuka, but it was difficult. There was a twelve-hour time difference. Japan, being on the other side of the globe, made communication expensive and nearly impossible. But he had hope and faith that things were going to work themselves out. Sincere took all the necessary steps to bring his daughter and her mother to the States. He even asked Asuka to marry him in Japan, but she turned down his proposal.

While in the back seat, he stared at the only picture he had of his baby girl and her mother. He smiled. The cab arrived at his home, and he climbed out to see Maurice leaving from the front door. Sincere quickly paid the driver and hopped out of the cab to catch up with his brother.

"Maurice," he called out.

Maurice frowned. He still didn't want anything to do with him.

"What you want?" Maurice griped, walking away.

"We need to talk," said Sincere, catching up to him.

"There's nothing to talk about."

"Where are you going?"

"That's none of your business," Maurice replied.

Sincere was fed up with his attitude. He grabbed Maurice by his arm and spun him around. Maurice scowled and shouted, "Get the fuck off me, man."

"What the fuck is wrong with you? You can't be that mad at me," Sincere exclaimed. "I did what I needed to do to stay alive and out of jail. But I'm back now. I want to make things right with you. How can I go about that?"

Maurice continued to scowl at him. Finally, he uttered, "Just stay the fuck outta my way."

"No, I'm not going to do that," Sincere said.

"I'm not a kid anymore, Sincere. I'm a grown fuckin' man, and you can't tell me what to do anymore," Maurice chided.

"I see that. But being 19 and on these streets doesn't make you a man," Sincere proclaimed.

"Don't belittle me. I'm more of a man than you think. And I don't need to fly across the world to find myself. South Side is my home, and I take care of business here. I'm makin' money now and doin' me, bro . . . You feel me? We don't need you. *I* don't need you."

Sincere scoffed. "You always gonna need your family, Maurice."

"You would believe that, wouldn't you? Look, nigga, just go back where you came from. You ain't my brother, muthafucka. You just some nigga pretending to be him. Because the Sincere *I* knew said he would always have my back and be there for me. The Sincere *I* knew, he got money on these streets and had a crew that respected him. The Sincere *I* knew would never leave his family behind," Maurice wholeheartedly proclaimed.

"There's more to life than this place, believe me," said Sincere.

Now it was Maurice who scoffed at Sincere. "You's a fuckin' fool, nigga. The army planted some bullshit in your head, right? Them fools brainwashed you. *That's* your family now, *not* us."

The two brothers looked at each other. Then Maurice's pager went off against his hip. He glanced at the number and returned his hard look at his brother. Maurice was becoming a hard nut to crack.

"We done here, nigga? 'Cause I got someplace to be," Maurice said.

Sincere remained silent.

"I thought so," Maurice added. Then he pivoted and marched away.

Sincere sighed. It was the second time his little brother gave him the cold shoulder and stormed off bitterly. But he wasn't about to give up on him. No matter what, Sincere was determined to get through to Maurice. Family was everything to him.

# Chapter Seven

The Q Club was the place to be tonight. It was packed with people, and the ladies came out in droves to celebrate Mob Allah's release from state prison. You couldn't see the dance floor because it was wall-to-wall people dancing. The R&B music moved everyone like they were puppets on strings. The good vibes flowed like a virus.

Mob Allah watched the revelers from the elevated VIP section inside the club. He was dressed sharply in a Giorgio Armani suit and wingtips. He clutched a bottle of Moët, took a swig from it, and nodded his head in approval. It was his night. It was a celebration. Mob Allah looked and felt like a million dollars. Occupying the large VIP area with him were Zulu, Big Will, Zodiac, Mackie, Donny, Julie, Freddie, and Queenie. They were his inner circle, the people he trusted. Everyone was dressed to the nines, enjoying expensive champagne and success.

"Yo, I wanna give a shout-out to Mob Allah," the DJ announced. "Welcome home, Mob Allah. We all love you, my nigga."

The crowd roared. Mob Allah smiled and raised the Moët bottle to salute the DJ. He then scanned the crowd below. Everyone was jiving, twisting, turning, holding hands, and grinding against one another. The strobe light masked many of their movements and sweaty skin. A few beautiful and sexy ladies caught Allah's attention, and he smiled their way. It had been a long time since he had sex, and a thirst was swirling inside him.

"You liking it?" Zulu asked him, placing his arm around his day one homie.

"Yeah, this is cool. I respect it," Mob Allah answered. "But we need to talk in private."

"Now?"

"Yeah, now. I got shit on my mind," he said.

Zulu nodded; no problem. "We can talk in the manager's office," Zulu said.

Zulu turned and walked away. Mob Allah lingered near the edge of the VIP section. His attention was fixed on a lovely-looking lady wearing a sexy, black cocktail dress that showed off her long legs and ample cleavage. She smiled at him. He gave her a head nod indicating that she had his attention. Then he turned and followed behind Zulu.

The two men entered the manager's office, and Zulu closed the door behind him. The office was spacious and neat. A desk and a high-back leather chair with a safe stood in the room. And security monitors were showing the club's activity everywhere.

Mob Allah looked around and said, "Are we good to talk here?"

"Yeah, we're good. I have a silent stake in this club. And I have my security peoples sweep it twice a month," Zulu replied. "What do you need to talk to me about?"

Mob Allah stared at Zulu expressionless. He then proclaimed, "I've been home almost forty-eight hours, and I don't see any retribution for one of our spots being hit. Where's Voltron? Where's the information, Zulu? The longer this shit lingers, the weaker we look out there."

"I told you, I'm on it, Allah. Just relax."

"Relax? This shit should have been handled yesterday," replied Mob Allah. "I respect this party, but I wanna get shit done."

Zulu huffed.

"Why you blowing out your mouth, nigga? You got a fuckin' problem, Zulu? Huh?" Mob Allah chided.

"Nah, nigga . . . but I don't appreciate how you out here questioning my actions," Zulu griped. "I've been holdin' shit down for eight years while you were gone. I took this organization to the next level and continued to put money in your pockets. So, don't come at me like I'm some off-brand muthafucka, Allah."

"I respect that, but what I always told you, don't get too comfortable out there," Mob Allah returned. "We have a problem. And if we don't handle it now, it's gonna snowball into a fuckin' avalanche. There's a snitch in our circle."

"You think so?"

"How many people knew about the Long Island stash house?"

"Maybe eight," Zulu answered.

"And why do you make all of your drops late at night?"

"Because traffic is sparse, so it's easy to see if you're being followed in the dark. I tell my men to take note of every car on the block, and if they believe they're being followed, take a longer route," Zulu said.

"Whoever hit the stash house knew you make your drops late at night. They were waiting. Didn't need to follow your drivers. Someone gave it up," Mob Allah stated.

"Keys did mention to me that he heard one of 'em say, 'He said no bodies,'" Zulu uttered.

"We don't need any more hiccups. Find this muthafucka Voltron and get him to talk. Force this fool to give up his source. And then make this nigga die slow and painful for fuckin' with our business. Put the full-court press out on these streets."

The two men exited the office and headed back to the action inside the club. The alcohol continued to flow like an IV drip, and Reggae music was blaring throughout the nightclub. Mob Allah took a seat in VIP, and he stared at every one of his comrades closely. He figured one of them was a traitor. He was going to find out who it was and kill them himself. But for now, he sat back and continued to become indulged.

Mob Allah noticed the beautiful woman in the cocktail dress weaving through the crowded dance floor. She had an aura about her that he liked from afar. She looked his way and smiled. He nodded. Then he called Zodiac over.

"You see shorty down there in the black cocktail dress?" Mob Allah pointed out.

"Yeah," Zodiac said.

"Invite her to join us in VIP."

Zodiac smiled. "No doubt. I got you."

He walked away to do what he was instructed. Mob Allah sat back and watched him work. He had a penchant for petite, light-skinned women, and she fit the template to his desire. Right away, the young lady followed Zodiac through the crowd and toward the VIP section. Mob Allah kept cool. When she stood in front of him, he said, "You're beautiful. What's your name?"

"Melody," she replied.

"That's a lovely name. Care to have a seat and talk?"

She grinned. "Sure."

Melody nestled against Mob Allah, and she was pretty with green eyes. He placed his arm around her, and they already looked like a couple. While she laughed and flirted with him, Mob Allah stared at everyone in VIP with him, scrutinizing them in silence and wondering about their loyalty. Someone in his clique had betrayed the organization, and they would pay with their life.

# Chapter Eight

Drip-Drip, Voltron, and Maurice had divided up the cash between them. In total, their take from the robbery was nearly $120,000. It was a successful payday for them and split three ways, that was $40,000 apiece. Drip-Drip planned the theft, and his two associates went along for the ride. They decided to celebrate a week after the heist. So, they went to an underground strip club in Brooklyn. It was a place where anything goes, where the strippers got butt-naked and were willing to do anything strange for a nice piece of change.

The hole-in-the-wall spot was as grimy as they came. It was in a basement, underneath a local bar on Broadway Avenue in Bushwick. Men paid a cover charge of twenty dollars and were allowed downstairs into a world of debauchery where naked girls, liquor, music, gambling, and weed abounded . . . all the vices needed to have a good time. And that's what the trio planned to do . . . have a really great time. Voltron had a penchant for strippers and whores. He knew where all the spots were in Queens and Brooklyn. They decided to party in Brooklyn because Queens had become too hot for them. And they didn't want to draw any attention to themselves around familiar faces.

Biggie's "Big Poppa" blared throughout the spot. Nearly two dozen naked or scantily clad ladies walked around the impromptu strip club with the makeshift bar and stage. The basement was swollen with men of all ages and sizes . . . thugs, drug dealers, and goons mixed in with squares, locals, and blue-collared men looking to have a great time and snatch themselves a piece of pussy tonight.

Voltron's eyes lit up as he eyed the bootylicious and curvy young girl on the stage who was naked like the day she was born.

"This what it's all about, my niggas," said Voltron. He pulled out a wad of bills and began throwing money at her. "It's party time. You lookin' good, shorty. What's ya name?"

She smiled and replied, "Delicious."

"Delicious, huh? I like that. You definitely lookin' delicious right now," he joked.

She was all his. Maurice and Drip-Drip hit the bar and got a few beers. Maurice took a few swigs from the Corona and then said to Drip-Drip, "You sure we should be doin' this?"

"What?"

"I'm sayin', drawing attention to ourselves in here. We ain't rob no off-brand niggas, Drip-Drip. That was Zulu's spot."

Right away, Drip-Drip glared at him and pushed him into a corner. He then griped, "Nigga, you talk too fuckin' much. Keep ya mouth shut, nigga. You crazy? You forget where we at? Just because we in Brooklyn don't mean muthafuckas don't know what went down in Queens."

Maurice knew he messed up. "I'm sorry."

"Fuck your sorry, and just shut the fuck up," Drip-Drip cautioned him.

Drip-Drip pivoted and walked away. Maurice sighed. Though he looked tough, he was nervous and scared. He couldn't stop thinking about the bodies they'd left behind. He'd taken someone's life, and he couldn't get her out of his mind. Maurice was having nightmares about the woman. It felt as if she were haunting him. It was his first body, and he felt absolutely awful. But of course, he couldn't confess his sins to anyone. Even though Maurice had felt immense peer pressure to go through with the murder, he couldn't be seen as weak, especially when roaming with wolves. He had a reputation to uphold. But now, he felt like a coward because it was a woman.

Maurice took another swig from his beer. He looked around, and everyone was either engaged in pussy, drinking, or gambling.

"You want a dance, cutie?" a naked stripper asked him.

In all of her glory, she stood in front of Maurice, smiling at him like he was a winning lottery ticket. She was petite, light-skinned, and bright with beauty. Maurice looked to his left and noticed Drip-Drip was watching him. It creeped him out. The last thing he needed was anyone doubting his loyalty or thinking he was weak and shaken up about the murders.

"Yeah, I would love a dance wit' you," he said.

Immediately, she turned around and backed her ass up against him. Then she started to grind against his crotch. She was ready to put on a show for him and make him yearn for more of her time and attention.

"You can touch me wherever you like. Let me take your mind off your troubles tonight, baby. I got you," she said temptingly.

Maurice cupped her breast and became aroused. "What's ya name?"

"Holiday," she replied.

*Holiday, cute,* he thought. Holiday continued to entice him. She was soft from head to toe, and her tits were supple. She was the complete package. Holiday felt Maurice's erection against her butt and grinned.

"Ooh, I see someone else is happy tonight," she cooed.

Maurice looked to his left again to see if Drip-Drip was still watching him. Strangely, he was. It made him uncomfortable, sending a deep chill down Maurice's spine.

"You want some private time with me, baby? We got rooms to fuck in if you want," said Holiday. "I know you want to be in this pussy."

"How much?"

"One hundred," she replied.

Maurice thought about it for a moment and then said, "Fuck it. I'm down."

Holiday grinned. She then took Maurice by his hand and led him to another part of the basement with a narrow corridor. There were several rooms on both sides of the passage. A man clad in black stood at the edge of the hall.

"Give him a twenty for one of the rooms," Holiday told Maurice.

Maurice removed a wad of cash, and Holiday's eyes lit up like Times Square, New York. She knew it was payday for her. Maurice handed the man a twenty bill, and Holiday continued to guide him to one of the rooms.

Maurice was taken aback by the décor of the small room. It was small but comfortable with a futon bed, a wall mirror, and a chair. Holiday closed the door behind her and instantly went for his crotch and zipper.

"It's a hundred for fifteen minutes. If you want a half hour, give me $150," she said.

Maurice had money to splurge, and besides, he didn't want to be in the central area with everyone else. So, he handed her $160. Holiday beamed. She pushed him on the futon, dropped to her knees, grabbed his dick, and started sucking it. Maurice threw his head back and moaned.

"Oh shit. Damn."

***

It was three a.m. when the trio arrived back in the hood of Queens. Everyone looked like they had the time of their lives tonight. Drip-Drip steered his Jeep to the curb of the projects, and Voltron climbed out from the passenger front seat.

"Yo, I'ma holla at ya niggas tomorrow, a'ight?" said Voltron.

"Do that," Drip-Drip said. He then looked back at Maurice and uttered, "Nigga, get ya ass in the front seat. I ain't a fuckin' taxi."

Silently, Maurice climbed into the front seat. Then Drip-Drip drove off.

Voltron was a bit tipsy, but he was able to focus. It was the devil's hour, and the 40 Projects were as quiet as a mouse. When he neared the lobby, he heard someone call out, "Yo, Voltron, let me holla at you."

He turned around to see Mackie calling out to him from the front seat of a Toyota 4Runner. It was clear to see that he wasn't alone. Voltron knew seeing Mackie wasn't good news for him. He frowned and replied, "Nah, I'm good."

Mackie got out of the 4Runner and exclaimed, "Nigga, we ain't asking."

The other doors opened, and several other men climbed out of the vehicle. Voltron knew they weren't there for a friendly chitchat. So he spun around and took off running. Three men, including Mackie, gave chase. Guns were drawn, but they were ordered to bring Voltron back alive.

Voltron tried to zigzag through the projects. He sloppily tried to jump over one of the short iron fences, but he botched it and fell on his side. Mackie and his goons were looming. Voltron hurriedly reached for the pistol in his waistband. He aimed it at them and fired.

*Boom boom boom!*

But he missed. He stood up and continued to run. Mackie scowled. He hated being shot at. Now, it was personal. They continued to chase Voltron through the projects. Fortunately for them, Voltron wasn't a sprinter, and the alcohol in his system made him a bit disoriented. He shot at his assailants again but missed. One of the goons shot back and struck Voltron in the back of his leg, and he dropped. Before Voltron could fire his gun again, they all were on top of him, beating him senseless.

"You shoot at me, nigga?" Mackie shouted, kicking him in the side.

Voltron howled in pain. He couldn't move. When they were done beating his ass, they dragged him to the 4Runner and stuffed him into the back compartment.

"Mob Allah wants a word with you," said Mackie.

"Fuck y'all niggas," Voltron growled.

"Keep acting tough, nigga . . . See how long that shit gonna last," Mackie replied. "You fucked with the wrong crew, muthafucka."

# Chapter Nine

Voltron was crippled with pain. His breathing was labored, and he could barely see because of the blood flowing into his eyes. He looked grotesque. His eyes were swollen, and bloody spit drooled from his slacked jaws. His body was damaged almost beyond the point at which recovery was possible. Voltron was lucky to remember his own name.

"Give us a fuckin' name, muthafucka," Mackie shouted. He punched him in the face, and then he extinguished a cigarette against his cheek.

Voltron howled in pain.

"Talk, nigga. If not, I can do this all night with you," Mackie exclaimed.

Voltron continued to remain silent and stubborn. Finally, he managed to utter, "Fuck you."

"This muthafucka," Mackie said in disbelief. It had been nearly two hours of torture, and Voltron still wasn't breaking. "You a tough sonofabitch, nigga. I'll give you that."

Voltron was tied to a chair and stripped down to his underwear. He was held captive in a concrete basement with no windows, surrounded by goons. He'd been burned with cigarettes, had his fingers broken, ribs broken, and assaulted with a baseball bat. Still, he remained tight-lipped. Mackie was growing tired and impatient.

"We know you ain't rob our stash house by yourself. So, who put you up to it, nigga? Give us a name, and I promise you, all this pain will end," said Mackie.

"Fuck you," Voltron spat defiantly once again.

"Yo, I swear, I'm 'bout to go biblical on this nigga." Mackie tightened his fists and was ready to strike him again.

"Hold on," Mob Allah said. He appeared in front of Voltron, carrying a deadpan expression. "I got this."

Mackie nodded and stepped aside. No problem. Mob Allah placed a folding chair opposite Voltron and took a seat. Though his look was expressionless, Mob Allah still looked like a menacing figure.

"The problem with y'all young niggas, you all are self-ish . . . just think about yourselves. You don't think about your mother, grandmother, or sister. Because if you did, you wouldn't have done something so stupid like rob one of our stash houses and kill my peoples," Mob Allah coolly proclaimed.

Voltron remained silent.

"I mean, if I were you," Mob Allah continued, "I would always think about my family first before I do some stupid shit on these streets. Now, if I didn't have any family, maybe I wouldn't give a fuck. Probably steal, pillage, and live recklessly. But you have a big family, a nice family, and most of them live in the projects. So, that makes you one stupid muthafucka to steal from us."

Voltron squirmed in his seat while Mob Allah glared at him now.

"I'm going to ask you some questions, and before you disrespect me and repeat, 'Fuck you,' I want you to think about your family. I want you to picture this. I send a couple of goons to confront your lovely grandmother, Ms. Lane, and have 'em shoot that bitch in the head. And then I send some men to kidnap your young sister and baby mother. Throw them into the trunk of a car, drive them somewhere desolated where my men will rape them repeatedly and probably in front of your child. It'll get so bad they'll be begging to die. And your son, he's 4, right? I don't kill kids. I'm not that coldhearted. But imagine how fucked up that kid's gonna be seeing his mama and aunt repeatedly raped and abused. Gonna fuck him up for life. Little nigga gonna need therapy for a long time," Mob Allah proclaimed convincingly. "Save yourself the headache, nigga, and save your family by helping us."

Mob Allah had put Voltron between a rock and a hard place. But, unfortunately, he didn't give him any wiggle room to be adamant.

"Now, give us some fuckin' names," Mob Allah said sternly. He fixed his eyes on Voltron, knowing he was about to crack open with information.

"Maurice and Drip-Drip," Voltron uttered, defeated.

"Drip-Drip? That's Rafe's little brother," Mackie chimed in.

Mob Allah smiled and said, "You're doing good. Now, another question. I know y'all little niggas didn't come about that location by chance. So, who put y'all up to it?"

"I-I don't know. Whoever it was reached out to Drip-Drip. And they said, 'Take the cash, but no bodies.'"

Mob Allah nodded. He believed him. He stood up and stared at Voltron. It was that time. Voltron was defeated, and he knew what his fate was. He stared up at Mob Allah and asked, "You gonna let my family be . . . leave 'em alone?"

Mob Allah smirked, and then he replied, "I don't know. I'll think about it."

Those were his final words to Voltron. Then he lifted a pistol to Voltron's head and fired twice. *Bak, bak!*

Mob Allah stood there in silence, staring at Voltron's body, now slumped in the chair. It was as if he were an artist admiring a piece of artwork. Instead, however, there was something sadistic in his gaze. He turned to Mackie and said, "Get him out of here."

"You want us to make him disappear?" asked Mackie.

"Nah, put that fool out on front street. Show everyone what happens when you rob from us," Mob Allah instructed.

Mackie nodded and smirked. "No doubt. And what about Drip-Drip and that other nigga he named?"

"Get in contact with Rafe. Tell him we need to talk about his little brother and find out who the fuck Maurice is."

"I'm on it," Mackie replied, eager to get things done.

A few goons untied Voltron and removed his body from the room. Mob Allah sat back in the folding chair and lit a cigar. It was time for him to become king of kings.

It was early in the morning. Gray clouds loomed above, indicating rain was coming. It was a bit windy for spring and cool. It wasn't the perfect day for the beach. A black Mercedes-Benz E-Class with tinted windows arrived at the boardwalk pier and parked. The front passenger door opened, and Rafe climbed out of it. There was an air of power about Rafe. He was slim and black with chiseled features. He had dark, deep-set eyes, and his head was as bald as a baby's bum. He wore jeans that covered his white Nikes and a black, collared, button-down.

With his right-hand man, Malik, they walked toward the boardwalk where Mob Allah, Zulu, and Mackie waited for them near a bench. Since it was early with an overcast, the boardwalk and the beach were deserted. Rafe and Malik coolly approached the three men for a meeting.

"I'm glad you could make it, Rafe," said Mob Allah.

"Why the fuck am I here?" Rafe asked bluntly.

"A man that gets straight to the point. I respect that," replied Mob Allah. "We have a problem. And I figured us as men and leaders, we can address this issue and fix it."

"I'm listening," Rafe returned.

"I'm sure you're aware that one of our stash houses was raided, and four of my peoples were executed in cold blood. Word on the streets is that Drip-Drip was involved."

"My little brother?" Rafe voiced, disbelieving. "Who put his name out there?"

"A reliable source that's no longer with us. Three men were involved, and we're now looking for the third man."

"I'm not giving him up, Mob Allah. You know that. He's my little brother," Rafe said gruffly.

"I expected that. He's family to you. But you see, that puts a dilemma between you and me, Rafe. And as you know, I just came home, and the last thing I need is a war between us because these little niggas got stupid," Mob Allah proclaimed. "I don't need that kind of spotlight on me right now."

"So, what's your solution?" Rafe asked.

"Compensation. A quarter of a million," Mob Allah answered.

Rafe scoffed at the number. "What?"

"And you clean up your house, and I'll clean up mines. Your little brother gives us the information needed on this nigga named Maurice. I want him to tell us who provided him the address to our stash house in my organization. So let's keep things amicable between us," Mob Allah announced nonchalantly.

"Two hundred and fifty thousand is not happening, Mob Allah. Besides, I heard you got hit for a little over a hundred. One fifty, and I'll definitely get my little brother to talk. He'll correct his stupidity," said Rafe.

Mob Allah glanced at Zulu, a silent understanding between the two. He then looked at Rafe and replied, "We can work with that."

"By tonight, you'll have all that info and your money," said Rafe.

"I'm glad we could work things out between us, Rafe," Mob Allah expressed.

"Yeah, welcome home," he replied dryly.

Mob Allah smiled. Rafe pivoted and walked away with Malik behind him. Mob Allah and Zulu lingered on the boardwalk. Zulu looked at Mob and asked, "You trust he'll come up with the information and cash?"

"He doesn't have a choice. His little brother put him in a situation that could rock the boat. And besides, he can't afford a war with us."

"What happened to that shit you were talkin' out of prison, about you ain't wit' that peace and UN shit?"

Mob Allah grinned slightly. "Plan for what is difficult while it is easy; do what is great while it is small," he stated.

The statement went over Zulu's head. Huh? But it was evident that Mob Allah did a lot of reading while locked up.

"This is chess, not checkers, Zulu. One move at a time," Mob Allah said.


An old gray Lincoln Town Car sat on Union Hall Street and 108th Avenue with its hazard lights on. It had been left there overnight, and the locals started to take notice of the vehicle. They had never seen the car before, and they wondered who'd left it behind with its blinking lights still on. It was a hot spring day, and soon, a pungent smell started to come from the vehicle, which bothered everyone. Someone called the police, and a marked police car arrived that evening. Two cops walked toward the Town Car and coolly inspected it. The smell was strong, and they winced. It came from the trunk of the vehicle.

They managed to pry open the trunk, and what they saw inside made both officers cringe in horror.

"What the fuck," one cop cried out.

It was a mutilated body contorted inside the trunk. The face was unrecognizable, and whoever it was, was in their underwear.

"Get on the horn with homicide. Tell them we have a situation."

The neighborhood would soon learn that the decomposing body inside the trunk was Voltron.

# Chapter Ten

Detectives Acosta and Emerson arrived at another gruesome crime scene in Flushing Meadows Park. Emerson frowned, being in another park. It was a gloomy morning with the clouds diffusing the daylight to a soft, gentle breeze. The detectives stepped on the grassy field and knew this scene wouldn't be pretty. Flushing Meadows Park was a public park in the northern part of Queens. It was bounded by the I-678 on the east, Grand Central Parkway on the west, Flushing Bay on the north, and Union Turnpike on the south.

"Lots of highways and roads around. And we're what, five miles away from Forest Park. Couldn't be a coincidence," Emerson pointed out.

"Our killer definitely is familiar with the area," said Acosta.

The crime scene/area was already bustling with CSI collecting evidence and taking pictures, police officers roaming about, and other detectives were already on the scene. Acosta and Emerson could see the body sprawled across the grass from their short distance. It was an open area. There was a lake on one side and the highway on the other. They approached the body and saw that she was naked.

"What do we have here?" Emerson asked the primary detective on the scene.

"It's the same MO. A young girl, pretty, naked, with her tongue, eyes, and fingers missing," Detective Anthony Quinn answered.

Acosta huffed. He approached the body and crouched near it. He examined her from head to toe. This one was young, and all eyes were on her.

"You're nobody 'til somebody kills you," Acosta murmured, quoting the late Biggie. "She had to be 17 or 18."

"The last victim in Forest Park, did y'all ever get an ID on her?" Quinn asked them.

Emerson nodded. "Natasha Henderson, 20 years old. She had a record for prostitution and theft. One of our officers remembered her from a year back. So, chances are, this one's a prostitute too," Emerson pointed out about the victim.

"But where was she taken from?" Acosta chimed in.

"And what's the thing with removing the eyes, tongue, and fingers?" Quinn questioned.

"I believe it's some kind of ritual," replied Acosta.

"Ritual . . .?" Quinn questioned.

"Yes. I don't know if it's visionary or missionary," Acosta stated.

"You're losing me here, Acosta," Quinn uttered.

Michael Acosta stared at the young victim with his soft eyes and sharp perception. His mind was spinning. This was their second victim within two weeks, but he thought, were there more out there that they *didn't* know about? There was definitely a serial killer in Queens, making things more troubling and complicated. This kind of killer doesn't just "go crazy" one day and kill lots of people. They don't kill out of greed or jealousy. This was someone who worked alone, killed strangers, and killed for the sake of killing. They didn't kill in a crime of passion.

He rose to his feet, turned to Quinn, and proclaimed, "Serial killers can be act-focused, meaning they kill quickly, or process-focused, meaning they kill slowly. For act-focused killers, killing is simply the act itself.

And within this group, you have two different types: the visionary and the missionary. The visionary murders because he hears voices or has visions that direct him to do so. The missionary murders because he believes he is meant to get rid of a particular group of people. Process-focused serial killers get enjoyment from torture and the slow death of their victims."

Quinn was taken aback by his knowledge. "When did you become an expert on serial killers?"

"I do a lot of reading," Acosta replied and smirked. "I think we're dealing with someone who derives sexual pleasure from killing or murders them because they believe they will profit somehow."

Acosta stared at the body again, then took in the surrounding area. It was a big park, but the highway and roads were visible, unlike the last crime scene where it was secluded. He knew the killer was definitely comfortable and familiar with the area, and the victim was dumped there sometime in the wee hours of the morning.

But the first thing they needed to do was identify the victim, notify the family, and dig into her life.


Maurice checked the 9 mm Beretta clip in his hand and saw that it was fully loaded. He then went to the window and stared out at the block. It was late evening, and things were quiet. No anomalies about. However, he'd heard about Voltron, and he was scared. If they got Voltron, he knew they were coming after him. He had called Drip-Drip nearly a dozen times but didn't get a response. He continued to be paranoid and stared out the window again. Then he heard, "What are you doing with that gun?"

Maurice spun around to see Sincere standing at the threshold of his bedroom. He looked at him for a moment and then uttered, "It ain't your business."

"Like hell, it isn't," said Sincere, stepping farther into the room. "What's going on with you, Maurice?"

"Look, I can handle myself." Maurice continued to be stubborn.

"It doesn't look like it to me. It looks like you're scared of something or someone. What's going on? What did you do?"

Sincere wasn't going anywhere. He was steadfast in finding out the truth from his little brother.

"Talk to me. You can trust me, Maurice. Whatever trouble you're in, I'm here to help," said Sincere.

Maurice wanted to be stubborn, but he knew he needed someone's help, even if it came from his brother. He huffed and pouted but gradually relented. "I got into some shit, okay?" he stated, being vague.

"What kind of shit? Is someone after you?"

"I don't know."

"What you mean you don't know?"

"I don't know, all right?" Maurice shouted, becoming frustrated. "They found one of my friends dead. They killed him, but I don't know why."

Sincere stared intently at his little brother, knowing he wasn't telling him everything. Maurice paced around the room, still clutching the gun. He stared out the window again. "I need to get the fuck outta here," he said.

"And go where?"

"I don't know, but I can't stay here."

"You're better off here for the moment than out there," Sincere suggested. "And if you can't be truthful with me about what you have done, I can't help you, Maurice. I know you're scared. I see it in your eyes. But the last thing you need to do is do something stupid and irrational. So, let's sit down, talk, and assess the situation."

"How are you gonna help me?" Maurice seethed.

"If this is a life-or-death situation, maybe we can go to the police."

Maurice glared at Sincere and exclaimed, "Are you fuckin' crazy? I don't do fuckin' cops, Sincere. You from the streets, nigga. Why would you even suggest that dumb shit? See, you've been gone too long to help me. The government got you brainwashed, and you want me to become a fuckin' snitch."

Sincere had enough of Maurice's equivocation about the trouble he was in. He scolded, "It's time for you to stop beating around the bush and tell me what the fuck happened out there. Because right now, it looks like *I'm* the only one here to help you, and I'm *not* going away. I didn't come home only to lose you in these streets to some bullshit."

Sincere stared at Maurice like an angry and concerned father rather than a brother. He wasn't about to let anyone destroy his family. If they had to barricade themselves inside the room until they figured out something, so be it. Maurice needed help, and that's what Sincere was determined to do.

"Did you kill someone?" Sincere frankly asked him.

"No one was supposed to get hurt," Maurice voiced faintly. "It was just supposed to be a strong-arm robbery—in and out. That's it. I needed the money."

Sincere felt deflated like a balloon. He was disappointed with his brother's poor decision, knowing someone did get hurt or killed. He stood in front of Maurice with his eyes burning into his little brother, and he compellingly stated, "Who was killed? I'm not leaving this room until you tell me the entire truth, Maurice."

Maurice sighed and relented. "Like I said, I needed the money. Drip-Drip had gotten information on this stash house in Long Island. It belonged to Zulu. We robbed it and killed everyone inside."

Sincere was taken aback. "What?"

"It wasn't the plan. Whoever told Drip-Drip about the stash house told him no bodies. But Drip-Drip and Voltron went crazy and started shooting everyone. I was against it. But they made me do it . . . They made me shoot her."

Sincere couldn't believe what he was hearing. It felt like he couldn't breathe because he knew his little brother had stepped into some shit that couldn't be easily wiped away.

"What the fuck, Maurice? Are you *kidding* me?"

"I wish I was," Maurice replied sheepishly.

"Okay, look, from now on, you don't talk to anyone, and you don't trust no one. Not even Drip-Drip," Sincere advised.

"But I *need* to talk to him," Maurice uttered.

"No, you don't. You stay away from him, Maurice. You can't trust him. You think he's gonna have your back? You think he's going to look out for you? Wake up, Maurice. That's Rafe's little brother, and they will use you as a scapegoat and sell you out," Sincere proclaimed on high emotions.

"So, what I'm supposed to do? Just sit around here and wait for them to come after me?"

"No. But I'm gonna figure something out. I promise you, Maurice. I'm here for you. And I'm not gonna let anyone take you away from me. I promise you that." Sincere replied wholeheartedly.

# Chapter Eleven

"I love you," Trina cried out from the sensation of Coffee's big dick rubbing her pussy lips, sliding in and out of her as she rode him like a stallion. She clutched his chest as he spread her ass cheeks. The instant she felt him inside of her, they became one.

The sensation of feeling his thick, hard dick thrusting into her, pumping her, filled Trina with ecstasy.

"Damn, baby, your pussy is definitely platinum. That's why you're my bottom bitch," Coffee uttered.

"Fuck me, daddy, fuck me."

Coffee flipped Trina onto her back, into the missionary position. If there was a heaven, it was having the total weight of her man on top of her, hearing him whisper in her ear, "Damn, your pussy is good."

She dug her nails into his ass, pulling him deeper and deeper inside of her. She craved him deeper, harder, faster, as he was fucking her with all his might.

Trina was Coffee's bottom bitch. She had been with him for nearly a decade, and she sat atop the hierarchy of prostitutes working for him. She'd been there with her pimp through the thick and thin. Trina was in love with Coffee, and she would do anything for him.

Coffee grabbed her hips from behind to feel her tits swinging while he thrust with all his might, and he put his fingers in her ass. Trina was a freak like that. While the two were in the heat of the moment, a loud knock at the bedroom door interrupted their rendezvous.

"Coffee, there are two cops downstairs asking for you," one of his girls shouted out.

"What the fuck?" he grumbled.

He removed himself from the pussy and reached for his pants. Coffee was a bearded man who stood six-one with a lean body, a narrow face, intense eyes, and a raspy cigarette voice.

"Everything okay, baby?" Trina asked him.

"How the fuck would I know?" he griped.

He exited the bedroom shirtless and only wearing jeans. Trina was right behind him, naked. She didn't care. He marched downstairs and into the front room, where two suit-and-tie-wearing detectives were waiting for him.

"What the fuck y'all want?" Coffee exclaimed.

"I'm Detective Acosta, and this is my partner, Detective Emerson."

Instantly, Trina's stark nakedness caught the attention of both men. Trina smirked and uttered, "What, y'all fools got a problem? Y'all ain't never seen pussy before?"

"Can she put some clothes on?" Detective Acosta asked.

"Y'all can fuckin' leave if I make you feel uncomfortable," Trina retorted.

"Trina, chill," Coffee remarked. "I got this."

Trina frowned and huffed. She then turned and removed herself from the room. Once she was out of the room, Coffee asked, "Y'all here for business or pleasure?"

"We're here about one of your girls, Diamond," Emerson spoke.

"Yeah, what about her? I haven't seen Diamond in like two weeks. So, I figured she took off," said Coffee.

"Are you aware she's dead? Her body was found in Forest Park," Acosta mentioned.

"Nah, damn. I'm sorry to hear about that."

"We know she was working for you, Coffee. She was only twenty years old."

"Listen, I don't control these bitches. They just happened to like staying here and being around me. You feel me, Detective? I give 'em shelter, clothes, food, protection, and some dick once in a while," Coffee said.

"Protection?" Emerson chuckled. "How well did that work out for Diamond, or shall I say, Natasha? That was the name her mama gave her. So, you wanna know what happened to her? Huh? What someone did to her?"

"Look, I can't be everywhere all the time. It's a crazy world out there. And besides, the bitch was a runaway, and she came to me lookin' for help and a job. I'ma miss her. She knew how to make that money," Coffee proclaimed arrogantly.

Emerson fumed. He didn't like the pimp's attitude and arrogance.

"How about we make things difficult for you, huh? I'll give a Vice a call, have every cop in this area harass your girls and lock them up for the smallest violations," Emerson expressed.

"I'm a man of business, Detective. I'm not a killer. So, why this visit?"

"We want you to put the word out to everyone, let them know there's a killer out there targeting young prostitutes. And any details you can give, no matter how small you think it is, contact us," Acosta proclaimed.

He handed Coffee his card.

"You can either help us or keep having your girls go missing, which will be bad for business. I'll let you decide," Acosta stated.

Coffee sighed. He was reluctant to work with the police, but he knew he couldn't afford to have any of his girls go missing or murdered. If a serial killer in Queens were going after young prostitutes, it would be bad for business, and his girls wouldn't want to work.

"I'll see what I can do," he replied dryly.

"That's all we ask," Acosta said.

"We'll see you soon," Emerson uttered smartly and winked at Coffee.

The two detectives pivoted and left the premises, leaving a bad taste in Coffee's mouth. He frowned and immediately made a call from his mobile phone. It rang a few times until someone answered.

"Yeah, what's up?"

"We need to talk. Some cops just came to see me about Diamond. I can't be having cops in my business," Coffee stated.

"I'll reach out to Zulu or Mob Allah, set up a meeting."

"You need to do that."

The call ended, and Coffee stood there in a sour mood. Trina came back into the room clothed this time. She approached her pimp and asked, "You wanna finish our business upstairs?"

Coffee shunned her and spewed, "Bitch, you think I'm in the mood to fuck right now? Get the fuck outta my face, bitch."

Trina did what she was told and left the room. Coffee needed some time to himself to think.

# Chapter Twelve

Sincere wanted to concentrate on becoming a police officer, but he couldn't. He was distracted by the fact that people wanted to kill his little brother. Although he'd promised Maurice that he wouldn't let anything happen to him, he was scared. He didn't know what to do. He wanted to beat the shit out of Maurice for being so stupid and getting involved with home invasions and murders. Not only did Maurice jeopardize his own safety, but he also jeopardized his family's safety. The streets didn't care about collateral damage, and a bullet didn't have anyone's name on it. So, Maurice had a target on his back. And Sincere understood that even with Maurice in hiding, they would try to get him through their mother or baby sister.

Sincere had passed the civil service exam and the medical examination with flying colors. Next was his character assessment. Clad in a dark blue suit, Sincere sat in front of a board of cops for his panel interview. He was nervous, distracted, and ambivalent all at the same time. They were going to ask him some tough questions, and he was advised to answer every question honestly.

"Why do you want to work in this industry?" one cop asked.

"Tell us about yourself," another said.

"Where do you see yourself in five years?"

"Why are you leaving your current job?"

"What's your greatest weakness?"

"Why should we hire you?"

The questions came at Sincere like a massive flood. They were precise. And a few questions were asked again but phrased differently. When the panel interview was over and he was asked to leave, Sincere felt deflated. He thought that he did his best, though there were times when he had been caught off guard and sidetracked. Next was the written psychological assessment if he made it past the panel interview.

Sincere arrived back in Queens that evening. It was hot when he emerged from the subway on Sutphin and Archer Blvd. The intersection was active with people and gypsy cabdrivers parked near the station. The drivers wanted Sincere's business, but he waved them off. He decided to walk home instead. His mother's home was only a few blocks away. Sincere needed to walk and think. For now, Maurice was staying with a cousin in the Bronx, and Sincere wondered how long he would be able to keep his little brother in hiding.

The hardest part was lying to their mother and little sister about why Maurice had to stay in the Bronx for a while. The explanation Sincere gave was that there was a warrant out for Maurice's arrest. Sincere felt it was better for their mother to worry about the police than for her to worry about thugs coming after her son. The last thing he wanted was for his mother to relapse and start using drugs again. She was doing well.

Sincere made it home to an active block. The spring weather made everyone come outside, and he was the oddball wearing a suit and shoes on a hot day. Kids were playing, the residents were lingering on the front steps chatting and taking in the day, and the thugs were gambling or selling dope on the side. While walking toward his mother's row house, Sincere noticed a tan Ford Explorer parked on the opposite side of the block. From his viewpoint, he couldn't make out the occupants inside. But his gut instincts told him that the vehicle was trouble. They were watching the house. He frowned and boldly approached the car, but when he got close, it hastily drove away. Sincere tried to look at the occupants inside but couldn't see clearly. He only saw the silhouettes of two men in the front seat.

Thinking about his family, Sincere pivoted and hurried to the row house. He stormed inside, calling out for his mother and sister.

"Denise, Ma, where are y'all?" he shouted.

"We're in the kitchen," his mother replied.

Sincere felt relieved. He entered the kitchen to see Denise was cooking dinner, and their mother was sitting at the table paying some bills.

"Why are you yelling like something done happened?" Janet questioned him.

"No reason," he said. "It's just been a long day."

"You sure?"

He nodded.

"Here, bro, taste this," Denise said, trying to shove a spoonful of sauce into her brother's mouth.

"Damn, that's good. What you cooking?" he asked her.

"Spaghetti with fried eggs," she mentioned.

Hearing the two mixtures would make anyone cringe, but tasting it gave Sincere second thoughts. "That's different," he uttered.

Denise smiled and went back to cooking. Sincere stood there taking everything in. Everyone was in a happy place. If it had been like this a few years ago, Sincere felt he would have never left to join the army. But before he left for boot camp, everything was in turmoil. Janet would prostitute herself on the streets or steal to support her drug habit. There had been times when she stole from her own children. And there had been times when

Sincere caught his mother in vile, sexual acts, from sucking dick in her own home to being fucked by multiple
men on the streets. Crack made his mother destructive
and promiscuous. So, it was ironic that Sincere had to
sell crack on the streets to survive and pay the bills.

This is what home was supposed to look like. Now,
Sincere was worried that Maurice's foolish actions would
bring it all to an end.

Janet smiled at her son and said, "I can't believe you
want to become a cop. How did it go today?"

"It went okay," he answered halfheartedly.

"That's good to hear."

"Let me get comfortable and take off this suit. I'm
hungry," he smiled.

"You do that, big bro, and come back down and eat,"
said Denise.

Before Sincere went upstairs, he went to the living
room window and looked outside to see if the Explorer
had come back. It didn't. He sighed, knowing that if
they didn't show up today, they would most likely come
back tomorrow and the next day. They were looking for
Maurice.


Sincere downed his beer and signaled for the bar-
tender. She smiled his way and uttered, "Another beer?"

He nodded. "Yeah."

They locked eyes for a fleeting moment. She was an attractive girl with a shapely figure. Her hair was midnight
black, and it flowed over her shoulders. She wore grun-
gy-styled clothing like she was from Seattle in the '90s,
which stood out, and it was apparent she had a crush on
Sincere.

She placed another beer in front of him and asked,
"Are you okay?"

"I just have a lot on my mind right now," Sincere coolly responded.

"I can see that. Never saw you in here before. I'm Ashley, by the way."

"Sincere."

She smiled. "Beautiful name."

"Thanks," he replied indifferently.

While they were conversing and getting to know each other, Nasir entered the bar and sat next to Sincere. Sincere gave Ashley a look, and she took the hint. "I'll let y'all talk."

When she was out of ear distance, Sincere said to Nasir. "Talk to me. What did you find out?"

"It's not good," Nasir stated. "Maurice's name is hotter than fish grease on these streets. Word is, Zulu put out a $10,000 bounty on his head."

Sincere groaned. "Fuck."

"And now that Mob Allah is home, shit isn't going to be pretty. I was informed that Mob Allah and Rafe had met, talked some shit out, and—"

"Maurice is going to become the scapegoat," Sincere said.

"They're looking for him."

Sincere sighed heavily. It was awful news.

"I'm sorry," Nasir added. "Maybe he needs to leave town."

"And go where? We don't have any family elsewhere. And besides, that's a short-term solution. When they can't find him, who do you think they will come after next? His family. And I can't allow that to happen," Sincere proclaimed.

Nasir was sympathetic. He looked at Sincere and said, "You trying to go to war with these niggas?"

"I'm one man, Nasir," he replied. "I just came home from the army, and I'm trying to become a cop. Do

something good with my life. I just want to live in peace
with my family. I don't need the violence."

"Unfortunately, Maurice's actions put a dent into that
plan of yours. Mob Allah and Zulu, they're gonna come
after him. You know they're not gonna let it go. They
need to prove a point like they did with Voltron," said
Nasir.

It was the harsh truth, and Sincere knew it.

"Whatever you decide to do, let me know. I don't like
them niggas anyway," uttered Nasir.

Sincere sighed and took another swig of his beer. He
was stuck between a rock and a hard place, trying to
protect his little brother. But, on the other hand, how
could he protect Maurice and his mother and sister
simultaneously? It was a hard choice. One alternative
was better in some ways, the other was better in different
ways, and neither was better overall.

# Chapter Thirteen

Drip-Drip was lost in the enchanted haze of mind-blowing oral sex that never seemed to end. The young, curvy, and endowed girl was on her knees sucking dick. Her suction and salivating mouth continued to bring Drip-Drip closer to an orgasm. One of her hands was cupping his balls; her nails tickled the backside of his scrotum. Her other hand gripped the base of his dick and became like a vice, not allowing anything to get past her fingers as she sucked his dick harder and aggressively.

"Oh shit. Damn. Aah," Drip-Drip groaned, feeling his knees nearly buckle from the fiery pleasure he was feeling.

They were in the backroom of a social club in Hollis, Queens. A birthday party was happening on the main floor while a sexual rendezvous was happening away from it.

The girl moaned while giving Drip-Drip head. The vibrations flowed along his dick, past her fingers, and into his balls.

"Shit, I'm 'bout to come," he announced.

He continued to moan as well and move with her. Soon, he couldn't keep his flood from rushing forward. Drip-Drip squirmed and could feel his knees becoming weaker. This girl was a pro at giving head, and he was about to succumb to an intense orgasm. He quickly released while her suction was concentrated, and she didn't flinch. Instead, she gulped and swallowed every last drop of him.

She grinned and uttered, "I see why they call you Drip-Drip."

Suddenly, the door to the room flew open, and the lights snapped on. Rafe glared at his exposed little brother with the pretty girl still on her knees. Embarrassed, she quickly stood up, fixed her clothing, and marched out of the room.

"What the fuck are you doing?" Rafe griped.

"Chill. I was just having some fun with her."

"That was Malik's little sister," Rafe exclaimed.

"And? That bitch can suck dick like the rest of them. In fact, she was the best of them," Drip-Drip mocked. "C'mon, bro, you know his little sister is a fuckin' freak. The bitch been eye-fuckin' me all night anyway."

Agitated, Rafe shut the door and charged at his brother. He forcefully grabbed Drip-Drip by his shirt and slammed him against the wall. Rafe's eyes burned into his little brother.

"That's your fuckin' problem. You don't have any respect for anything," Rafe bellowed. "Because of you, I had to spew out over a hundred grand for your stupidity."

"Yo, get off me, big bro," Drip-Drip voiced coolly. "Why you trippin' anyway? Fuck Mob Allah and Zulu. I don't fear them niggas, and you shouldn't either."

"It's not about fear, nigga. It's about respect and boundaries," Rafe returned. "And the money I had to cough up, that's now *your* debt owed to me."

"What?"

"Two hundred thousand is your price for ambition," Rafe said.

"Nah, fuck that," Drip-Drip cursed.

"You're reckless, Drip-Drip. And if you want to refute it, then fuck with me," Rafe growled. "I'm tired of your bullshit and stupidity. If it wasn't for me, you would have been in the back of a trunk by now like your fuckin' friend."

Drip-Drip scowled. Voltron was his friend, and he felt he didn't deserve that kind of fate. And since Rafe and Mob Allah met, Drip-Drip had to suffer minor consequences from his actions. He'd been demoted from a chief to a subordinate inside the organization. And he was placed elsewhere, at an off-brand location at the edge of Queens where business was slow.

"You wanna make it up and rebrand yourself? Help us find your third accomplice, Maurice," said Rafe. "You fuck up; you make it right. Until then, you stay where you are."

Rafe turned and left the room, leaving Drip-Drip to contemplate his next move. He definitely didn't want to stay in the position that he was in. And word on the streets was that Maurice hadn't been seen in a week. He was in hiding.

Drip-Drip exited the back room and returned to the party. The birthday party was for their great-aunt, Joy. She had turned 72 years old, and music, balloons, liquor, food, and people abounded. It was a family affair, but a few of Rafe's men were in attendance, including Malik and his little sister, Tea.

Drip-Drip was in a foul mood. The last place he wanted to be was at an old woman's birthday party. Having Tea suck his dick was the highlight of his night. But he felt disrespected by his older brother. Drip-Drip felt Rafe was becoming out-of-touch and soft—disconnected from the streets. He also felt that when Rafe agreed to pay Mob Allah and Zulu the money taken from the stash house, it brought a bad look to their crew. Rafe was more concerned with keeping the peace and making money than going to war. Drip-Drip was ready for war.

He stood there scowling, hearing the old-school music blaring. Everyone was dancing and laughing, including Rafe. And Tea was showing out in front of everyone, booty popping. He shook his head in disgust and muttered, "Fuck this."

Drip-Drip went marching toward the exit with his angry attitude palpable to everyone. Rafe turned to see his little brother leaving abruptly. He frowned at his brother's rudeness. Then he and Malik exchanged glances.

# Chapter Fourteen

The Wolf watched a batch of scantily-clad prostitutes walk the track in their high heels and toying smiles. The hookers filled the streets along the fringes of Queens Blvd. under the Queensboro Bridge, with their pimps keeping watch from the sidewalks. Then, when darkness had set in, it was time for the illegal after-hours sex trade in Long Island City. Prostitutes and Queens Plaza went together like peanut butter and jelly. Lookouts were roaming around; hookers were having sex on stoops, alleyways, and in parked cars—using the streets as bedrooms.

The traffic was heavy in an eight-block radius. The Wolf watched an assortment of hookers climb in and out of cars. He eyed the pimps strolling the sidewalks and the hookers walking in the street. His urges were strong, and he couldn't control them. He needed to fulfill his fantasy and curve his lust. They were all beautiful creatures, and their flesh was teasing—and they were sinners too. There was no cure for him. The lust he felt was overwhelming, and the Wolf needed it—his nourishment. He focused on the girls turning tricks and waited patiently for the right one.

It didn't take him long to find her. She was young and petite. Her hairstyle was in a high puff, and she was beautiful. She wore a short skirt and a skimpy halter top that left nothing to the imagination. The Wolf spotted her climbing out of a blue Lexus where she had just finished a date with the driver. He fixed his eyes on her as she approached her pimp on the sidewalk and handed him some cash. She then pivoted and went back to work.

The Wolf started the engine to the burgundy Honda Civic he was driving. It was unassuming. He waited until she was away from her pimp and the other batch of ladies, and then he steered the Civic away from the curb, determined to pick her up. He watched her cross the streets in her high heels, smiling and waving at passing cars. He hoped no one picked her up until he could introduce himself. He moved closer to her, and she turned the corner onto a less active block to his luck. The entire area was industrial, and even though it was late and closed, the traffic in the area mirrored rush hour because of the hookers.

He turned the corner and continued to watch her work the track. There was a vehicle ahead of him, a Toyota Camry. It slowed down to get the girl's attention, and the Wolf believed he'd missed his opportunity. The young hooker walked closer to the Camry, and a few words were exchanged, and to his surprise, the Camry drove away without her. He beamed. She continued to walk, and the Wolf wasn't about to miss his chance.

He maneuvered the Civic parallel to the young hooker with the passenger window already rolled down. Then, with his clean white teeth, he smiled her way and uttered, "Hello, beautiful."

She turned to take a peek inside the Civic to see a handsome, casually dressed Black male. He looked like a hardworking, married man, and he looked harmless.

"You lookin' for a date tonight?" she asked.

"I am," he replied brightly. "How much for your time?"

The young hooker moved closer to the car. She leaned into the passenger window to get a better look and feel him out. She noticed the wedding ring on his left hand and the car seat in the back. She deduced he was married with children and looking for some pussy before going home to his wife.

"It's $150 for everything, baby. You wanna feel paradise tonight?"

"Of course," he continued to beam.

He removed the cash from his person, which sealed the deal for her. She climbed into the passenger seat, and he drove away from the area.

"Where to?" he asked her.

"I know a quiet area."

She directed him to a secluded area in the vicinity where they could do their business. He parked at an isolated and dead-end street near the East River five minutes later. It was the perfect location. He paid her the $150 for her services, and she uttered, "You got fifteen minutes to bust a nut."

"What's your name?" he asked her.

"Coco."

"Lovely name."

She didn't care for the friendliness. It was strictly business. She unzipped his pants, slid a magnum condom on his erection, opened her mouth, and went to work on him. Immediately, the Wolf was thrust into absolute bliss. He moaned softly as more of his big dick went into her firm mouth. He watched her cheeks hollow, and he closed his eyes. He didn't move. She glanced up at him, and it was the typical reaction from her customers. Anytime now, she believed.

"I will not look with approval on anything vile. I hate what faithless people do. I will have no part in it," he uttered out of the blue with his eyes closed.

Coco thought it was weird, but she believed it was an odd perversion he had. She continued to suck his dick in the front seat until it was time for them to fuck in the back seat. She climbed into the back seat, but he hesitated for a moment, maybe having second thoughts. Then, the Wolf coolly exited from the front seat and moved into the back seat with Coco. As she was about to straddle him, she said, "You got eight minutes to come."

He nodded.

She straddled him, lowering herself on his dick, and he slid in deep. The Wolf started to groan as she rode him hard, bouncing up and down using her thighs and the headrest for support. Moans continued to rise from the back seat. He lifted her top to suckle her nipples and caress her breasts as she raised and lowered against him.

"Do not lust in your heart after her beauty or let her beauty captivate you with her eyes," he uttered another wacky verse.

The Wolf continued to keep his eyes closed. He gripped her riding hips and continued to groan and moan. He was about to come inside of her. Instead, he casually moved his hands from her hips and placed them around her neck. With his hands around Coco's neck, still penetrating her, facing forward, he uttered, "Do not lust in your heart after her beauty or let her beauty captivate you with her eyes."

"Nigga, you're getting weird on me," Coco voiced.

Their sexual tryst started to become rough. The Wolf began to squeeze as he fucked her, and Coco started to panic.

"Stop it," she cried out. "Get off me!"

Instead, he started to choke her while he was inside of her and expressed, "This is sin . . . This is death."

"Muthafucka, get the fuck off me," she yelled. She could feel him crushing the muscles in her neck, and her breathing was becoming restricted.

Coca clawed at his face to no avail. The Wolf was determined to strangle her to death while still fucking her. She started to thrash around in the back seat, fighting for her life. But her petite frame was no match for his bulging physique and his thirst to kill. And within a minute of his attack, she was dead. He snapped her neck like it was a twig, and her body slumped against him. Then, sickeningly, he continued to fuck her with her body limp and came inside her.

"See no evil, speak no evil," stated the Wolf.

It was an awakening for him as he relished her death. He then coolly climbed out of the back seat and opened the trunk of the car already lined with a tarp. He removed her body from the back seat and gently placed Coco into the trunk of the Civic onto the tarp. The Wolf briefly inspected the area and saw he was still alone. He took a deep breath and climbed back into the Civic.

He was soon long gone from the area with his newest victim.

# Chapter Fifteen

Mob Allah climbed out of the Mercedes-Benz E320 on Flatbush Avenue in downtown Brooklyn looking like he was on his way to court. The area was a compacted urban nucleus in the Brooklyn suburb of New York City. The sidewalks were crowded, and the shops were bustling with customers. Mob Allah was wearing a dark blue three-piece suit and black shoes. He moved from the Benz toward the restaurant with a purpose. It was a beautiful night, with the sky a tranquil black and the warm weather hugging you no matter what.

Mastro's Steakhouse was a high-end minichain serving steak, seafood, and sushi. It was flushed with customers enjoying the finest cuisine. Though he wore an expensive suit in the sea of respected faces, Mob Allah still carried that street's essence and a hard look. He searched the restaurant for two patrons and quickly found them seated to the far right in a stylish booth draped with cloth and flowers.

Sonja D'Agostino stood from the table to greet him. She was a beautiful woman with rich olive skin and long legs. She was a skilled defense attorney, and she was kept on retainer by Mob Allah and Zulu. Sonja smiled at Allah. The two locked eyes, indicating there was some history between them. When Allah faced a lengthy prison sentence, D'Agostino negotiated eight years instead of twenty.

"Allah, I want you to meet Michael Kostroff," she introduced.

Michael Kostroff stood from the table to greet him.

"Mr. Allah, it's good to meet you," Michael greeted, shaking his hand. "Sonja has told me many great things about you."

Mob Allah nodded slightly, remaining expressionless.

Kostroff was a Jewish property developer and corrupt political donor known for his shady business practices. He was a man who loved making money by any means necessary. Kostroff was immaculately dressed in a Brooks Brothers suit, and he knew how to work a room and make money.

"Gentlemen, let's sit and talk," D'Agostino suggested.

A lovely waitress walked to their table carrying a bottle of wine which she placed on the table.

"Adrianna Vineyard," Michael uttered. "Best overall wine."

Mob Allah didn't know too much about wine or Michael Kostroff; therefore, he was skeptical, sizing him up. However, Sonja vouched for him. Mob Allah had a vision, and he needed help, so he was ready to trust this meeting.

"I have two words for you," said Michael. "Economic feasibility. This city is changing and growing, and you can either grow with it and make some money or become one of the ones being pushed out and forgotten."

Sonja smiled.

Mob Allah nodded. He was listening. Then he asked, "And what is it that you do again, Michael?"

"I'm a property developer. My company is World Capital, and we take nothing and make it into something. It's called raw land development. Most people purchase land for the opportunity to build their dream home. But men like us, we see beyond the typical four-wall dwelling.

We have a vision . . . an out-of-the-box visionary who really wants to see our money go the distance," Michael Kostroff wholeheartedly proclaimed.

"Do you know where I come from, where my money comes from?" Mob Allah asked.

Michael smiled. "I don't care where it comes from. I only care where you invest it. Whether you're from the ghetto or Wall Street, everybody wants to get rich, right?"

"And with you just being released from prison, Allah, you should keep a low profile and stay away from the day-to-day activities," Sonja chimed.

"You can't be a drug dealer forever," said Michael.

Mob Allah sat there quietly for a moment, contemplating what was being said to him. Although Michael was Jewish and Sonja was Italian, Allah was a convicted felon, so a rainbow coalition was sitting at the table. And ironically, money and greed brought everyone together.

"I want to insulate you from further prosecution," Sonja expressed. "This is just the beginning of bigger things to come. We'll make it where you'll become larger than Donald Trump in this city."

Michael then added, "When it comes to flipping land, bigger is better. And with your money and my resources, we can own this city. They're changing the zoning laws in this city, and property value will triple within ten years. And flipping raw land is quicker and cheaper than any home remodel."

Mob Allah knew he was out of his element, but he was willing to learn, and he had his lawyer, Sonja, to guide him. He was a 29-year-old drug kingpin with tons of money to invest. In the past decade, Sonja represented him and members of her clients' organizations at various criminal trials, advising them on a defense strategy on charges from drug trafficking, murder, and unlawful possession of a weapon to parole violation. She was the real deal and great at her job. She also acted and advised for Mob Allah and Zulu's front organizations and now for Allah's real estate business. Sonja was corrupt and unscrupulous and very willing to aid her clients in furthering their criminal activities.

The trio continued to enjoy dinner at the steakhouse and talk business.

"This is your time to shine, Allah," Michael declared. "The information coming from city hall is accurate. It's about to become a new century in a few months, and this city will expand like a balloon. Sometimes, you don't need to do anything to make money with vacant land. The land will just sit there and behave while the rest of the market does the work."

Michael Kostroff had said a mouthful this evening. He was convincing, and Allah believed him.

"I'm in," Mob Allah said. "If Sonja trusts your vision, then I'll trust your vision. But don't fuck me. That's all I ask from you."

Michael and Sonja were excited. "You won't regret it," Michael assured him.

They raised their glasses and toasted to their new business opportunity. Mob Allah and Sonja stared at each other. The chemistry between them was strong, and she blushed.

After dinner, the trio exited the restaurant. Michael said his goodbyes and climbed into the back seat of a Lincoln Town Car. Mob Allah stared at Sonja in her black blazer and sophisticated skirt, with her expensive pearls shining. He said, "So, is this gonna be simply business or pleasure too?"

Sonja smiled. She stepped intimately closer to him, wrapped her arms around his neck, and uttered, "I missed you."

\*\*\*

Mob Allah followed Sonja into the lavish 1,800 square foot split-level suite with a large roof deck off the second-floor bedroom with views of the World Trade Center and the Empire State Building. The hotel's top-floor Sixty Loft was a dreamy urban retreat.

"Nice setup," he said.

"I knew you would like it," she replied.

It was a $4,500-a-night suite. Sonja pulled out all the stops for Mob Allah. She wanted to please and impress him. Not only was she his attorney, but the two had been in love and fucking each other for a decade. So, when Mob Allah was indicted for murder in 1990, Sonja D'Agostino came to his rescue. She was referred, took a liking to Mob Allah, and immediately went to work getting him acquitted on first-degree murder charges.

Sonja had the gift of gab and a razor-sharp tongue. Mob Allah had shot a man during an altercation outside of a nightclub. And the deceased happened to be a rival of his. The prosecutor tried to bring down the full hammer of justice on Mob Allah, but Sonja was there to curtail a "Guilty" verdict.

"I apologize for not making it to your welcome home party at the Q Club. I was out of town," she said. "And besides, I know you like to keep things low-key between us."

"You didn't miss much," Allah replied. "But I've been looking forward to this since I came home."

"I know you have."

Their mouths hungrily devoured each other's lips as their tongues battled for dominance. Finally, she undid his pants, and he unzipped her skirt. Right away, Sonja was on her back against the bed with Mob Allah climbing between her legs and thrusting himself inside of her. She gasped and held him tight.

"Fuck me," she cried out.

He felt her jerk around his dick with each deep penetration and her pussy pulsed nonstop. Sonja cooed underneath him. Her arms and legs tightened in a grip on his body. It felt like a greedy, gulping throat was sucking on his dick. Momentarily, her body shook beneath his as she orgasmed along with him.

When their orgasm finally rode its course, the two remained snuggled on the bed, and then Mob Allah's mobile phone rang. He answered. It was Zulu.

"What's up?"

"I figured you might want to talk to him before the inevitable happens," said Zulu.

"Where was he?" Mob Allah asked.

"Staying with a relative."

"I'll be there in an hour." Mob Allah ended the call and looked at Sonja.

"Business?" she asked him.

"Yeah."

She understood what "business" meant in his world. She didn't want to represent him in another murder case. Sonja wanted her lover to remain a free man. The two shared a passionate kiss, and then Mob Allah broke off the kiss and looked sadly into her eyes. Sonja still paraded the sight of devoted love and unadulterated hunger.

While he got dressed, she was smiling happily up at him.

# Chapter Sixteen

When Mob Allah descended into the concrete basement, the dungeon, he saw that their victim had already been severely beaten. Mob Allah looked fiercely at the naked, subdued man chained to a chair. This one he took personally because it was a betrayal to their organization. Big Will sat hunched over, bloody and beaten. He was barely breathing but still conscious. Finally, Drip-Drip gave up Big Will as his insider, and when he'd found out, Big Will fled the city and went hiding at his uncle's place in Philly.

The moment Big Will saw Mob Allah enter the basement, he cried out, "I'm . . . I'm sorry."

"You sorry, nigga? Yeah, you're sorry, muthafucka. You steal from us and think we wouldn't link it back to you?" Mob Allah uttered with contempt. "And to think, you was one of the first faces I saw when I was released from prison. It was all love. And the entire time, you was fuckin' me."

Big Will whimpered. "No one was supposed to get hurt."

"Yeah, well, your ambition is about to cost you your life," Mob Allah stated. "Fuck that. I want this nigga to suffer. You were *family*, nigga."

Mob Allah gave a head nod to one individual in the room, and he walked closer to Big Will. This man started to cut Big Will's face with a box cutter, and he shrieked in pain. But it was only the beginning of worse things to come. With deep lacerations on his face and blood running down, a cage filled with hungry rats was placed over his head. Their only source of food or escape was by eating their way through Big Will's face.

Right away, everyone in the basement heard the excruciating screams coming from Big Will as several rats gnawed and tore apart his face. It was nearly deafening to hear, and some cringed.

"Shit," Mackie uttered, wincing at the display.

Mob Allah angrily stared at everyone and shouted, "I'm not fuckin' around. You fuck with me or betray this organization and steal from us, I'm gonna go biblical and medieval on you. Now, find me this fool named Maurice."

They were listening and knew he meant it. Big Will's screams diminished and soon ended, indicating that he was dead. He no longer moved and slumped, but everyone could still hear the rats chewing his face.

No one wanted to see the outcome of the torture.

Sincere sat in the back seat of the cab for a moment and stared at a beautiful young mother picking up her son from school. The boy looked 4 years old. He was handsome and cheerful as he walked, holding his mother's hand. It was early afternoon in Hempstead, Long Island, and the nice weather brought the parents and kids to the parks. The town had a dense suburban feel with many bars, restaurants, coffee shops, and parks.

"What are we doing? Are we staying or leaving?" the cabbie asked Sincere.

Sincere reached into his pocket and pulled out a fifty-dollar bill. "Here," he uttered.

"It's your time and money," replied the cabbie.

It was more than enough to keep the cabbie idling nearby. Sincere continued to watch the mother and child cross the street, going toward the playground. Excited, the boy released himself from his mother's hand and raced toward the playground to play with the other children. His mother watched from the side, smiling.

*She's more beautiful than ever,* Sincere thought. *And she looks peaceful and happy with her son.*

It had been four years, and Monica was still beautiful. His mind and thoughts were racing with so many things. Did she have someone in her life? Did she think about him? Did she miss him? What was her son like? And was that *his* son?

Sincere watched her move about the playground wearing a vibrant printed maxi dress and sandals. Monica was just the sort of woman blessed with heavenly curves in all the right places. She was five foot eight, with skin the color of bronze, almond-shaped eyes, and hair styled in Bantu knots. He watched her be a mother by pushing her son on the swings, playfully chasing him around the playground, and lightly wrestling with him. He was captivated by them in even the little moments.

Sincere smiled at the playful action. He was nervous about showing up suddenly and was concerned about Monica's reaction. If it weren't for her little sister, Sincere wouldn't know where she had relocated. Monica's sister, Theresa, always had a soft spot for Sincere. He believed Theresa had a crush on him. So, when he ran into her on Jamaica Avenue, the two conversed, and, of course, Sincere asked about Monica. Theresa was happy to tell him where she was.

"You know, you either do it or don't. But you can't wait around here watching that woman with her son forever," the cabbie stated.

Sincere knew he was right. He took a deep breath, opened the rear door, and climbed out of the taxi. Clad in beige cargo shorts, a T-shirt, and sneakers, Sincere nervously headed toward the playground carrying a toy truck with him. While watching her son go down the slide, Monica turned to see Sincere approaching them, and she recognized him immediately. But enthusiasm didn't show across her face. Instead, she frowned.

Right away, she asked Sincere, "How did you find me?"

He nervously smiled and replied, "Your sister, Theresa. She told me."

"She always did like you."

"You still look beautiful," he said.

"Don't," Monica quickly voiced. "You think you can win me over with compliments and a toy truck for your son?"

"So, he *is* my son?"

Monica huffed. "Yes. I never fucked Mighty, no matter what people thought. And it's been four years. So you just up and leave, Sincere . . . join the army and get to see the world and leave me behind pregnant and in tears. So what do you want from us?"

"I just wanna talk, Monica."

"Now, you wanna talk," she griped.

"Yes. I'm sorry for the way I left things; I truly am. A lot was going on, and I just needed to go. I couldn't handle it."

Monica bit her lip, trying very hard not to show the anger or distress she was feeling. He had abandoned them.

"And so, you just leave," she uttered.

"Mommy," her son cried out, running toward her. He immediately clung to his mother's leg and stared up at Sincere. "Who's he?"

"He's just a friend of Mommy's," Monica replied.

"Hey, there, little guy. What's your name?" asked Sincere.

"Tyriq," he answered.

"I like that name," said Sincere. "I got something for you."

Sincere handed him the toy truck, and Tyriq's eyes lit up.

"Thank you," said Tyriq.

"Tyriq, go play and let Mommy finish talking to her friend."

Tyriq nodded and ran off with his new toy in his hands. Monica stared at her son with a smile for a fleeting moment. Then she shifted her irate gaze back to Sincere. "What do you want from us, Sincere?"

"I wanna be in his life. I wanna be in *your* life," he answered honestly.

"Don't you think it's too late for that? You wanted me to get an abortion. You believed I was with Mighty, and you were gone for four years. *Now,* you want to make things right?"

"It's never too late, Monica. Let me become a father to my son," Sincere uttered earnestly.

Monica sighed and stared at him. She was upset, but it was clear that she still had strong feelings for him.

# Chapter Seventeen

Sincere followed Monica and Tyriq into the two-bedroom apartment on Front Street. It was a modest apartment attractively decorated with a woman's touch. It was a home, and it was comfortable.

"Nice place," Sincere complimented.

"It's affordable," Monica returned nonchalantly.

"I like it."

Tyriq ran into his bedroom to play with his new toy. Sincere and Monica stayed in the living room. Being sarcastic, Monica uttered, "Do you want a tour of the place?"

Sincere chuckled. "Sure."

Monica pointed, "There's the kitchen, the hallway, the bathroom, and the bedrooms are down the hall."

"You always had a sardonic sense of humor," he said.

"And you always got on my damn nerves," Monica countered. "Would you like something to drink . . . soda, juice, water?"

"I'll take water."

Monica turned and went into the kitchen, and Sincere's attention lingered on her curvy backside. He slightly exhaled, knowing it would hurt to find out if she was in a relationship. And he wondered if he should tell Monica about his daughter in Japan. Would she be upset with him about Asuka and his daughter, Akari?

Sincere took a seat on her couch and looked around. He was happy that Monica was in a better place and away from Jamaica, Queens. He wanted to put the drama behind them and start fresh if possible. He'd missed four years of his son's life. Now, ironically, with him being back in the States, he would miss out on Akari's life. Sincere huffed, thinking about his dilemma. If only things could be so simple, but they weren't.

Monica walked out of the kitchen carrying bottled water and a bottle of wine. She handed Sincere his water and then took a seat opposite of him.

"Wine, huh?" Sincere uttered.

"Yes, it relaxes me. And don't worry, I'm a casual drinker."

"I'm not judging you."

"You shouldn't."

Sincere sighed, having something on his mind. "Listen, there's something I need to tell you," he voiced uneasily.

"I'm listening," Monica replied solemnly.

He decided not to sugarcoat things and beat around the bush. Instead, he confessed, "While I was stationed in Japan, I had a daughter."

Monica was taken aback. "You had a what?" she uttered in disbelief.

"I wanted to be honest with you."

"You have a daughter? Wow." She groaned. "I didn't see *that* coming."

"Her name is Akari."

"A-kari," Monica tried to pronounce. "So, you left us, fucked some Asian bitch, and now you have an Asian kid."

*That was rude,* he thought. But he knew Monica was hurt. She couldn't hide it.

"What's the mother's name?" she asked him.

"Asuka."

Monica marginally chuckled at the name. "Asuka. You're just full of surprises today, Sincere."

Sincere heaved a sigh and said, "I want another chance with you, Monica. I wanna start over, be a family. This time, I'm not going anywhere."

"Be a family?" Monica expressed irately. "So, I'm supposed to tell Tyriq that he's got a half-chink sister on the other side of the fuckin' planet?"

"Monica, that's *not* nice. She's *still* my daughter," he chided.

"You know what?" Monica uttered, standing to her feet, clearly emotional from the news. "Just leave, Sincere. Please."

"Look, I know you're upset."

"Oh, I'm far past upset. Look, nigga, you didn't even want Tyriq to be born, and you left like I wasn't shit to you. So, now you come back here and tell me that you have a daughter in Japan, and I'm supposed to forgive you and play family and house with you?" Monica exclaimed. "Fuck you, Sincere."

Hearing his mother shout brought Tyriq into the living room. "Mommy, are you okay?" he asked.

"No, your mommy is not okay," Monica uttered, tears trickling down her cheeks.

Tyriq went to his mother to hug her. Monica hugged him back. It was an emotional moment that Sincere witnessed. He sighed.

"I didn't come here to cause any trouble. So I'll leave," he said.

Sincere walked toward the door, but before he could leave, he heard Monica say to him, "I'm still in love with you, Sincere. I have *always* been in love with you."

He stopped, pivoted, and Monica stared at him with her tear-stained face and watery eyes. The two looked at each other, knowing they had some unresolved issues that they needed to fix if they were going to work out. But Sincere was torn too, thinking about Asuka and his daughter. Could both these worlds coincide with each other?

# Chapter Eighteen

Maurice ascended from the subway station at the intersection of Sutphin and Archer and looked around for the nearest cab. Then, with a handgun tucked snuggly in his waistband, he climbed into the back seat of a dollar cab and gave the driver twenty dollars.

"Fuck them other fares. I'm paying you to take me to a certain location," said Maurice.

The driver nodded. Twenty dollars was more than enough for him to drive Maurice wherever he wanted to go. So, he started the vehicle and drove off. Maurice sat back but remained alert. He wasn't supposed to be in Queens, but he needed to see his girlfriend, Shawanda. He hadn't seen her in two weeks, and he missed her. Sincere advised him to never come to Queens until he could figure something out, but Maurice defied his brother's instructions. Besides, Shawanda had called him earlier, and she seemed troubled by something. She told Maurice that she needed to see him. It was urgent.

Maurice knew that being back in Jamaica, Queens, he was back in the lions' den. The Bronx wasn't the safest place for him to lie low, but no one knew him there. He was staying with their older cousin, Sean, who was a square and a postal worker. Sean didn't have a problem with Maurice, as long as Maurice didn't bring any trouble into his home.

The cab moved down Sutphin Blvd. with Maurice's attention on a swivel. It was late in the evening with a warm breeze, and the wispy clouds above seemed to be painted, making it look unreal with the sun in the process of setting. Yet, with summer right around the corner, the neighborhood was acting like a Saturday at Great Adventures.

The cab maneuvered through the neighborhood as Maurice remained quiet in the back seat and stared aimlessly out the window. He had a lot on his mind, and his conversation earlier with Shawanda troubled him.

He soon arrived at Shawanda's place in Queens. She lived in Hollis with her grandmother and nephew. Maurice climbed out of the dollar cab and walked toward the apartment building. He moved through the lobby and pressed for the elevator. He kept his gun close the entire time, and his head continued on a swivel. Though he was in Hollis, it was still Queens, and Mob Allah and Zulu had reach, money, and influence.

Maurice stepped off onto the fifth floor and continued toward Shawanda's apartment. He felt apprehensive as he knocked on her door and waited. He wished he could go back to that night and change the past. But it was impossible to do so. Now, he was dealing with the consequences. Finally, the door opened, and Shawanda appeared, smiling.

"Hey, you," she greeted him.

"You okay?" he asked.

Shawanda nodded. "Yes. But we need to talk."

Everything seemed copasetic. Shawanda opened the door wider and stepped aside. Maurice entered the apartment . . . and the moment he did so, he saw that it was a mistake. Zulu's goons were present, holding Shawanda and her grandmother hostage. Maurice's eyes widened with fear, and he quickly reached for his gun. One of Zulu's goons tackled him like a linebacker drilling a quarterback from the blindside, a clean shoulder-to-shoulder hit. The weapon clattered from Maurice's hand and skittered on the floor. Three men suddenly attacked

Maurice. Then someone smashed an elbow into the side of his skull.

They had caught him off guard and beat him sense-lessly.

Shawanda cried as she witnessed the beating. "I'm sorry, Maurice," she cried out.

Maurice could barely move. He lay in the middle of the living room like a rag doll.

"Pick that nigga up and get him the fuck outta here," Mackie said.

Two men dragged Maurice out of the apartment as Shawanda and her grandmother helplessly looked on. They couldn't do anything about it. Then finally, Mackie turned and stared at them. They were at his mercy.

"What are you gonna do with him?" Shawanda fright-fully asked.

"Fuck him. Y'all need to be concerned about y'all selves," Mackie replied.

"They saw what went down here, and they saw our faces," one goon said to Mackie. "I'm not tryin'a have anything linked back to us."

Mackie nodded, knowing what was being said—no witnesses. He stared at the two women, aimed his gun at the grandmother first, and fired—*Bak, bak!* He then shot Shawanda in the head twice. Finished, they left the apart-ment with Shawanda slumped against her grandmother. It was a cold-blooded murder.

It was a romantic moment between Sincere and Monica. The two took a bubble bath together, with Tyriq asleep in his bedroom. The two had spent a week together, and they'd rekindled their relationship by making intense love and having great conversations. Sincere was blissful with Monica, and he was happy to spend some quality time with his son, getting to know him.

Sincere held Monica in his arms as they relaxed in the warm bubble bath. His heart began to pound. He felt a desire run from his heart to his chest and down toward his stomach. His fingers touched Monica's neck. He moved her hair away and kissed the back of her neck, giving her chills. Then he kissed her shoulder, ran his lips against her skin toward her ear, and nibbled at it.

Monica laughed. She tilted her head, closed her eyes, and exhaled. Sincere cupped her breast as he continued to nibble at her ear.

"I love you," he declared.

"You do?"

"Yes," he said.

"I love you too," she proclaimed.

It was a pleasant moment between them, and neither wanted it to end soon. Monica turned around in the tub so that they were facing each other. She stared into his eyes and smiled. Sincere's eyes exuded love, protection, patience, longing, and respect. He grabbed her hands gently yet firmly, placed them in front of her, and paused. He didn't say a word. Instead, he smiled and then let go of her hands. He ran his fingers through her hair with one hand and gently guided her face closer to his, eventually leaning her in to rest her head on his chest.

Monica then straddled him, and he was soon inside of her. His arms wrapped around her as they both moaned. The two became fastened together by penetrating passion. Sincere suckled at her breast and continued to hold her, never wanting to let her go.

"Aaaah," he moaned.

Monica's heart was about to beat out of her chest as she kept her eyes closed, feeling his erection swell inside of her. She exhaled deeply. And while she was pressed against his chest, she could feel his heart pound.

After their lovemaking inside the bathtub, the two toweled off and continued things inside the bedroom.

It was late, but Sincere had nowhere else to be. So they continued to fuck until they were exhausted. Then they snuggled together with pillow talk.

"Japanese people are all extremely polite and are very obedient to laws. You can leave a purse or wallet on a street corner during a parade and just walk around. Unless some other Americans steal it, it will still be there," he told Monica.

"Really?"

"It's a huge country, with plenty to do in the cities, and the countryside is beautiful with plenty of hiking and skiing and other outdoor sports."

Monica's head was against his chest, listening to him talk about his time in Japan.

"Bars, even in Tokyo, are hilariously small compared to American ones. Not a joke; dancing is illegal in Japan unless the club has a permit," said Sincere.

"Wow. Really?"

"Yeah . . . That's crazy. It makes you appreciate the liberties we have here," he said.

And then she asked, "And how did you meet her, Asuka?"

It was an uncomfortable question to answer with the woman he loved. But he'd already opened Pandora's box. What Monica didn't know, and what Sincere wasn't about to tell her, was that he'd asked Asuka to marry him, but she'd turned down his proposal.

"At a bar," he admitted.

"A bar . . . ?"

"Yeah. She spoke English, and I liked her conversation. One thing led to another, and our daughter was born," he explained it coolly to her.

Monica remained silent. Even though she accepted the situation with Asuka, it was difficult for her to hear about Sincere's foreign relations. But now they were together, and surprisingly, she was happy with him. And her attitude toward his daughter had changed. She even stated, "Well, one day, I would like for Tyriq to meet his sister."

Sincere smiled. "I would like that too."

While the two remained nestled in her bed, Sincere's mobile phone started to ring, interrupting their moment. He sighed and grudgingly answered the call. It was Nasir.

"What's up?"

"Yo, I got some bad news," said Nasir gloomily. "Maurice is dead."

The news was shocking to Sincere. It jolted him from the bed with the phone still glued to his ear. "What? What the fuck are you talking about, Nasir?"

"They found his body, and it's not pretty."

Monica stared at Sincere with concern and asked, "Sincere, what's going on?"

He ignored her. He was beside himself with grief. It felt like he had a panic attack. His heart started racing, and he was experiencing shortness of breath.

"Sincere, talk to me. What happened?"

He continued to ignore her. Then he said to Nasir, "I'll be back in Queens in twenty minutes. Meet me."

"No doubt."

Sincere ended the call, and his eyes were watery like a river. The look he had on his face was disbelief and heartbreak. He looked at Monica and said, "Maurice is dead."

Monica gasped. "Oh my god! What happened?"

"I don't know, but I'm gonna definitely find out."

Monica leaped from the bed and went to him to console him. She wrapped her arms around Sincere and held him as he collapsed to the floor in deep grief.

"I'm here, baby. I'm here," she said with her arms around Sincere like a blanket.

# Chapter Nineteen

Maurice's body was found in the trunk of a car in Queens, and it was the same MO as Voltron's demise. He had been tortured and mutilated with cigarette burns, broken bones, cavernous cuts, and deep bruises. It was gruesome to look at.

"Damn, they killed this kid six different times," an officer stated.

It was apparent that the cause of death was a gunshot wound to the head; stippling and powder burns surrounded the wound, indicating close contact. They tortured him first, then shot him.

The entire area was restricted and isolated with yellow crime scene tape as onlookers stared from a safe distance. There was gossip amongst the crowd. Another body was found in the trunk of a car within two weeks. It definitely wasn't a coincidence. CSI collected evidence and snapped pictures as homicide detectives were investigating the scene, knowing the body was dumped there to leave a message in the community.

"Do we have an identification of the body?" a detective asked.

"No," an officer replied.

It was a spectacle. When the body was removed from the trunk to be transferred for physical examination, an onlooker uttered, "Yo, I think that's Maurice, Sincere's little brother."

"What?" someone replied.

"I know that jacket."

Everyone was putting two and two together, knowing Maurice was friends with Voltron and Drip-Drip. The streets were talking, and it became public knowledge about the home invasion and killings of four people at a stash house on Long Island. Maurice's fingerprints were all over that one. And since Mob Allah's release from state prison, bodies started dropping.

The body was removed from the trunk, placed into a body bag, and transported to the examiner's office. Then the car that the body was in was towed away.

Sincere arrived at the scene too late. The coroners had already removed his brother's body. So, he did a hundred-yard dash from Monica's Ford Taurus to the restricted crime scene. Seeing the remnants of a crime scene sent Sincere into hyperdrive. He was about to charge through the area like a bull, but uniformed officers immediately grabbed and stopped him.

"You can't go any farther," said a cop, trying to hold him back.

"Get the fuck off me! That's my little brother they found," Sincere yelled.

Sincere fought with them as they continued to hold him back. He had the strength of a bull as he was overwhelmed with grief. He pushed forward while tears welled up in his eyes.

"Get off me," he continued to yell.

More cops were needed to restrain him, and finally, he was forced to the ground and overpowered. But his cries echoed throughout the street, with him sounding like a wounded animal. Sincere's grief felt endless, and it was displayed for everyone to see.

"Just calm down, sir," an officer shouted.

But they didn't understand; his little brother was dead. All at once, Sincere felt shocked, denial, and disbelief.

And then came the anger and hostility. *How did this happen?* His brother was supposed to be in the Bronx. *So why did he come back to Queens?* He tried to make sense of it, but he couldn't. He wanted to blame something or someone for his brother's death.

At that very moment, Sincere vowed revenge. He wanted to kill anyone that had a hand in his little brother's death.


The last thing Sincere wanted to do was tell his mother about Maurice. He was afraid that Janet would fall into bottomless grief and relapse into drug use. But there was no easy way to tell a mother that her son was dead. However, when he walked through the front door to his home, two detectives had already beaten him to the punch. Janet was sitting on the couch in tears, and Denise was grieving uncontrollably. Janet stared at Sincere and exclaimed, "Oh my god! Oh my god! No."

Right away, Sincere hurried to console his mother and sister. Both detectives stood up to give them some space. It was something the detectives did too many times, informing the family about the tragic loss of a loved one. Still, it was something they could never get used to doing. It didn't get easier.

"We're sorry for your loss," said Detective McMillian.

The detectives were polite, professional, and they seemed like they cared about the case. But no matter what Maurice had been into, he was still a victim. He was murdered, and they had a case to solve.

"Did your son have any enemies that y'all knew about?" Detective Benjamin asked.

Of course, he did.

"He was a good kid," Janet cried out.

Sincere knew who was responsible, but he refused to tell the detectives anything. Instead, he replied, "Nah, I don't know. I just came back home from the army. And besides, now is not the time, Detectives."

"We understand. Unfortunately, we're going to need someone to come down to the morgue to identify the body and retrieve his possessions."

Sincere nodded.

"Here's my card in case you have any questions or further information," said Detective Benjamin.

The two detectives exited the home while Sincere was left behind to console his family. But they were inconsolable. Maurice was gone, and everyone wondered how they would fill the gap left in their lives. Heartache had hit them immediately and with full force. And for Sincere, he was experiencing a sense of changed identity.

Sincere was tasked with identifying his brother's body at the morgue. He sat in a bland room with no religious iconography like crosses. They weren't allowed anywhere there to not upset families. Although they'd gotten the news that Maurice was dead, it still didn't feel real for Sincere until he saw his brother's body. A morgue attendant entered the room carrying a photograph, and he took a seat opposite Sincere.

He calmly explained to Sincere what he would see to minimize shock.

"I'm simply here to help," said the attendant.

Sincere sat there indifferently. The morgue attendant then placed the photograph face down in front of him and said, "Just take your time and view it at your own pace."

Sincere took a deep breath. He understood that there was no turning back once he flipped over the photograph to identify the body. Janet and Denise refused to do it. He was given all the time needed to work up his courage. It was all about making the experience as nontraumatic as possible. He closed his eyes briefly, maybe hoping this wasn't real. Finally, Sincere reached for the photograph and turned it over. His eyes rested on the picture of Maurice with his eyes closed on a table. There was a tattoo on his right chest and one on his right arm. Sincere could identify him.

He nodded. "Yeah, it's him."

He flipped the photograph back over and remained unruffled.

Subsequently, the morgue attendant offered to direct him and his family to grief counseling if needed. But instead, Sincere coolly lifted himself from the chair and walked out of the room. He left the building feeling a mixture of sadness, anger, guilt, and everything in between. Some people seek help immediately by showing their emotions and talking to people. But Sincere decided to deal with his grief his own way . . . slowly, quietly, and by himself—and lethally.

He wanted revenge.

# Chapter Twenty

An associate named Bings walked up to Drip-Drip as he sat at the bar inside the pool hall with his drink and conversed with a lovely young lady. While Drip-Drip was engaged in a conversation, Bings leaned into his ear and said, "Maurice is dead. They found his body."

Drip-Drip remained apathetic to the news. He simply shrugged it off and went back to talking to the girl next to him. He didn't want to think about it because he only wanted to think about pussy tonight.

Big Pockets was a pool hall/bar owned by Rafe. It was a place to go to kill time or win some money. It was a smoky place in Queens occupied by an assortment of characters. Rafe was a skilled pool player with a passion for the game, and sometimes he would host pool tournaments at his establishment.

The place was magic for Drip-Drip if he wanted to idle away an evening. He loved the atmosphere with the sounds of colliding balls and winners shit-talking. At Big Pockets, nearly everyone knew everyone there. It was a place where someone could quickly get a nickname or feel a sense of kin. But there was also a dark side to the pool hall. It was a place where Rafe cultivated his disciples into a crew experienced with the process of murdering and dismembering victims in the basement. The streets dubbed the basement to the pool hall "No-man's-land" because down in the cellar, for men and women, once you entered it, there was a pervading atmosphere of "fear or uncertainty."

While Drip-Drip was conversing with the young lady and Rafe was engaged in a game of pool, Detectives Arron McMillian and Spencer Benjamin entered the pool hall on business. They both were white males in their mid-thirties. Detective McMillian was grizzled and capable, and Benjamin was reserved, sharp, and assertive.

Right away, the detectives stood out like Muslims at a Klan rally. All eyes were glued on them. The detectives scanned the room looking for someone while Rafe stopped playing his game and grilled both cops like they were some kind of antichrist. They immediately spotted Drip-Drip by the bar and made a beeline his way. Rafe was right behind them when he saw them going for his little brother.

"Drip-Drip, right?" Detective Benjamin asked.

"What the fuck y'all want?" Drip-Drip griped.

"We'll need you to come down to the station to answer a few questions for us," McMillian chimed in.

"Fuck y'all," Drip-Drip cursed. "I ain't goin' nowhere."

"You wanna play this game with us?" Detective McMillian said.

Rafe walked behind the detectives and asked, "What y'all want with my little brother?"

Detective Benjamin turned to Rafe and replied, "You can come down to the precinct with him to find out."

"This is a place of business, Detective. My business. Do y'all have an arrest warrant for him?" asked Rafe.

"No, we don't. But I'm sure if you want to make things difficult for us, we can come back here tomorrow with a search warrant for the entire place and turn over some rocks and see what we can find. Or maybe we can place this pool hall under investigation. I've heard the stories," Detective Benjamin sternly countered.

Rafe pouted and huffed. The last thing he needed was cops in his business. He glanced at Drip-Drip with reluctance and uttered, "Go with them."

"Are you fuckin' crazy?" Drip-Drip contested. "Fuck these pigs."

He was defiant and hardheaded. Rafe glared at him and sternly stated, "I *said* go with them for now, and I'll send a lawyer to meet you there."

Drip-Drip scowled like he'd swallowed an onion. He leaped from the barstool with an attitude and unwillingness. Everyone was watching them as the detectives escorted him out of the building and into the back seat of an unmarked police car. Rafe watched as his little brother was being driven away. When the vehicle turned the corner and disappeared from his view, he turned to Malik and said, "Get in contact with our fuckin' lawyer and tell that fool to meet me at the police station. These clowns wanna fuck with my little brother." Then Rafe heaved a worried sigh, and Malik nodded. He was on it right away.

Mob Allah, Sonja D'Agostino, Michael Kostroff, and an investment banker named Anthony Patrick walked the lengthy boardwalk in Far Rockaway, Queens, discussing business. It was a beautiful evening with a gorgeous sunset that blossomed upon the horizon with red and gold. Far Rockaway was one of the farthest-flung parts of the city, isolated and nearly forgotten. It was plagued with more poor and poverty-stricken neighborhoods than wealthy, with a growing crime rate and underdeveloped areas. But the advantages of Far Rockaway were the beaches along the ten-mile peninsula.

Summer was encroaching. The area would blossom into an unlikely beach town with cafes, boardwalk snack shacks, and surf shops catering to locals and visitors coming en masse from Brooklyn and Manhattan by subway, car, or ferry.

"This entire area will be unrecognizable in the next ten to twenty years," Michael Kostroff stated. "Some big-name developers are taking notice of the area's investment potential. This is the time to get in while we can."

Mob Allah was listening.

"The majority of this area will be rezoned for commercial use, meaning we're about to make a part of this town look like South Beach, Miami," said Michael. "Picture it . . . luxury condos, high-risers, nightclubs, and cafes. And not just here. We're talking *everywhere* in this city, downtown Brooklyn, Harlem, the Bronx . . . Gentrification on such a wide scale, you'll be making money even when you're fucking or taking a shit."

Everyone laughed. Mob Allah remained quiet. He pictured what Michael was saying to him. It was the opportunity he needed to expand and become untouchable. What is wealth without power and influence? Wealth is, simply put, an accumulation of resources. And power is the ability to exert control over one's environment or other entities. He controlled the streets. Now, he wanted to control society. He wanted the best of both worlds—to become a Black real estate developer *and* drug kingpin.

"Owning waterfront property is the way to the future, gentlemen," uttered Michael wholeheartedly.

Sonja smiled at Mob Allah and asked, "Are you feeling the proposal?"

"I am," he replied.

Michael concluded his pitch, and Mob Allah and Sonja walked toward Mackie, waiting by the SUV on the street. Before Mob Allah could climb into the back seat of the SUV, Mackie said to him, "Detectives picked up Drip-Drip. Probably want to question him about Maurice."

"And what does that have to do with me?" Mob Allah replied.

"I just figured you would want to know."

"That thing with Rafe and his brother is old news. Look around you, Mackie. This is our future, not some bullshit," Mob Allah stated.

Mob Allah got into the back seat of the SUV with Sonya climbing in right behind him.

Mackie was Mob Allah's chief lieutenant, and he was extremely loyal. He was a street nigga, not a businessman, and he had no clue about real estate or investments. He did what he was told, including murder. He got behind the wheel of the Escalade and drove away.

While Mob Allah and Sonja were in the back seat overhearing what Mackie had said, Sonja looked at Allah. Then she asked, "Should I be worried about something?"

"About what?"

"A woman and her grandmother were found murdered inside their apartment in Hollis. And there was a second body found in the trunk of a car in your old neighborhood," Sonja mentioned.

"People are savages, Sonja. Unfortunately, it's the world we live in."

"But try not to let it become *your* world anymore, Allah. As your lawyer, I advise you to separate yourself from it if you're serious about doing business with Michael. The last thing we need is to scare him off and everyone else. They like you. I can tell. But if they become spooked by anything, especially murders, they'll drop you like a bad habit," she proclaimed.

"There's nothing for you to worry about, baby. I got this," Mob Allah assured her. "We just had to tie up some loose ends. And from here on, it's all business."

"I don't need to hear anything incriminating, though I'm bonded by the attorney-client privilege. I just want you to be protected and safe," she uttered.

"Enough business talk, bae. It's an hour until we get to the city, meaning we have some spare time, right?"

Sonja grinned. "And what do you have in mind?"

Mob Allah unzipped his pants and pulled out his big dick. Sonja beamed. And in her dark blue pencil skirt suit set, she leaned forward into his lap. She took his erection into her mouth, right away deep throating him, creating a sensual moan from Allah.

"That's my girl," he moaned.

Mackie continued to drive, minding his own business while hearing the sexual deed take place right behind him. He occasionally glanced in the rearview mirror to see an $800-an-hour criminal and business attorney sucking dick. Mob Allah had the best of both worlds for real.

"Ugh, I'm gonna come," Mob Allah announced.

Sonja didn't let up and swallowed every ounce of his semen so none would get on her expensive suit.

# Chapter Twenty-one

Sincere sighed as he stared at his image in the mirror. He was dressed in a black suit, preparing himself for his little brother's funeral. He felt that he had no more tears left to shed, but the pain and grief he felt continued to wrap around him like the skin he was in. It flowed through him like a river in mountain passes, eroding him from the inside. Sincere was in a pit of darkness, and there was no escaping it. It had been a week since Maurice was murdered, and the family had to scrape every last dime together to bury him. Nasir helped with the funeral expenses, and the family was grateful.

Sincere stepped out of his bedroom with a deadpan look. Everyone was waiting for him downstairs—everyone except Janet. He went to her room and opened her door to find his mother still grieving alone on her bed. The blinds were closed, and the bedroom was dark. Janet hid underneath the covers suffering from severe depression. It was clear to Sincere that she didn't want to go to her son's funeral.

"Ma, are you coming?" he asked.

"Leave me the fuck alone and close my fuckin' door," she yelled.

Sincere sighed. This is what he was afraid of. He feared his mother might fall into a deep depression and relapse into drug use. He didn't want his mother to be alone.

"You need to say goodbye to him," he expressed.

"They killed him. They fuckin' killed my baby. My baby, he's gone," Janet cried out. "Get the fuck out."

There was no changing her mind. Janet refused to attend her son's funeral. Defeated, Sincere backed out of the bedroom and closed her door. He lingered there for a moment knowing the inevitable was coming. He clenched his fists and punched the wall with rage, creating a gaping hole in it. What they did to Maurice was overkill. They'd tortured him for no reason but just to do it. And then they disposed of his body like trash on the street. Quickly, Sincere collected himself, knowing he couldn't attend Maurice's funeral filled with rage. Besides, everyone was waiting for him, and Monica and Tyriq were downstairs.

Sincere pivoted and went down to see everyone. Monica and Tyriq were his core. The moment Monica saw Sincere, she stood up from the couch to greet him with a warm and calm hug. He breathed in her arms and remained composed. Nasir, Denise, and a few relatives and friends were standing in the living room waiting to leave to bury Maurice.

"Let's just go and get it over with," Sincere said half-heartedly.

Springfield Cemetery in Queens was a sprawling, old Jewish cemetery. Over a dozen people gathered around the burial site. Maurice's casket was an oversized twenty-six-inch cloth-covered blue coffin. His funeral and burial weren't over-the-top but straightforward, with a few flowers and grieving mourners.

While the groundskeepers lowered the casket into the ground, the pastor recited a few words, saying, "Death is an event, not a destination. His end here on earth is the beginning of an eternity in the presence of our God. Find comfort in God. Many of God's blessings . . . all through our lives . . . are delivered in our circumstances, events, and, most importantly, in the people He places in our lives. For God so loved the world, that He gave His only begotten Son, that whoever believes in Him shall not perish but have everlasting life."

Sincere's eyes were covered by dark shades, but his attention was fixed on the casket lowered into the ground. Monica was by his side with their son, with dismay on their faces. Not once did Sincere shed a tear. He heard the preacher talk about God, but he didn't believe in God right now. Instead, he believed in vengeance and retribution. His little brother's killers took away something meaningful from Sincere—a second chance with Maurice.

With Maurice's casket in the ground, the preacher completed the service, and everyone started to depart. But Sincere lingered by his brother's grave in silence. He then quietly said, "I won't let them forget you, little brother. I promise you that. They'll pay for what they did to you."

Saying that, he finally pivoted and left.

Everyone arrived home that evening, ready to unwind the best they could. The house was quiet, and the first thing Sincere did was hurry upstairs to check on his mother. He pushed open her bedroom door to find her gone.

"Shit," he mumbled to himself.

Sincere feared the worst, knowing his mother left to get high somewhere. He took a seat at the edge of the bed and hunched over with his elbows against his knees. When he thought he couldn't cry anymore, tears welled up in his eyes, and a few tears streamed down his cheeks.

The sadness raided his heart as if it were his emotional piggy bank, then smashed it with rage when it was all gone. Sincere's sadness was evidence that he absolutely loved his family. Now, he felt not only did he lose his brother, but he lost his mother once again.

# Chapter Twenty-two

Tucked beneath the dark gray sky was a gloomy summer day. Nevertheless, Drip-Drip walked out of the Queens precinct in good spirits. Though he'd been detained twenty-four hours for questioning, he was finally released and ready to start his day. As he trekked down the stairs to the precinct, he shouted, "Fuck the police. All y'all pigs can suck my dick."

Rafe was standing on the sidewalk, waiting for his release. He frowned at Drip-Drip's loud comment in front of the police station. He thought his little brother would never learn. He was naïve and reckless.

"What is *wrong* with you?" Rafe asked his brother.

"What you mean?"

"Why do you have to be so fuckin' stupid and reckless?"

"What? You mean when I shouted, 'Fuck the police'?" Drip-Drip repeated loudly. "I ain't scared of these fuckin' racist pigs."

"Get the fuck in the car, nigga," Rafe scolded him.

Drip-Drip smirked as he climbed into the passenger seat of the Lexus RX 300. Rafe got behind the wheel and left from in front of the precinct, chop-chop. As he drove, the sky opened up. Next came a tapping on the window, and then it became a pitter-patter—a downpour. The rain rudely thumped on the Lexus's roof as people ran for cover outside and opened umbrellas. Puddles began plinking as the rainfall became heavier.

Drip-Drip watched the poor suckers who had been caught in the rain and scoffed at them.

"What did they want to question you about?" Rafe asked out of the blue.

"Some murder," Drip-Drip replied indifferently. "I ain't had shit to do with it, though."

"Who's?"

"Maurice."

Rafe sighed. "Look, I want you to start keeping a low profile," he suggested.

"For what? I'm not running from anyone or anything," Drip-Drip argued.

"This isn't about running, muthafucka. It's about being smart. Things are changing with Mob Allah home, and I don't trust him."

"I thought y'all had an understanding between you two. Y'all niggas had that meeting, right? And fuck that fool. He can get got too."

"And what about the cops? They can get got too?" Rafe uttered to his brother sarcastically.

"I don't give a fuck 'bout the cops."

"But they give a fuck about you. And they'll find any excuse to lock your dumb, black ass up," said Rafe.

Drip-Drip scowled. He didn't want to be told what to do.

The rain continued to cascade down on the city, sounding like a buzzing of angry bees as the raw wind whistled through the air. Vehicles skated through the roads with their lights on to guide them, and the rainwater rushed into drains, lost forever from the world above. The city was full of life, yet dead when it was raining.

"Where you taking me?" Drip-Drip asked.

"Home. And I want you to stay there."

"What, I'm five years old now?"

"Listen, nigga, I'm tired of bailing you out and saving your ass. You're becoming more trouble than you're fuckin' worth. And if you weren't my little fuckin' brother, they would've found *you* in the trunk of a car too," Rafe heatedly proclaimed.

"Everything's squashed, right? You wanted me to help them find Maurice. I did that. The cops ain't got shit on me, and Mob Allah took care of business. So, why the fuck I gotta lie low for? I ain't fuckin' built like that," Drip-Drip angrily refuted. "These *my* fuckin' streets."

Rafe grumbled. "So, you're ready to be out there on your own, huh?"

"Bro, I take care of business. I got bodies on my name, and I make y'all money. And I get respect out here. I'm tired of playin' second fiddle to niggas out here that ain't fuckin' wit' me, and that ain't doin' the shit that I'm doin'."

Rafe chuckled. "Oh, so you're a general now."

"I've *been* a fuckin' general."

"Generals are loyal soldiers first," Rafe said.

Souls continued to scatter throughout the city as the rain persisted. No one stopped to look at anyone or anything. Unfortunately, rain had that effect on people.

Rafe's Lexus arrived at Rochdale Village, a housing cooperative in the southeastern corner of Queens. It was a sprawling and towering housing complex that stood out from Baisley to Guy R. Brewer Blvd. Rafe brought the Lexus to a stop in front of one of the thirteen-story buildings grouped in a circle. The rain had finally stopped with the Lexus idling.

"You're not coming up?" Drip-Drip asked.

"Nah, you go ahead. I got a few things to take care of," said Rafe. "Just stay tight here for a few hours and get your head right."

"I need some pussy or something, nigga."

Rafe shook his head at the comment. Then he handed Drip-Drip a pistol and said, "Just chill, nigga. And be careful out here."

Drip-Drip nodded and got out of the vehicle. Rafe drove off, and Drip-Drip headed toward the lobby with the gun tucked in his waistband. The rain made the area seem isolated. Drip-Drip was the only soul entering the building.

Drip-Drip lit a blunt as he sat on the high balcony that overlooked the neighborhood. It was a picturesque view from the eleventh floor. It had stopped raining, and it became a beautiful sunset with the sky bold, brilliant, and rich in color. Drip-Drip took a pull from the blunt and eyed Queens. He wanted to wear the crown and control it all someday. He felt that he deserved it. While he continued to smoke, his pager went off. He checked the number and recognized who was trying to contact him.

Drip-Drip called back from his mobile phone. His pager was for business, while his mobile phone was for personal use and emergencies.

"Yo, Bings, you paged me?" asked Drip-Drip.

"Yeah, I heard they cut you loose," said Bings.

"You know they ain't got shit on me. But what's up? Why the page? We good?"

"Yeah, we good. But I figured you might want to relax and chill, get your mind off shit. I got these two bitches that wanna meet up tonight. You down?"

"Say no more. I'm there," Drip-Drip quickly acquiesced.

"Come by my place, and we'll drive out to Brooklyn together," he suggested.

"These hoes in Brooklyn?"

"Melody and Tasha," Bings mentioned. "And they're down for whatever."

"Definitely. I'm gonna need some pussy after what these pigs put me through."

Drip-Drip immediately went into his bedroom to shower and change clothes for the evening. He smelled like pigs, bacon, and weed. And within the hour, he was out the front door with his gun tucked and concealed in his waistband. He refused to keep a low profile because he felt he was untouchable. After all, he was a prince waiting to be crowned king.

Drip-Drip arrived at Bings' basement apartment on Sutphin Blvd., intending to unwind by pussy and smoking tonight. When he went to knock on the door, he noticed it was open. So, he took it upon himself to enter.

"Yo, Bings, where you at?" he called out.

The place was dark and silent. Right away, Drip-Drip knew something wasn't right. He reached for his gun, but the moment he did so, he felt the cold steel of a 9 mm pressed against the back of his head and the chilling words, "You move, and I'm gonna blow your fucking brains out."

Drip-Drip stopped dead and frowned. "Nigga, you know who the fuck I am?"

"Yeah, I do. Why do you think I'm here?" the stranger said.

The man relieved Drip-Drip of his pistol, and then he tried incapacitating him with chloroform. Sincere firmly pressed a heavily soaked rag against Drip-Drip's mouth and nose. Surprisingly, he didn't become unconscious quick enough. Drip-Drip fought and struggled to keep from passing out, kicking and flailing to break free, but to no avail. Sincere was stronger and determined, and eventually, Drip-Drip collapsed with Sincere standing over him, scowling.

Drip-Drip became conscious an hour later. His eyes gradually opened, and he tried to move. But to his horror, he had been strung up wearing only his underwear with his arms behind his head. He had no idea where he was, but the area was dim, grim, and windowless. Drip-Drip struggled against his chained restraints, but he wasn't going anywhere anytime soon.

"What the fuck?" he cursed.

"The more you resist, the tighter those chains become," said Sincere.

Drip-Drip scowled and yelled, "Muthafucka, are you crazy? You know what my brother's gonna do to you when he finds out about this?"

"I'm hoping he does find out," Sincere replied.

"What the fuck you want?"

"Payback," Sincere uttered chillingly.

"Who the fuck are you, nigga? Huh? You know who the fuck *I* am?"

"An arrogant bitch living on borrowed time," Sincere mocked.

"Fuck you."

Drip-Drip struggled with his restraints once more, and as Sincere said, they became tighter around his wrists. He then scowled at Sincere and asked, "Bings gave me up?"

"It took him some time, but eventually, he told me what I needed to know to get to you."

"What you do to him? He's dead?"

"I would be more concerned with yourself than him," said Sincere nonchalantly. He picked up a sharp blade, and Drip-Drip's eyes widened with fear.

"What the fuck you gonna do with that knife?"

"I ain't cutting fuckin' apples, nigga," Sincere taunted, moving closer to his target.

"C'mon, man, I don't even fuckin' know you," Sincere shouted.

"But you knew my little brother. You and Voltron befriended him, got him into some shit, and got him killed. So now they're dead, and you get to live . . .? Nah, that isn't justice."

"Who was ya fuckin' brother?"

"Maurice."

The recognition showed on Drip-Drip's face. "You his brother? Look, I didn't kill him. That was Mob Allah and Zulu. *They* did that to your brother."

"But you sold him out to save your own ass. You gave them the information needed to find him. So, now, he and two ladies are dead because of you. I'm sick and tired of your kind," Sincere proclaimed.

"C'mon, look, let's work something out," Drip-Drip desperately begged.

"I'm done talking," were Sincere's final words.

Sincere placed the sharp blade against Drip-Drip's chest and nipples, and he began a torture called flaying or skinning. He slowly peeled away Drip-Drip's skin with the blade as if he were skinning an apple. The pain was traumatizing and excruciating, and the screams that Drip-Drip produced sounded unearthly.

"They tortured him, so I'm gonna torture you," Sincere said and continued skinning Drip-Drip.

# Chapter Twenty-three

Rafe was bent against the pool table with the pool stick in his hands, lined toward the cue ball.

"Eight ball, far corner pocket," he announced.

He was focused and ready to strike. And then he struck, applying a sidespin to the cue ball. It was an advanced technique that affected the curve and throws of the cue ball hitting against the eight ball, and the eight ball rolled down the table and disappeared into the far corner pocket.

"And that's game. So, pay up, fool," Rafe said to one of his cohorts.

The man placed $1,000 into Rafe's hands and uttered, "Double or nothing."

"You like losing money to me, don't you?" Rafe joked. "And you know what? I like taking it too."

The pool hall was opened for Rafe and his crew, Malik, Olay, Spring, Foolish, and Dwight. A few ladies were in their presence, but tonight was a private party with free endless drinks. Business was good, so everyone wanted to celebrate the good life and unwind with liquor, party favors, and beautiful women.

"Rack 'em up again," Rafe told Olay.

Olay quickly grouped the balls into a triangle on the table, and they were ready to play another game.

"Two grand this time," Rafe uttered. "You gonna put your money where your mouth is?"

"Let's go," Olay replied.

Rafe had a special bond with his crew. Though he could be feared and ruthless, he treated those loyal to him like his family.

Rafe loved playing pool. He came up hustling in pool halls when he was 15 years old. While teens his age were on the basketball courts, he was hustling and scheming in the pool halls until he opened his own billiards one day. If you didn't know anything about Rafe, you knew one thing . . . He was a pool shark.

The cue ball collided with the grouped balls, scattering them across the pool table, and right away, Rafe sank two highs into different pockets. Then he circled the table looking for his next shot. While doing so, Malik's mobile phone rang.

"Who this?" he asked.

"Put Rafe on the phone," the caller demanded.

"Who the fuck is you? And why are you calling?" Malik exclaimed.

His raised voice caught the attention of Rafe and others. Rafe stopped making his shot and asked, "Yo, Malik, who's that on the phone?"

"Don't know, but they're asking for you," he replied.

"Give me the fuckin' phone," Rafe gestured.

Malik handed him the phone, and the moment it was to his ear, Rafe could hear someone screaming in the background.

"Keep listening," said the caller.

"Is this a joke?" asked Rafe.

"Unfortunately for your little brother, it isn't," Sincere replied.

When Rafe heard that, his heart sank to his stomach. It couldn't be Drip-Drip screaming like that. So he believed it was a scam and countered, "You're lying."

Then Rafe heard the unthinkable. Sincere had put Drip-Drip on the phone, and he said, "Help me, bro. He's killing me."

The look on Rafe's face was palpable to everyone in the room—fear, shock, and anger. "Muthafucka, I swear to you, whoever you are, I'm gonna fuck up your entire world."

Rafe heard his brother's agonizing screams again. His heart continued to sink into his stomach like it was in quicksand. And he feared the worst. There wasn't anything he could do to help Drip-Drip. It was one of the few moments where he felt utterly helpless.

"What do you want—money?"

"You can have more money than God, and it wouldn't help your little brother's fate," Sincere replied.

"Then what the fuck is this about?"

"You took away something from me. So now, I take away something from you. And you can thank Mob Allah and Zulu for that," Sincere uttered.

Rafe could still hear Drip-Drip's sobbing and his tormented cries. Finally, he shouted, "Hang in there, bro. I'm gonna find this muthafucka."

"No, you won't," Sincere taunted.

Next, Rafe's worst nightmare came true, and Sincere executed Drip-Drip while he was listening.

*Bang . . .*

"No, noooo!" Rafe screamed in horror.

The call ended, and Rafe was beside himself with anger. His crew stared at him in shock. He threw the phone against the wall, then flipped over the pool table, destroying it. Everyone stood there aghast.

"They got Drip-Drip," Rafe exclaimed.

"What you wanna do?" asked Malik.

Rafe spun and made a beeline for the exit. Everyone followed behind him. His gun was visible when he stormed out of the pool hall and climbed into the driver's seat of the SUV. Malik hurriedly climbed into the passenger seat, and they were gone that fast with a caravan of vehicles right behind them.

Rafe arrived at the apartment in Rochdale. He charged into the place like the police would do conducting a raid. He hurried from room to room, hoping to find Drip-Drip and that fool on the phone. But, unfortunately, the place was empty. Upset, he turned to Malik and exclaimed, "Find my fuckin' brother and that nigga who was on the phone. I don't give a fuck if you gotta burn this entire neighborhood down."

"I got you," Malik replied committedly.


Hatred is what Sincere felt, and it was changing the chemistry in his brain, stimulating brutality against his brother's killers. First, Sincere stared at Drip-Drip's mutilated body and frowned. Then he spat on the body as it was still dangling from the chains and uttered, "Burn in hell, muthafucka."

Killing Drip-Drip wouldn't bring his little brother back, but knowing his victim suffered gave him some satisfaction. He planned on leaving the body hanging with portions of its skin removed. Sincere wanted Rafe to find his little brother just like that. He wanted the brutal image of Drip-Drip's torture to linger inside of Rafe's mind like a growing tumor. So, he collected any evidence with his DNA, wiped down the area, and left the premises that night.

When he climbed into Monica's car, he finally called Rafe and told him where to find his little brother. "Go to this address in Canarsie, and you'll find that bitch-ass nigga in the basement of a row house. And once again, thank Mob Allah and Zulu for his fate."

Sincere started the car and left. He knew they couldn't trace anything back to him because he was careful. He couldn't afford to make any mistakes. In his mind, he was at war, and he didn't plan on taking any prisoners.

Forty minutes later, a Nissan Pathfinder came to a screeching stop at the address Sincere had provided. Right away, Rafe sprang from the car like a track star and rushed into the abandoned building near the projects. Malik and a few other goons were right behind him. Everyone went looking for Drip-Drip, frantically screaming out his name. Finally, Rafe found his brother in the basement, still restrained by the chains around his wrists, with his body slumped and a pool of blood underneath his feet. It was a horrific sight, and immediately, Rafe was hit with crushing grief.

"Get him down—now," he ordered his men.

Three men struggled to release the body from its restraints. Rafe pushed them out of the way, pulled his brother's dead body into his arms, and cried. Each man stood around Rafe in silence, knowing the devil himself would fear Rafe right now. It was about to become hell on earth.

Rafe glared at Malik and growled, "Find this muthafucka and everything he loves—and kill them."

# Chapter Twenty-four

She was beautiful, even in death. She was a prostitute, but she was still God's child. She was young but mature. The victim lay there naked but peaceful. Like she was in her own bed. The Wolf stared at the girl and wondered about her last thoughts before killing her. They could have been of family or unfulfilled goals. Before he fucked her and then strangled her. The young girl experienced sheer panic. Her survival instincts went into overdrive, and there was this desperate but futile search for some reprieve, unfortunately, to no avail. Her last moments were of consummate terror. This one fought hard. She was determined to live, but the Wolf snapped her neck like a twig, ending her battle.

The Wolf picked up this one in Brooklyn. She was 17, and he enjoyed her unequivocally. He'd become hypnotized by her beauty and engorged by her insides as she satisfied him with an intense orgasm, followed by guilt and anger. He couldn't control himself. He was suffering from one of God's seven deadly sins: lust. He was unable to resist the temptation. Even when he got down on his knees to pray, his heart would be filled with strong emotions, and it was becoming very difficult to resist the urge to sin.

The Wolf started to undress. It was time for him to cleanse his sins. He removed his jacket, unbuttoned his white shirt, and placed his clothing to the side, not getting them wrinkled or dirty. He now stood stark naked

over the body, and he stared at his work . . . or weakness—
*his* sin. He was a complex man. He was unable to resist
the temptation and found himself thinking about it and
experiencing feelings of guilt.

The Wolf's physique was masterful, like God, Himself
perfectly took His time to design every single inch of him.
He was in great shape, inside and out. His rich, black skin
shimmered like oil. The Wolf picked up the sharp blade
and stepped on the tarp where she lay. He then crouched
closer to his victim and voiced, "I pray, Lord, you will
destroy any passion for lust inside of me. I pray against
the lust of the flesh. It covers me. And I wish for you to
cover me in righteousness and fill me with self-control
to stand firm against temptation in Jesus' name. Amen."

Before he started to cut her up, he added, "See no evil,
speak no evil, touch no evil."

He took the blade and started with her eyes by surgically
removing them from their sockets. He then cut out her
tongue, and with a pair of shears, he cut off her fingertips
like he was snapping peas. He placed her eyes, tongue,
and fingertips into a liquored jar and tightened it. The
Wolf then carefully packaged his victim inside of the tarp.
Finally, she was ready for removal. While he was still
naked, he tossed the body over his shoulder and carried it
back to the car nearby. He placed her into the trunk and
went back to the ritual site to clean himself and dress.

The Wolf looked like any average human clad in a
dark blue suit, polished wingtip shoes, and wire-rimmed
glasses. Then, with his sins forgiven and his victim inside
the trunk, he got behind the wheel of the Ford and left
his lair to dispose of the evidence. This time, he dumped
the remnants of his victim in a Brooklyn park. When he
carried the body into Prospect Park, it was the middle of
the night. He displayed her body across the grass fittingly
for all to see when dawn came.

The Wolf then disappeared into the night.

The following morning, the Wolf, now wearing a charcoal-gray suit, looked like the epitome of a Dapper Dan. But, on the contrary, he was a new-age gentleman with class, poise, and style like no other. He was the standard of what Adonis strives to be—a real man, not a nigga.

His apartment was neat and decorated tastefully with African and religious artifacts. He was a man that took pride in his appearance, religion, and his home. He was a bachelor with a purpose. The Wolf stared at his image in the bedroom mirror one final time and nodded with approval. He then picked up his Bible and left the apartment.

The Wolf arrived at the First Baptist Church in Flatbush, Brooklyn. It was a beautiful Sunday morning when he walked into the church. And the first thing he heard was, "Good morning, Deacon."

"Good morning, Sister Knowles," the Wolf replied with a smile.

The Sunday morning services were about to start. The Wolf, whose real name was Christopher Mathews, was the church deacon. He was a respected and loved member of the church and community. He knew nearly every member of the congregation, and they adored him. He was an important figure at First Baptist Church. The church's mission was not a single act but a process—to preach the gospel, proclaim the kerygma, deepen faith and sacramental life, and bring Christ to those who do not know Him.

"Good morning, Deacon Mathews," the pastor of the church, Malcolm Wright, said.

"Morning, Paster Wright." The Wolf smiled.

"Are you ready to have another glorious sermon?"

"Always, Pastor." The Wolf continued to smile.

"Great. Every day the Lord gives us is a blessing," said the pastor.

"Yes, indeed. Yes, indeed."

Christopher, a.k.a. the Wolf, took his place on the platform near the pastor overlooking the congregation. It was a packed house. Pastor Wright was a popular and well liked man with a gift for spreading the message— God's words. The church's first lady sat near the Wolf and smiled at him. She was a beautiful woman in her early forties, filled with grace and personality.

"You're looking quite handsome today, Deacon Mathews," she said.

"And you're magnificent as always, First Lady. Too bad the pastor got to you first," he flirted.

The first lady chuckled while her husband stood at the podium and stared at everyone.

"Good morning, everyone," the pastor greeted the congregation.

"Good morning," the congregation replied loudly.

"God is good, right?"

"All the time," they exclaimed.

"Let me hear you repeat it . . . God is good."

"All the time," the congregation shouted out loudly and joyfully.

"Amen, amen," the wolf shouted in praise and joy, even standing to his feet with his hands raised to the ceiling.

# Chapter Twenty-five

The penthouse apartment in Manhattan was a place for Mob Allah and Zulu to escape the urban jungle. With the help of their lawyer, Sonja, they were able to purchase the site via money-laundering services. For a hefty percentage, their lawyer and certain acquaintances of theirs provided a service by putting their cash through several shell companies and fronts she'd set up to make their money appear legitimate at first glance. Some might say that Sonja D'Agostino was the brains of the organization. And if it weren't for her, Mob Allah and Zulu would have remained two-bit drug dealers on the streets. But Mob Allah had always been intelligent and ambitious. Sonja was the tool and motivation he needed to advance his business. Unfortunately, he had a setback, spending eight years in prison. Still, while he was incarcerated, Sonja and Zulu kept the vehicle moving.

Mob Allah was one of the intelligent percentages of drug kingpins who weren't looking to glorify wearing the crown and squander their money on frivolous things like jewelry, flashy cars, and pussy. The bulk of his problem came because he had too much money and not enough ways to launder it. On paper, he was able to pay himself a very handsome salary by overreporting how much they earned from their businesses. But he knew that he couldn't overstep the mark and arouse too much suspicion.

Mob Allah poured himself a glass of expensive scotch and downed it, savoring the taste. Then he poured himself another glass and looked at Zulu. Finally, he raised his glass and said, "To the good life."

"You keep playing them away games with Sonja while shit is happening on the streets, Mob Allah," said Zulu. "I thought you were coming home on some takeover shit. Now, you're the one keeping the peace in the UN."

"It's those away games that will keep the Feds and IRS off our asses, nigga. We need these deals, and we need her," he replied.

"*You* need her. I don't trust her. I never did," Zulu admitted. "But you're so busy keeping your dick between her legs and down her throat that you can't see she's fuckin' using you . . . using *us*."

"How? If it weren't for her, we wouldn't have any of this shit," Mob Allah replied. "She helped you keep things in motion while I was locked down. And now that I'm home and making moves with her, you don't trust her."

"All I'm saying, she knows a lot about our organization . . . too much. And what happens one day when the Feds come knocking on her door with a subpoena and some questions? You think she's gonna be that ride-or-die bitch because you're fuckin' her. She *ain't* one of us, bro. She's a white, scheming, go-getter bitch with a few niggers under her thumb," Zulu sharply proclaimed.

Mob Allah simply replied, "I know what I'm doing. And *I* trust her."

"I thought you said never trust anybody. And now you trust this white bitch, huh? That pussy must be platinum," Zulu chuckled.

Mob Allah poured himself another glass of scotch, pivoted, and stared out the floor-to-ceiling windows with a scenic view of Central Park.

"But listen, we got other problems," said Mob Allah. "Coffee had two of his bitches murdered in the past two weeks. So, people say there might be a serial killer in Queens murdering young prostitutes."

"And that's our problem, why?" Zulu replied.

"Coffee is paying us for protection, right? He does business in our territory for a percentage. And if there's a serial killer in Queens killing young girls, it will bring media attention to the area, and that's the *last* thing we need," he said.

"And if that happens, the Feds will get involved," said Zulu.

"Bingo."

The last thing they needed was the Feds coming into Queens sniffing around, turning over rocks to find some serial killer, and then encroaching on their businesses.

"And how are we supposed to find this nigga? You know these sick muthafuckas don't exactly advertise their shit. A nigga like that could be right next door to us, and we wouldn't even know it," said Zulu.

"When it rains, it pours, right?" Mob Allah uttered.

Suddenly, there was a knock at the penthouse door, and they both heard, "It's Mackie."

Zulu went to answer the door, and Mackie entered the place with more troubling news to announce.

"What is it?" asked Zulu.

Mackie looked at both men with despair written on his face. Then he bluntly uttered, "It's Drip-Drip. He's dead."

It was shocking news to Mob Allah and Zulu. "What the fuck are you talkin' about?" Mob Allah asked.

"Someone kidnapped him, tortured him, and then shot him in the head. Rafe is up in arms right now, ready to kill anything moving out there."

"Fuck," Mob Allah uttered.

"They know who did it?" Zulu asked.

"No. But he wants a meeting with you two . . . like right now," Mackie informed them.

"He's upset and emotional, and he will want someone to blame for his brother's death," said Mob Allah.

"Muthafucka better not be blaming us," uttered Zulu.

Mob Allah looked at Mackie and said, "Set up the meeting with him. We'll figure this shit out."

Mackie nodded. "A'ight."

Mob Allah turned around and walked back to the makeshift bar in the room, and once again, he poured himself another shot of scotch. Then he said to Zulu, "We don't need for anything else to go wrong."

"In this business, something *always* goes wrong," Zulu replied.


Rafe, Malik, and Olay were already waiting for Mob Allah and Zulu to show up at the meeting place on the boardwalk in Far Rockaway, Queens. It was early in the morning, and the sky was still dark with the salty air blowing in the men's faces, cooling and dampening their skin. The tide hit the shore, and the seagulls peacefully squawked as they soared overhead, singing and searching for food.

Finally, Mob Allah, Zulu, and Mackie arrived on the boardwalk. And the moment Mob Allah was face-to-face with Rafe, he uttered, "My condolences for what happened to your brother."

"Fuck them apologies. I want fuckin' blood," Rafe exclaimed.

"And you'll get it," said Mob Allah.

"You damn right I'ma get it because I'm about to put every soldier I have on them streets, and there ain't gonna be no rest until I find my brother's killers. Dead on."

"Think rationally, Rafe, and don't do anything stupid," Mob Allah said.

Rafe couldn't believe what he was hearing. The nerve of Mob Allah to tell him, *don't do anything stupid.*

"What? What the fuck you talkin' about, nigga? It ain't *your* fuckin' kin in the fuckin' morgue right now," Rafe retorted. "And whoever killed my brother mention y'all names. Said his fate was because of you and this nigga." He pointed out Zulu.

"My peoples had nothing to do with your brother's death," said Mob Allah.

"Then who?"

"That's why we're here to find out," Zulu chimed.

"Whoever it was, they tortured and skinned off pieces of Drip-Drip like he was some fuckin' science project," Rafe exclaimed.

"Rafe, you know we both have enemies out there, and it could be anyone that came after your brother," said Mob Allah.

"I heard there's a serial killer in Queens," Olay mentioned out of the blue.

Everyone looked his way, like . . . *"What?"*

"It was on the news yesterday," he said.

"Nigga, he killing bitches, not our peoples," Malik responded. "Fuck you talkin' about?"

Embarrassed, Olay shrugged and shut his mouth.

"Look, both of our camps been on good terms for a few years now, and the last thing we need is trouble and war, Rafe. You start putting a spotlight on you, and then you will put one on us. Subsequently, the authorities come in, and no one makes any money," Mob Allah coolly proclaimed. "How about this . . .? I'll send a few of my men to you to help you find this nigga, and I'll pay for the funeral. That's the best I can do for you right now."

Rafe contemplated the proposal. He glanced at his right-hand, Malik, and they shared a silent agreement. Then he looked back at Mob Allah and replied, "I appreciate it . . . for now."

"Good. It's done then," said Mob Allah.

With an understanding between both organizations, Rafe and his people left the boardwalk while Mob Allah stood behind. When they were out of sight, Zulu said, "Whoever came at his brother might come at us too."

"I know," Mob Allah uttered.

"Who do you think it was?"

"I don't know. But we definitely need to find out. And amp up security everywhere and put everyone on alert," Mob Allah instructed. "Better to be safe than sorry."

# Chapter Twenty-six

Sincere bowed his head as the shower water cascaded down on him. He was lost in thought and isolation. It seemed like overnight, everything came to an abrupt end. He was once ambitious about becoming a cop, but that stopped. His opportunity to better himself ceased to happen, or it looked dead to him if it did. There wasn't any shine in his eyes about anything. They had become like a plastic doll's. His eyes were in a daze, distant. It was as if he were somewhere else.

He hadn't seen his mother in over a week. But Sincere knew where she was . . . in the pit of her addiction. Janet would rather get high than deal with her grief. It was easier to separate from reality by habit than drown in sorrow. So, for now, it was he and Denise. And he wasn't trying to lose her too. In fact, Sincere wanted Denise to move out of their row house in Queens and stay with Monica on Long Island. He felt it was too dangerous to remain at their old place because it wasn't over. Sincere wanted to kill them all. Killing Drip-Drip had awakened something inside of him, and there was no putting it back to sleep.

The water was running full blast, soaking him from head to toe. The shower curtain opened, but he didn't pay any attention to it as Monica joined him in the shower. He felt the touch of a soft hand start at his hip, and it worked its way up the right side of his body as she pressed her naked frame against his. Then she put kisses all over his neck and back. Sincere turned around to face her. He stared at her angelic features, and without a word, he kissed her deeply and passionately. His hand rose to the back of her head, pushing his tongue deeper into her mouth.

Monica wanted to pull Sincere back from his mental isolation and depression. And the best way she knew how was sex. Sincere hoisted her into his arms with her legs straddling around him, and he was soon inside her.

"Ugh . . . Ugh," she moaned. "Fuck me."

Her body lit up with pleasure as their tongues became entwined once again. Her arms and legs tightened in the grip of his body as she cooed underneath the pouring shower. With each thrust, her body tensed, and her moans altered into screams of delight. The intense passion of their encounter was beginning to take over her body. Soon, he came inside of her, and her body shook against him as she orgasmed along with him. The two lingered in the shower for a moment, collecting themselves from the intense gratification.

"You okay, baby?" Monica asked him.

Sincere nodded. "I'll be okay."

"Are you hungry?"

"No."

Monica continued to be sensual with her man, trying to prevent him from going somewhere dark. She knew his history and how much he loved his little brother.

"I'm always here if you need to talk . . . or if you need something else again," she chuckled.

He slightly smiled.

Then Monica pulled back the shower curtain and stepped out of the water to towel off.

"I'll be out in a minute," he said.

Sincere spent another five minutes in the shower before he stepped out to dry off. He stared at his reflection in the bathroom mirror and what he saw was a man not wanting to be pulled back from the darkness. Yes, sex with Monica was nice, and it momentarily took him away from his hell. But like his mother with her crack addiction, he was in his own pit of darkness, and it was easier to react with violence than to drown with grief and regret.

Sincere heard his family in the next room, but he went into the bedroom and shut the door. Then he reached for the phone and called Nasir.

Nasir answered with, "I was just about to call you. We need to talk."

"Where do you want to meet?"

"I'll be at this school, PS 160, in an hour. Meet me there," said Nasir.

"Okay."

The school yard was crammed with noisy and active kids. Several kids played dodgeball while a young girl with glasses was writing in a notebook on the concrete. A few other young girls were playing jump rope and double Dutch. Two long ropes were turning in the opposite direction, with another girl jumping between the ropes simultaneously while the staff walked through the school yard monitoring the kids. It was the children's favorite time of the day, lunch and outdoors.

Nasir sat in his Accord parked across the street. His attention was fixed on the kids playing in the school yard. But his eyes were hooked on one particular child, a 6-year-old girl with pigtails chasing behind her friends playing tag. Nasir smiled at the cheerful little girl. He took a pull from the cigarette in his hand and then sighed.

A moment later, Sincere climbed into the passenger seat of the Accord and asked, "Why did you want me to meet you here?"

"You remember my daughter, Jazzman, right?" Nasir said, still staring at his daughter playing with her friends. "She's 6 years old now. I come here sometimes to watch her play. It feels like it's the only time I get to see her. Baby moms trying to keep me out of her life because of what I do. She don't like me being in these streets and don't want our little girl around my mess. Like I'm gonna have my daughter around some bullshit."

Nasir took another pull from the cigarette and continued with, "Bitch met me while I was in these streets. So now she wants to act differently. But the bitch doesn't have a problem taking my money to take care of her and Jazzman, living comfortably off my drug money. And she won't even let me see my daughter like that."

"I'm sorry to hear that, Nasir," said Sincere.

"It's all good. That's my angel, though . . . best thing to ever happen to me," he said, finishing off his cigarette and flicking it out the window. He finally turned to Sincere and said, "I heard about Drip-Drip. Was that you?"

Sincere didn't answer him. Where he was from, if you kill a man, you never speak on it ever again. It was self-snitching in his book. But by his silence, Nasir knew what time it was and uttered, "You opened Pandora's box, my nigga. And Rafe is ready to burn this entire neighborhood down to find his brother's killer. You even spooked Mob Allah and Zulu. Word on the street is that they amped their security everywhere."

"Fuck every last one of them," Sincere finally spoke. "I'm coming for all of them."

"How, nigga? They got soldiers, and with the snap of their fingers, they can take out you *and* your entire fuckin' family."

"After what they took from me, Nasir, I'm already in hell."

"I'll tell you this. You won't get close to any of them . . . especially Mob Allah."

"He gave the order to have Maurice killed."

"Even if he did, he's like a god in this hood. Muthafuckas fear that man, and if you come upon his radar, he won't stop until everything you love is destroyed," Nasir stated.

"And I won't stop until everything *he* loves is destroyed," Sincere chillingly replied.

The look in Sincere's eyes was equivalent to hellfire. It was going to burn forever. He was undaunted by Mob Allah and Rafe's violent reputation.

"When I came home from the army, I saw my mother was finally clean and happy, and my sister was doing good in school, so I was happy. Our house finally became a home, Nasir. You know the hell I've been through before I enlisted. And yeah, Maurice was becoming a headache, but I understood why he was mad at me. I wasn't there for him. And what Mob Allah and these fools took away from me was reconciliation and having a second chance of happiness with my baby brother. And now my mother is back to smoking crack again because of this shit," Sincere zealously proclaimed.

"But now you have a second chance with Monica and your son," Nasir replied. "I gotta sit parked across the street from a school to see my daughter. And what happened to 'I'm one man, Nasir. I'm trying to become a cop and do something with my life'?"

"That changed after they tortured Maurice like he was in some POW camp," Sincere replied.

There was no changing his mind.

"Either you're with me or not, Nasir," Sincere added.

"It's a suicide mission going against two organizations, and I'm trying to get money, my nigga. I had love for Maurice too, but you're not thinking rationally at all and ready to do something stupid."

"Like this is the first time we got into some stupid shit. Remember what we did when we were with the Gotti Boys," Sincere reminded him.

"We did what we had to do."

"You understand then. And I need to do what I have to do. I refuse to let Maurice's death be in vain. I owe him vengeance, Nasir. Maurice believed I abandoned him by enlisting in the army. I can't rest knowing that," he unequivocally proclaimed. "We're survivors, Nasir. We control our fear."

Nasir managed to grin. "That, we do. But I see this course of your life is changing right in front of you, and you don't even see it. You start coming for them, and they will come for you and your family."

"I'm no fool. I know," Sincere replied. He then released a deep sigh and continued with, "It is not the violence that sets a man apart. But it's the distance he's prepared to go."

With that, Nasir handed him a piece of paper with something written on it. He said, "Those are two addresses to stash houses belonging to Rafe and Mob Allah. Don't ask me how I got 'em; I just have 'em. And since you're not going to back down, I'm with you. But you can't come at them directly. You need to hit 'em where it's going to hurt . . . and that's in their pockets. You start fuckin' with their money, and they might start unraveling. And that's a big *if*."

Sincere stared at the addresses and nodded. "Thanks for this. And I'll be careful."

Sincere then climbed out of the Honda and walked away, leaving Nasir to sit and contemplate if he did the right thing. Finally, he exhaled and continued to watch his daughter run around with her friends in the school yard.

# Chapter Twenty-seven

It was a clear, warm night in Soho, a neighborhood in Lower Manhattan. The noble area was known for many artists' lofts, art galleries, and its variety of shops ranging from trendy, upscale boutiques to national and international chain store outlets. Many of the side streets in the district were paved with Belgian blocks or cobblestone.

A 1999 black Range Rover stopped in front of one of the four-story, cast-iron architectural buildings lining the street. Mob Allah and Mackie climbed out of the vehicle and approached the attractive building. While Mob Allah was dressed handsomely in a dark Armani suit, Mackie was clad in a Nike tracksuit. Mob Allah looked relaxed, but Mackie looked uneasy.

"This ain't my cup of tea, Mob Allah," he griped.

"Just chill and shut the fuck up. This is business," Mob Allah chastised.

The two were let into the building. They entered the elevator and ascended to the top floor, where they were introduced to an art gallery—art in the loft. The place was spacious and ultrasophisticated, oozing style and class in every room adorned with huge windows. It looked like a world away from Jamaica, Queens. The people in the room were dressed stylishly in suits, gowns, and lovely dresses. Uniformed servants walked around carrying silver trays with champagne and hors d'oeuvres for everyone to enjoy. The artwork displayed on the walls were aristocratic masterpieces from many different artists with various expressions.

Right away, Mob Allah started to look for someone. He was invited to the event, and he didn't want to let this person down. So, he removed a champagne flute from one of the passing trays. At the same time, Mackie remained deadpan and uncomfortable around the aristocrats. He too snatched a flute and some hors d'oeuvre from the tray like a brute. Then he downed the champagne and devoured the food.

Mob Allah looked at him and uttered, "Don't embarrass me, Mackie."

"I won't."

Finally, Mob Allah saw who he was there to see, Bobby Spyros. He was an ambitious multimillionaire coming from humble beginnings in Brooklyn. Bobby was in his early fifties and a Hofstra University graduate. He was sharp, handsome, charitable, and generous in public when it came to donations, but he was ruthless with a particular distaste for disloyalty in his organization and snitches. Bobby Spyros was a shrewd businessman with connections to the Mexican cartel. He was one of the two top drug distributors in the city. He was extremely wealthy and a well-connected city/state power player who seemed too big to fail.

The man stood in the room with an air of power about him. Dressed in a three-piece suit, sipping on champagne, and standing near a large painting while talking to a pretty woman, Bobby turned to see Mob Allah looking his way. He simply nodded his head to Mob Allah, and Mob Allah coolly approached him.

When he was close, Bobby said to the pretty girl, "Excuse us, beautiful."

She smiled and walked away.

"I'm glad you could make it," Bobby Spyros said to Allah.

"You wanted to meet, right?"

Bobby smiled and said, "Let's talk outside." He then pivoted and walked away with Mob Allah right behind him.

They stepped out onto the colorful rooftop terrace overlooking some parts of Soho. A full moon shone, and all seemed peaceful. Other guests were out on the deck, but Bobby looked at everyone and sternly but politely said, "I need everyone to leave right now."

He didn't have to repeat himself. Immediately, guests started to depart from the rooftop terrace. When the last one left, Bobby closed the door behind him. They now had all the privacy they needed.

"I see you brought your loyal dog with you," said Bobby.

"You mean, Mackie? I keep him on a leash," Mob Allah replied.

Bobby chuckled at the remark, then uttered, "I respect loyalty and commitment, Mob Allah. It's the reason why I wanted to meet with you."

"I'm listening, Bobby."

Bobby took a sip of champagne and gazed out at the city. Everything was calm between them.

"You do clean up nice," Bobby mentioned. "I like the suit."

"You always told me, 'A man dressed in a nice, tailored suit will always shine brighter than a guy in an off-the-rack suit,'" Mob Allah said.

"That's why I always liked you because you listen and take heed of the advice I give . . . unlike some people in my organization. As a result, you're becoming a business-man instead of a gangster."

"I want the best of both worlds," Mob Allah replied.

"We all do. I remember when I first met you in '88, '89. You were a young drug dealer in Queens trying not to get yourself arrested."

"I remember," Mob Allah replied.

Bobby Spyros took another swig of champagne and stared into the night. The area was bright, full of life, and partying with tons of tourists.

"I want you to become my number two, my New York distributor," Bobby finally said.

Mob Allah was utterly taken aback. "Whoa. That's a game-changer," he uttered.

"Yes, it is."

"I didn't know you were looking for someone to take that position," he said.

"And you weren't supposed to know. If the company boss lets his employees know that he's coming in for an inspection ahead of time, it gives them time to prepare. But you come in unannounced, and then you get to see the bullshit everyone does on your dime," Bobby said.

"And why me?"

"You bring a level of professionalism. And you're a man that has been confined for eight years. I'm to believe that a man imprisoned for eight years isn't trying to go back. So therefore, he's a cautious man with some skin in the game. And you carry a level of respect in this city that I admire," Bobby proclaimed. "Your reputation precedes you, Mob Allah. People fear you in this city."

Mob Allah nodded. "I'm honored that you're considering me. But is there something that I need to know before I decide to walk into this?"

Bobby smiled. "I have a situation with the SEC, insider trading, bribery . . . something I can handle. No big deal. But I need to limit myself and keep my interaction with certain people at a minimum. And I feel you can guarantee me a safe and secure pipeline with no interruptions."

"I can," said Mob Allah.

"We'll do business with each other two or three times a year. And no one else is to meet me or see my face."

Mob Allah nodded. Ironically, Bobby already placed him into the position without him actually saying yes to the position.

"Think about it. In a few months, we'll be heading into an entirely new century . . . the year 2000. But unfortunately, not too many people can say they were there to witness the turn of a century. And with it, absolute power, my friend," Bobby proclaimed.

Mob Allah smiled. Bobby raised his flute for a toast, and Mob Allah did the same. "To a lengthy friendship and business."

They clinked glasses, and Bobby downed his drink. He then asked Mob Allah, "So, I hear you're trying to become a developer."

"This guy, Michael Kostroff, he's looking for investors," said Allah. "Are you familiar with him?"

"Vaguely. I hear he has his hands in a lot of people's pockets," said Bobby. "Just be careful."

Mob Allah nodded, understanding.

The two men rejoined the other guests in the loft. Bobby trailed off from Mob Allah and continued to mingle with his guests. It was like the two suddenly didn't know each other. Mob Allah looked around for Mackie, who was trying to flirt with one of the ladies in the room. He quickly interrupted their conversation by telling Mackie, "We're leaving."

Mackie nodded and uttered, "It's 'bout time."

The two quietly left the event. When they climbed into the Range Rover, Mackie asked him, "What was that about?"

"Business," Mob Allah replied aloofly.

# Chapter Twenty-eight

Sincere couldn't sleep. It was the middle of the night, and he lay in bed with Monica cuddled next to him. The bedroom was dark and quiet, and he was consumed by his thoughts. He stared up at the ceiling and thought back to four years ago, a week before leaving Queens to attend boot camp in Fort Sills, Oklahoma. He was 20 years old, and he had run into some problems at home. Maurice was a freshman in high school and still a good kid, while Sincere became a seasoned criminal. He and Nasir sold drugs for the Gotti Boys, but they also did things the ski-mask way—becoming stickup kids. They were the dynamic duo and went out to Brooklyn and Long Island to do their dirty work, which included B&Es (breaking and entering). Together, they seemed untouchable. But one night, shit went wrong. They went out to rob a drug dealer named Crunchy in Hempstead, Long Island. It was the same procedure: stalk Crunchy and get to know his routine, people, and weaknesses. Sincere made sure there were no loose ends, so there wouldn't be any problems when the time came to rob the nigga.

Unfortunately, there *were* problems. They ran up on Crunchy after midnight when he came out of the stash house. Before he could get into his car, Sincere put the tip of the .45 against the back of his head and warned him, "Don't move." But Crunchy was undaunted by two masked men holding him up at gunpoint. It angered Crunchy, and he resisted and fought back. He swung wildly at them and wrestled for one of their guns. Sincere didn't have a choice but to put him down with two shots. Shocked and frightened, both men ran away like track stars, jumped back into the stolen Civic, and sped away, leaving Crunchy bleeding to death in the street.

Killing Crunchy that night scared Sincere. He knew the authorities were coming for him. He embraced himself for the inevitable—twenty-five to life for first-degree murder. For weeks, he kept a low profile and stayed home. He became paranoid and started to pray. He took a man's life, and it haunted him. And then came the crackdown on the Gotti Boys in 1995—a sting operation with nearly two dozen arrests. Surprisingly, Sincere and Nasir weren't arrested. The two were too busy doing robberies to come across the authority's radar. And Sincere saw this as a blessing and decided to get his life together. He did a lot of dirt and seemed to have gotten away with it. Then he found out Monica was pregnant, and he didn't believe the baby was his.

Sincere enlisted in the army because he wanted, or he needed, to get away from it all. It felt like the walls were closing in around him. And he thought it was either the state prison or Uncle Sam's army. So, of course, he chose the latter. And with the conflict with Mighty escalating, Sincere felt he was doing the right thing by leaving Queens entirely.

The one thing Sincere regretted was not telling Maurice his reason for leaving Queens. It wasn't abandonment; it was survival. If Sincere had stayed in Queens, he would either be dead or in jail.

*Am I my brother's keeper?*

Sincere felt guilty about Maurice's death and that his little brother was the one to pay for his sins. He'd killed a man and had gotten away with it. Unfortunately, Maurice followed in his footsteps, and he wasn't so lucky.

Not being able to sleep, Sincere removed himself from the bed and started to get dressed. And while Monica and everyone else were still sleeping, he left the premises, climbed into her car, and drove off.

The NYPD was still calling him, and the opportunity to become a police officer was still open. He needed to schedule his psych exam and undergo a psychological evaluation. The agency wanted to evaluate him for psychological stability and mental fitness. But Sincere had no interest in scheduling it. He'd tortured and killed a man, and he wasn't mentally stable. He was still in a very dark place. And there was a possibility that he would be subjected to a polygraph test to cross-reference the answers provided in his application packet. And then there would be a one-on-one interview with a psychologist.

Sincere arrived at the Springfield Cemetery and crept on the grounds. The place looked like a memorial park during the day, quiet and still. But at night, it seemed like the cemetery's actual character came out. The headstones were the only thing visible in the dimmest of moonlight. He made his way to Maurice's grave. When he arrived, he stood over it for a moment, moping.

"I'm sorry, little bro, and I miss you. But I promise you this; I won't let them get away with it. And I'm going to make them remember your name," Sincere candidly stated.

# Chapter Twenty-nine

*Two months later . . .*

The full moon was a charming lady. She shined brightly in the sky and looked like a beacon in the dark. It was big and illuminated by a pure frosty light, glimpsing from out of the cloud to look at civilization—to witness the evil acts done by men. It was a bit breezy but a comfortable night with the sound of the wind in the trees rustling leaves. The city was alive but yet felt so still as it was nearing four a.m. It was a time when the bars and clubs were closing, but prostitution was still very active in all five boroughs.

A silver Toyota Camry arrived at Pugsley Creek Park in the Bronx. The Wolf killed the engine and climbed out of the car. For a brief moment, he inspected his surroundings. Not a soul was around. The Wolf stared at the wetlands and marshes and the wildlife that inhabited largely untouched areas. The site felt isolated. It was perfect for the Wolf. He opened the trunk of the Camry, where another body lay inside. She was 18, and he'd picked her up from Hunts Point. She was beautiful with angelic features and had a body softer than cotton. The Wolf felt he could stay inside of her forever, but then he was disturbed by his sins and lust, and he strangled her while he continued to fuck her.

It wasn't going to end. He wanted to stop, but he couldn't control himself. He couldn't handle it. It was taking over. Three weeks went by without him sinning and lusting, but those sexual urges came back twice as strong. It was in his head, screaming and shouting at him. The Bronx became his new stomping grounds for his sexual gratifications. He'd killed five young girls in Queens and four girls in Brooklyn. Vice, the Feds—everyone wanted to catch him. They'd placed undercover prostitutes on the tracks to catch him and sent alerts to all the prostitutes to be on the lookout. His works had made the national news . . . a serial killer in the city preying on young prostitutes and mutilating their bodies.

And though law enforcement was searching for him, the Wolf continued to kill. He removed the body from the trunk, effortlessly tossed it over his shoulder, and headed into Pugsley Creek Park. He carried his victim deep into the thickness of trees and marshland, where he came to an opening near Westchester Creek, the perfect spot to leave her. The Wolf placed his victim on the meadow and positioned her like it were a ritual. She was naked with her hands folded across her chest and her eyes, tongue, and fingers missing. He stared at his handiwork for a moment knowing someone would find her tomorrow.

As he stood there admiring and praying, suddenly, there was a sound behind him, a branch snapping underneath someone's feet. The Wolf quickly pivoted to see a young couple eyeing him in shock and horror. There was no denying what they were witnessing . . . a serial killer. A feeling of dread crept up from the pit of their stomachs, and their hearts were throbbing in their ears, loud and irregular.

Right away, the boy told his girl, "Baby, run!"

They ran, and the Wolf had no choice but to chase behind them. They were fast, but he was faster. He was desperate; they saw his face. The couple zigzagged through the trees in the dark with the boy clutching his girlfriend's hand. But it was becoming harder for her to keep up with him. The footsteps of their pursuer echoed behind them so much that they couldn't tell if he was near or directly behind them. There was a fleeting blurry glimpse from the girl as she snatched a look behind, the terror on her face palpable.

Suddenly, the girl tripped and fell to the ground. Her boyfriend turned to aid her, but the Wolf burst from the trees with something sharp in his hand. And before the girl could get back on her feet, he pounced on her. She shrieked in horror. She tried to fight him with her flailing arms and missed kicks, but he managed to plunge the knife into her stomach and then pushed it into her throat, killing her instantly. The boyfriend watched in horror a short distance away, fear crippling him, freezing every muscle in his body. There wasn't anything he could do. She was dead . . . and he was next. The look in the Wolf's eyes was diabolical. He couldn't allow the boyfriend to escape. So, the Wolf sprang to his feet and chased after the young man.

They were near the trail when the Wolf finally caught up with him, and a violent struggle ensued. The boyfriend slammed his fists against the Wolf but to no benefit. Swiftly, the sharp knife was plunged into the boyfriend's chest repeatedly, with the boyfriend choking on his own blood. The Wolf continued to stab him until his body went limp into his arms and dropped to his feet. The blood on the Wolf was thick and crimson. It was a mess, and it wasn't supposed to happen.

"Fuck," the Wolf cursed.

With the bloody knife still in his hand, he ran.

The next day, Pugsley Creek Park was flooded with every cop, detective, and agent in town. The media was on the scene like scavengers chasing a hot story. So, when word had gotten around that three bodies were found in the park, it was front-page news.

The air was cool and fresh as the morning sun rose. The breeze softly blew between the blades of grass as the sun reflected flawlessly off the pond since the water was still. It was a beautiful summer day, but in contrast, the entire park was closed off as detectives and cops combed through every inch of the area, looking for evidence. It was a gruesome crime scene. News of three bodies found in the park traveled fast, even to Queens.

Detectives Acosta and Emerson took a drive to the Bronx to see the scene. It was their guy; they knew it. But three bodies in one park boggled their minds. When they arrived at Pugsley Creek Park, it was a chaotic spectacle. News vans, reporters, and people were everywhere. They had to fight their way to the crime scene, where Bronx Detectives Hudson and Whyte met them.

"Is it our killer from Queens?" Acosta asked Hudson.

"We believe so," Detective Hudson replied.

"Three bodies, though, it's a crazy step up from his MO," Detective Emerson said.

"We believed the other two stumbled on him as he dumped the body," Detective Whyte stated. "He chased them down and killed them both."

The detectives viewed the couple's body which was some distance apart, and it made them sigh with sympathy and shake their heads.

"Damn, this muthafucka," Emerson cursed. "He's in the Bronx now. Fuck."

It didn't take a rocket scientist to deduce what happened. The couple was probably out for a late-night/early-morning walk, maybe doing some hanky-panky—and were caught off guard by the serial killer. They ran. He caught up to her first, butchered her, and then chased and butchered the boyfriend.

"He's fast," Detective Hudson uttered. "From where the girl's naked body was found, to the couple . . . He's in shape."

"And the victim?" Detective Acosta asked.

"A young prostitute from Hunts Point. She was eighteen," said Hudson.

Detectives Acosta and Emerson went to see the victim, and there she was, naked and disfigured. Acosta took in the grassy area, where it was isolated from the public roads.

"This killer, he likes parks for some reason," said Acosta.

"I wonder why," said Emerson.

"Maybe a history with public parks . . . some kind of nostalgia with them, a better time in his life," Acosta suggested. "How many public parks are there in this city?"

"Shit, quite a few," Detective Whyte replied. "Dozens, maybe hundreds or thousands of public parks."

"Yeah, but he picks bigger parks with a lot more acres and isolated areas. Easier for him to go unnoticed," said Acosta.

"To narrow it down then, I say about a dozen or so," Detective Hudson chimed in.

Detective Acosta crouched near the killer's latest victim, another pretty girl killed and defaced. He stared at her with compassion, then he uttered, "We need to find this muthafucka."

# Chapter Thirty

Rafe and Malik arrived at one of their stash houses in Springfield Gardens, Queens. A colonial-style home with three bedrooms, 2,300 square feet, and a finished basement. The place was nondescript, lovely to raise a family. However, it was one of Rafe's drug spots, where the product went in to be secured, then distributed—his coke mostly. Rafe was smart enough to have several stash houses throughout Queens and Long Island, separating cocaine, other dope, and money.

Rafe scowled and cursed. "Fuck."

He seethed as he stared at the house where the police were crawling in and out of it. His stash house was now a crime scene. It had been robbed, and two of his men had been killed. Unfortunately for him, this wasn't the first theft. Last week, another one of his stash houses was hit in Queens, and the culprit or culprits got away with nearly a hundred thousand dollars in drug money. Now, he was out of ten kilos of cocaine at this location.

"Second location in two weeks. What the fuck," he exclaimed.

"It gotta be an inside job," Malik uttered. "Ain't no way we get hit twice in two weeks. We got a rat in our organization."

Rafe nodded, agreeing. "First, my little brother two months ago. Now, this shit. I swear, Malik, I want this city running red with fuckin' blood. They fuckin' wit' me. Fuck an understanding, and fuck everybody else."

The two men observed the coroners removing two bodies from the property. They were carried down the concrete steps in body bags toward a white van. Rafe knew both men personally. Their names were James and Hendricks. They were good men, and they were loyal.

They continued to watch the activity surrounding the house for a few minutes. Then, "Fuck this. Get Mob Allah on the phone. Tell him we need to meet right now. And get me the fuck outta here."

Malik nodded. He put the Nissan Pathfinder into drive, and they drove away from the block.

The next day, Rafe arrived at Baisley Pond Park to meet with Mob Allah and Zulu. He and Malik stood by the trail near the pond, staring at the ducks. It was a nice, sunny day with a gentle breeze. But Rafe was in no mood to enjoy the summer day. He was becoming unhinged with emotions and anger. Someone dared to attack his organization, steal his money and drugs, and it was a bold move . . . but stupid. Rafe had his suspicion, but he didn't have any proof. Not yet, anyway.

"Where these muthafuckas at?" Rafe griped. "We been here twenty-five minutes already."

Right then, a black Benz pulled into the parking lot nearby, and Rafe knew it was them finally showing up. He fixed his eyes on the sleek vehicle as it came to a stop and the passenger door opened. He watched Zulu get out of the car, but there was no Mob Allah.

"I know this nigga didn't come alone," Rafe continued to gripe.

Zulu and another man walked toward the pond where Rafe and Malik waited. The moment Zulu was close, Rafe exclaimed, "Where the fuck is Mob Allah? I said I wanted to see both of y'all."

"He's busy with something else," Zulu replied.

"Nigga, are you fuckin' kidding me? That muthafucka is *too busy* to meet with me? I told y'all, this shit is important. Two of my spots got hit within two weeks, and that ain't no fuckin' coincidence. If I got a problem, y'all fuckin' got a problem too," Rafe heatedly exclaimed.

"I heard, but that has nothing to do with us. You need to look into your own house for the solution," said Zulu.

"You know what? Fuck that. My little brother's dead right after he hits one of y'all spots. I made it right, no problem. And now, I'm gettin' hit, and Mob Allah is suddenly *too busy* to meet with me?" Rafe uttered.

"What are you implying?" Zulu asked.

"You know what the fuck I'm sayin', nigga," Rafe uttered through clenched teeth. "Either I'm gettin' played, or I'm the unluckiest nigga in Queens right now. Your boy out there playing them fuckin' away games while my shit is suffering. He the fuckin' connect now, huh? He doesn't need to waste his time with me anymore? Well, fuck him. And fuck you too, nigga."

"You're upset, Rafe. I understand. But be careful with what the fuck comes out of your mouth," said Zulu.

"You threatening me, nigga?" Rafe glared at him.

The tension began to grow thick between the two men. Malik became on edge, and so did Zulu's goon. It was supposed to be a civil meeting, but tempers were flaring, and Rafe became ignited. He looked like he was ready to explode like dynamite.

"I'm telling you to check your emotions before you write a check your ass can't cash," Zulu replied.

"I see. Y'all two niggas feel like y'all on top of the fuckin' world right now. Mob Allah out there tryin'a play big-boy games like he's Bill fuckin' Gates, and you his fuckin' lapdog . . . his fuckin' bitch now, huh?" Rafe insulted. "What, you suckin' that nigga dick like that white bread bitch lawyer?"

Zulu's eyebrows lowered and pulled closer together, his jaw tense. Rafe was becoming disrespectful, and he wasn't about to tolerate it. The tension had become so thick that you could cut it with a knife. Rafe was becoming unhinged and violent. After the death of Drip-Drip, he hunted for the likely killers, leaving behind a body count like he was a plague.

"You're becoming reckless and stupid, Rafe. And if you disrespect me like that again, I guarantee you won't be missing your little brother for much longer," Zulu warned him. "You need to fuckin' chill."

"What, nigga?" Rafe exclaimed, stepping threateningly closer to Zulu with his fists clenched. "I don't fear y'all niggas. Fuck both of you. I'm taking losses while y'all niggas are flossing, and *I'm* supposed to chill?"

Both men heatedly locked eyes. Malik looked like he was ready to react. Rafe was his friend, and if it came down to it, he wouldn't hesitate to kill Zulu where he stood even though he knew there would be consequences. But before things escalated, Zulu became the cooler head by uttering, "Look, Mob Allah would want us to talk things out. Not go OK Corral and Dodge City in the middle of a park. I know you're upset. How about this, you buy from us twenty cents on the dollar for every kilo—"

"I don't want your fuckin' charity, nigga," Rafe argued. "What I want is justice for Drip-Drip, and I wanna talk to that muthafucka personally—not you. He promised me something, and I expect to receive it . . . paid in full. If not, I'll burn this entire borough down like fuckin' Rome. So, don't fuck with me."

With that said, Rafe and Malik turned and walked away, leaving Zulu standing there pondering. He had predicted that Rafe was going to become a problem for them.

Rafe and Malik climbed into the Pathfinder, and before they left, Malik asked, "So, what's next? We going to war with Mob Allah?"

"Not yet. Mob Allah thinks he's some fuckin' centurion of New York, and I don't trust that nigga. When the time comes, I'm personally gonna put a bullet in both of their fuckin' heads. And that's gonna be justice for Drip-Drip," Rafe clearly proclaimed.

Malik grinned and nodded.

"Now, take me to these stupid muthafuckas," Rafe said.

Big Pockets Billiards was closed for the evening. Rafe and Malik arrived at the venue and entered the pool hall through a side door. They were soon greeted by two of Rafe's men. One of the men handed Rafe a pistol with a silencer. Rafe marched to a rear portion of the building and descended into the basement. There, he saw two men being held captive and surrounded by several other men. When they saw Rafe, a pistol in one hand and a towel in the next, their eyes widened with fear, becoming terrified. His presence made their blood run cold.

"Rafe, look, man, it wasn't our fault," one of the men desperately pleaded. "We didn't betray you. C'mon, man, you *know* me."

Rafe marched to the man menacingly, raised the pistol, and shot him in the head point-blank. Then he immediately wrapped the towel around the victim's head wound like a turban to stanch the blood flow. The second man was beside himself with absolute horror. Seeing this, he fell to his knees and began to beg for his life.

"I don't wanna die," he exclaimed, terrified.

His pleas fell on deaf ears. Rafe shot him in the head too and repeated the procedure with the towel. Malik crouched near both bodies with a large knife and stabbed both victims in the heart to prevent more blood from pumping out of the gunshot wound. It was a method they'd learned from Mafia members. With both men dead, his men started to strip away their clothing. Then they dragged their bodies into the bathroom, where the remaining blood drained out or congealed within the body.

"Y'all niggas know what to do with the bodies," said Rafe to his crew.

They knew. The bodies were placed on plastic sheets laid out on the ground, and Rafe's crew proceeded to dismember both men, cutting off the arms, legs, and heads. Subsequently, their body parts were put into bags, then placed in cardboard boxes. They would be sent to some landfill to be discarded forever and where it would be nearly impossible for the bodies to be discovered and recognized.

Rafe was becoming unhinged and bloodthirsty.

# Chapter Thirty-one

It was a pleasant summer night. The violet twilight quietly died away, blurring along the distant horizon and dissolving into a light haze as a crescent moon rose in the sky. Parked in an isolated spot near Jamaica Bay, Sincere sat inside an old Plymouth and watched the planes take off and land at JFK Airport. He stared at the aircraft and wished he were on one of them, flying somewhere far with his family and never returning. But it was a pipe dream. Sincere had unfinished business in Queens, and he wasn't going anywhere anytime soon.

The place was his secret oasis, where he could think and plot and not be bothered by anyone. But while he sat and waited, a pair of headlights began to shine his way, moving closer. Sincere climbed out of the Plymouth with a 9 mm tucked snugly into his waistband as the car approached. He calmly stared at the vehicle. Finally, it stopped opposite where he parked, and the headlights cut off. Nasir got out of the Accord to greet him.

"Damn, I ain't been out this way in years. Forgot this place even existed," Nasir said, looking around. "What's up, Sincere? Why did you want me to come out this way?"

"I got something to show you," Sincere replied.

Nasir followed him to the trunk of the Plymouth. He opened it to reveal the treasures that were inside. Nasir was shocked and speechless as he gazed at money and drugs.

"Shit! That was you that hit both of Rafe's spots," he said.

Sincere nodded.

"I thought you gave up on that idea. I mean, it's been two months."

"Plotting and planning, that's what we do best, right?"

"So, why I'm here?" Nasir asked him.

"I've been out of the game for a while now. So, I figured you'd have better use for the kilos than me, Nasir. I know you're an independent out there."

Nasir smiled. "Merry Christmas to me, I guess."

Sincere sighed deeply. Then he profoundly expressed, "This wasn't supposed to be my life anymore. I was out. Fuck. I wanted something better when I came back home. I wanted to become better."

"Why? Because that night with Crunchy is still haunting you? You did what you had to do, right? It was either him or us. And that was years ago. But with this, I tried to talk you out of it, but you still wanted revenge. You wanna know why? It's because this is who we are. It's in our DNA," said Nasir. "You can't change the spots on a leopard."

Sincere stood there in silence, brooding.

"Don't fret, nigga," Nasir continued. "I heard you left two bodies at one of the locations. What happened?"

"They reacted, so I finished it."

Nasir chuckled. "You're a killer, Sincere. It's who you are. No one can change their innate nature."

Sincere knew his friend was right. He wanted to become a cop to disguise something diabolical inside of him. So he became a soldier for the United States Army—where he was trained to kill and sent overseas for combat. But Sincere saw little to no combat while he was in the service. Instead, the army made him become a better shooter and fighter and prepared him for all elements of service: physical, mental, and emotional. It gave Sincere the tools necessary to perform.

Being a soldier was completely different than being a civilian. Boot camp sharpened his abilities. Sincere learned how to pay attention to details. When it came to cleaning a weapon, a civilian would wipe down a clean rifle with a soft cloth. But a soldier would field strip his weapon, inspect every part and reassemble it as if his life depended on it because it does. It was how he could rob two of Rafe's stash houses in two weeks. He paid attention to the details and carefully stalked and observed everyone involved. Sincere was patient, and Rafe's men didn't see him coming.

"Why are you goin' after Rafe when Mob Allah and his people killed Maurice?" Nasir asked him.

"Like you said, I'm only one man going against two drug kingpins. And I need to be smart about it," Sincere replied.

Nasir grinned. "I see it. You go after Rafe's organization and continue to hit him where it hurts. Then, sooner or later, he'll think it's coming from Mob Allah. Word on the streets is there's tension between the two men."

The two conversed briefly, and then Nasir collected the ten kilos of cocaine from the trunk. He was holding a lot of money inside the black duffle bag, kilos stamped with a cartel seal.

"And what about the money?" Nasir brought up. "I heard you stole nearly a hundred K from one of Rafe's money stash houses."

"I'm putting some of it away for Denise's college education. She deserves that," said Sincere. "But you be careful with those kilos, Nasir. Sell them shits off slow and away from here. The last thing we need is word coming back on you."

"I got this. I know some people down in the South. I'ma take a trip, B-more first, and then Charlotte. You feel me?" Nasir said.

Sincere nodded.

Nasir looked at his friend and said, "You be careful too. Because I know that look. I don't wanna be at your funeral anytime soon, Sincere."

"There won't be a funeral for me."

"Revenge is your drug, I see."

"What did Dominque used to say? 'Real niggas ain't scared of shit . . .'" Sincere began.

"Real niggas take care of shit," Nasir finished the statement.

The two gave each other dap and embraced in a brotherly hug. Then Nasir walked away with the duffle bag and climbed back into his Honda Accord. Sincere watched him drive away. He continued to linger by the Plymouth. There was something on his mind. He was a man ruminating on something. He watched as another plane approached the airport and landed. Then he climbed into the car and left the area.

# Chapter Thirty-two

Sincere climbed out of the old Plymouth and stared at the run-down row house, his home, or what used to be his home. He stood near the steps, looking pensively about something. Since the funeral, he hadn't been back to the place. Instead, he decided to stay with Monica on Long Island, and he brought Denise with him. He believed they were safer out there because Queens was becoming a hotbed for violence, and the memories were too painful to bear. And Sincere had plans for both drug kingpins. He didn't want anything coming back to his family. The row house on 164th Street was too close to hell.

It was a late evening with the block active with kids playing and people living their unassuming lives. With a pistol concealed in his waistband, Sincere kept his attention on a swivel, but he was confident he was okay back at his old home. He marched up the steps and saw that the front door was unlocked; it was typical. He pushed open the door and stepped inside. Right away, he noticed that things were different. The big-screen TV was gone, some furniture too. The place looked empty, like it was up for sale. Apparently, his mother began selling off anything valuable inside the home to support her crack addiction.

He inspected the house with sadness. A few months ago, laughter and a home-cooked meal came from the kitchen. Comfort and closeness were inside the row house, where detachment and hollowness were years ago.

He noticed the empty crack vials on the floor, indicating his mother had turned the place into a crack den. He continued to walk around downstairs. Then he made his way to the second floor. It didn't take long for everything to turn to shit. The smell was pungent because of the hot weather.

While in the hallway, he heard a noise coming from his sister's bedroom. Sincere removed the gun from his waistband and carefully went toward the sound. He pushed open the bedroom door to find a crack whore sucking dick.

"Yo, what the fuck?" Sincere exclaimed. "Get the fuck outta here."

They both hurried from the bedroom, afraid. Sincere frowned. It was his little sister's bedroom, once decorated with posters of pop stars and rappers. There used to be a TV, DVD player, and a bright comforter. They were all gone. Sincere turned and moved to his mother's bedroom. When he opened the door, he was shocked to see his mother lying on a mattress with a male crackhead. They both were bottomless, and the floor was littered with empty crack vials and several crackpipes.

Upset, Sincere kicked the mattress they were lying on and uttered, "Get the fuck up!"

He kicked it again, and the male finally opened his eyes to see a gun pointed at him. Startled, he sprang from the mattress and begged, "Don't shoot me! Please!"

"Get your shit, get the fuck outta here, and don't come back," Sincere uttered gruffly.

The man quickly gathered his things and left the bedroom. Janet glared at her son and griped, "Nigga, what the fuck you think you doin'? Don't be coming into my home kicking people out."

"Home?" Sincere shot back, upset. "You call this shithole a home? Look at this place. Look at what you did to it. And put some fuckin' clothes on, Ma."

Janet scoffed. "Muthafucka, you came out of this pussy, so don't be telling me what to fuckin' do. If you ashamed, leave."

Janet stood up, still bottomless, and continued to mock her son. "Pussy is pussy, nigga."

Sincere turned his head, ashamed of his mother's actions. "You were doing so good, Ma," he stated.

"And I'm still doin' good, muthafucka," she mocked.

"There was a crackhead sucking dick in your daughter's room. Are you proud about *that?*"

Janet snickered and replied, "You should have seen what went down in here last night. And don't be judging me, nigga. This is who I am, Sincere. You either accept it or don't."

"I don't," he retorted.

"Then leave, nigga. This is *my* house. Not yours. What I do in my fuckin' house is *my* fuckin' business," Janet exclaimed. "So, get the fuck out."

Sincere felt helpless. It was hard to accept it and keep his emotions in check. Janet refused to put on any pants, offending her son with her indiscretion. She had backslid into hopelessness, and there wasn't anything he could do for her.

Despondent by what he saw, Sincere turned and left. As he walked out of the front door, a man came up the steps. It was apparent what he was coming to do inside the row house. Sincere scowled at the man and angrily pushed him away, yelling, "Get the fuck out of here! Leave."

The man tripped, but he didn't resist. The look on Sincere's face was a warning to him. Sincere couldn't strike his mother for her indiscretions, but he could strike this unknown crackhead. Sincere watched the man scurry away. He looked back at the front entrance and released a profound sigh. There was a weight on top of him that felt paralyzing. And a desolate look in his eyes, empty like a void and puzzling like a maze.

He walked toward his car, but he hesitated to get inside. He took one look at the area, and no one noticed him, not even the neighbors. It was like he was a ghost. Then, a Lexus drove by with blaring rap music and chromed rims. Two men inside the car screamed hustlers. The driver shot Sincere an unfriendly look but then turned away, indicating he was a nobody. Sincere smirked and thought . . . if they only knew.


It was a beautiful sunny day at the park. Sincere and Denise were out for a walk enjoying the afternoon together. Sincere wanted to spend some quality time with his little sister. It had been awhile since they sat together and talked. They'd gotten ice cream earlier, and it provided some normalcy for them despite their lives being uprooted. They took a seat on an old wooden bench underneath some beautiful trees, and for a moment, they watched the world around them go by.

"Listen, I want you to transfer schools this fall," Sincere uttered out of the blue. "I don't want you going back to school in Queens."

Denise was taken aback by this. "What? Why? I thought us staying out here with Monica would be temporary."

"Well, it's not."

Denise was upset by this. She frowned at her brother and snapped. "So, you get to tell me what to do now, huh? What about my friends? And Ma?"

"What about them?" Sincere replied nonchalantly. "You can find some new friends here. And, Ma, she's sick. She's not herself."

"That's why we need to be back in Queens to help her. We just can't abandon her, Sincere. Especially now with Maurice gone," Denise griped.

"She doesn't want our help. And it's not safe to go back home."

"Bullshit," she cursed. "You just can't come back here after fuckin' four years and suddenly tell me what to do. Everything was fine while you were gone."

"I'm not trying to tell you what to do, Denise."

"It sounds like it to me."

Sincere huffed. "You're my little sister, and I'm in charge of you now. And I'm just doing what's in our best interest."

"You mean what's in *your* best interest," Denise countered. "You have Monica and your son out here with you. And what the fuck do *I* have? Everything I know and love is back in Queens, and you just wanna swoop in on my life and take it away from me."

"I'm not, Denise. I want you to be happy."

"If you want me to be happy, then take me back to Queens," she insisted.

Sincere sighed and replied, "That's not happening."

The scowl on Denise's face could scare the devil. She shouted, "Fuck you, Sincere." Then she leaped from the bench and stormed away.

Sincere stood up and called out for her. "Denise, come back here. Denise."

She completely ignored him and continued walking away. Sincere grimaced, but he knew he was doing the right thing. The last thing he wanted was for any harm to come to his sister, and he was willing to protect her at any cost. He'd started something, and until he finished it, his family would stay on Long Island.

And he was really looking forward to a quiet, peaceful day at the park.

# Chapter Thirty-three

The room was filled with important people, a corporate gala for fundraising and investments. The event was hosted on the rooftop of a five-star hotel in Midtown Manhattan overlooking Central Park. The fantastic view was exquisite at night. There was live entertainment and refreshing cocktails. Mob Allah and Sonja were dressed attractively. He was in a sharp, black-tie suit, and she was wearing a beautiful blue gown—Ebony and Ivory at its finest.

The sea of faces was primarily white, and exuberant wealth was displayed.

"There are over $5 billion in this room right now," Sonja said.

Mob Allah looked the part, but he knew he was out of his element. Sonja had become his third party to the bigwigs inside the room. She was beautiful, connected, and respected.

"Events like these mainly focus on business and customers to boost a company's brand reputation and impress potential investors, donors, or high-end clients. So it's important to build relations and strengthen the clientele," she said to him. "I've been to my fair share of these."

Mob Allah nodded. Black-tie servants walked around carrying silver trays, and the scenery was so swank it was nearly intimidating.

"I want to introduce you to a few people in the room," she said. "They would like to meet you."

Mob Allah followed her lead. First, she removed two flutes from a silver tray and handed one to Mob Allah. Then, she approached a group of men already engaged in conversation.

"Gentlemen," she announced, "it's good to see everyone."

They all turned to see her coming with a bright smile. "Sonja, good to see you."

"And it's good to see you too, Henry. I want to introduce you to a good friend of mine. This is Jeffery Mathews, a potential investor for several upcoming development projects in Queens."

Mob Allah shook hands with the men, and he didn't flinch when Sonja uttered his real name. He was still a gangster, but it was time to branch out. He understood that true power wasn't in the streets but in owning real estate and significant investments and becoming connected politically.

"Queens? I hear certain areas are about to experience an explosion of economic redevelopment," a man named Marvin Ross uttered. "Now would be a good time to grab some land in that borough."

"Brooklyn too," someone chimed in.

"The economy is depreciating bit by bit," uttered a man named Timothy. "With Clinton in office, it will be the Whitewater scandal all over again."

"No need to be pessimistic, Timothy," Marvin chuckled. "He has one more year in office, and then Bush will become our guy. Watch and see."

"I'll toast to that," Henry chimed.

The men continued to talk, and Mob Allah was soaking in everything. And though he was new to their world, he proved to be intelligent and entertaining. He was a wolf in sheep's clothing, knowing how to play his part and conceal who he was. Mob Allah understood that to thrive and climb, he had to become a man of many faces.

He held his own with the group, and they liked him. It was hard to tell that he was a convicted gangster who killed people and had a level of fear on the streets equivalent to a brutal dictator.

"You know who you were talking to?" Sonja asked him.

Of course, he didn't. "No. Who?"

"Henry Levy, a real estate tycoon who makes Donald Trump look like Bob, the Builder. He's very connected, very great with development in this city, and someone you'll want to know well," she explained to him. "But do not go into a room alone with him. You'll want me in there with you. Believe me. He'll bleed you dry."

Mob Allah nodded, taking in the information.

"I want to introduce you to a few more people," said Sonja.

The night continued, and Mob Allah, with Sonja's help, continued to work the room. He was impressed by Sonja's ability to finesse these old white men. They drew to her like moths to a flame.

The two had a private moment with a lovely view of Central Park and its terrain, from flat grassy swards, gentle slopes, and shady glens to steep, rocky ravines.

"Are you enjoying yourself?" she asked him.

"Yeah, I am."

"So, what do you think?"

Mob Allah grinned. He raised his flute as she did, and he proclaimed, "I think you and me will own this fuckin' city."

Sonja beamed, agreeing with him. Then they clinked glasses and downed the champagne.

Mob Allah went from a swanky and posh five-star event to arriving at a dodgy Brooklyn warehouse to oversee a large number of drugs, 500 kilos of cocaine. He was the biggest drug dealer in New York City. His distribution network included twenty-two cities and grossed more than $400 million. He distributed cocaine to the Bloods, Crips, and Latin Kings, and he had employees by the thousands. Also, Mob Allah knew that wearing the crown and becoming the top man would always make him marked. With Sonja and a handful of respected people by his side, it became easier for him to launder millions and millions of dollars. He had many legitimate businesses on paper. He was making so much straight money it was becoming simpler for him to put his name on things and carry things out in the open.

Also, Mob Allah had an uncanny ability to keep his associates in the dark. No one knew where he lived, what phone number he used, or what vehicle he drove. He'd become good at hiding his whereabouts.

Mob Allah stood hidden in the warehouse's rafters, out of sight from the dozen or so workers below and entire pallets of kilos. Zulu and Mackie flanked him as he observed everything from afar.

"How are we looking?" he asked Mackie.

"Everything's tight and on schedule," Mackie replied.

Mob Allah nodded. He watched as one of many of their customers arrived to receive their product. They were men from throughout the city, each in control of their own empire and territories. The first was Blue, a Brooklyn Crip from Brownsville. He was a dangerous gangbanger who supplied the low-level dealers in the projects, and he grossed about $25,000 a week in drug sales. Mob Allah made it his business to know the math and profit of everyone he dealt with.

The men watched Blue arrive with his right-hand man, and they were in and out with no issues.

"Mackie, give me a minute with Zulu," Mob Allah said.

Mackie nodded and left the area.

"What's the verdict with Rafe?" Mob Allah asked him.

"It's not good. He's becoming unhinged, dropping bodies, and making unnecessary noise. He's going to become a problem. He was upset that you didn't show up to meet with him," Zulu proclaimed.

"That's not happening. It's becoming more of a risk to me," said Mob Allah.

"He's goin' to make a move on us. I know it. We need to take him out; end things with that nigga before it escalates. I offered him our product for twenty cents on the dollar, and he refused. The nigga ain't been right since his brother's death."

Mob Allah sighed. He knew Zulu was right. It was best to nip things in the bud before they become out of control.

"Listen, get it done but quietly. We can't afford a war," Mob Allah instructed. "Malik too. We can't kill one and leave him alive to come after us."

Zulu smiled.

"And listen, Zulu. From now on, I'm not here to oversee these transactions. This is your task, your responsibility," said Mob Allah firmly.

Zulu smirked and replied with, "King of kings, huh?"

He turned and walked away, leaving Mob Allah standing there in all his glory. Mob Allah, a.k.a. Jeffery Mathews, was on top of the world.

# Chapter Thirty-four

"It's a beautiful weapon," Jimmy uttered to Sincere. "You can get a lot done with that gun."

Sincere coolly inspected a MAC-10. It was an intimidating weapon, but Sincere knew it wasn't the best.

"The main problem with the MAC-10 is it isn't accurate at all," said Sincere. He placed the gun back into the trunk of the car and picked up an M-16. "Now, the M-16 boasts an effective range of no less than 500 yards, ten times that of a MAC-10."

Jimmy smiled. "I see you know your guns. Marines?"

"Army," Sincere answered.

"Marines for me . . . was in the Gulf War," said Jimmy.

The two men connected. They met in Newark, New Jersey, where Jimmy grew up. Jimmy was a tall, slender man with a narrow face and a cigarette-raspy voice. Sincere found out about him through an old friend from the neighborhood. He needed a supply of guns for a reasonable rate.

Sincere picked up a Glock 20 and inspected it.

"Now, you're talking about my kind of gun," Jimmy said. "The Glock 20, while it doesn't pack the same punch as some other Magnum pistol calibers I sell, it still packs a lot of heat behind that 10-mm round."

"I'll take two of these," said Sincere.

Jimmy smiled. He had a mobile arsenal. Inside the trunk of the 1975 Dodge Dart were more guns than some armies in a small country. In fact, Jimmy had the best firearms manufactured, from Glock 17s and 41s, a few .45 ACPs, 9 mm Berettas, Springfield Armory XD9s, and Springfield Armory XD(M) 40s. There were several shotguns and automatic weapons for Sincere to look at too.

Sincere removed more guns from the trunk. This time, he gripped a revolver.

"The .44 Rem Mag is a small but mighty revolver with some real stopping power," said Jimmy.

Sincere continued to fill a large duffle bag with the guns he desired. Jimmy was happy for the business, but he was baffled by it too.

"If you don't mind me asking, why do you need so many guns?" he asked.

Sincere shot him a not-so-nice look and replied, "I mind you asking."

Jimmy shrugged. Business was business.

"I'll give ten thousand for everything," said Sincere.

"Damn, you got that kind of money on you now?"

Sincere revealed a $10,000 stack, and Jimmy's eyes widened. He made the deal. Sincere tossed him the cash and then zipped up the duffle bag. There was no need for Jimmy to count it, and he didn't ask him any more questions.

"We're good," said Jimmy lightheartedly.

Sincere started to walk away, carrying the duffle bag. But with an afterthought, Jimmy said to him, "Listen, man, I know it isn't my business what you're going to do with that many guns. But whatever you got planned, you don't know me and seek counseling or Jesus."

Sincere didn't respond. He continued to walk away.

Open Tease was a strip club in Yonkers. Inside were nude girls, booze, hip-hop music, and hedonistic fun for the patrons looking to escape their reality and perhaps get into some debauchery shit. It was a Friday night, and the place was packed with a decent mix of people. The girls were well-tanned and buffed, and the men were all well-behaved . . . so far. It was a sizable place with four dancing areas, numerous lap dances, and naked workers everywhere.

Mackie and his crew were having the time of their lives in VIP. Their area was teeming with naked women: short, thick, tall, voluptuous, Black, white—you name it. There was something for everyone. One of the shot girls had her tongue pierced, and for the excitement of the men, she gave mock fellatio to a test tube shot. Everyone cheered her and tossed money her way. Mackie seemed untouchable, surrounded by his comrades. He was a top lieutenant in the drug organization. And he was feared and respected. But tonight, it wasn't about business; it was about having fun, unwinding. The past few months, business had been so good that everyone was swimming in money and praise.

On the stage was a stripper named Passion. She was thick, with her skin dripping in ebony chocolate. She climbed the pole in a pair of stilettos and a sheer pink minidress and began her show. All eyes were on her. Passion slowly, sensually removed her sheer pink minidress, revealing her plump, juicy breasts. She slid it down the length of her body and then stepped out of it.

Passion, with her soft, smooth, dark skin and electrifying performance, immediately caught Mackie's attention. He approached the stage with a wad of cash so large it could choke a horse. He fixed his eyes on Passion as she dangled her piece over his head for a bit, allowing him to take in its spicy scent. After that, she threw it back over her shoulder and gently lowered herself onto his lap. Mackie began to toss so much money at her; it was a monsoon of cash. Passion picked up his hands and placed them around her waist, pushing his face between her breasts. Lingering in that position, she leaned down and kissed his neck, then guided his mouth to her left breast, which he gently kissed and poked with his tongue. The action was repeated with her right breast. Passion rose and pushed his face into her belly, and he covered it with tiny kisses. Throughout the whole dance, she didn't turn around once. She seemed focused entirely on Mackie. Her eyes were locked into his, and her smile was as bright as the sun.

Everyone was jealous. Mackie had the respect and the cash, and Passion personally dried fucked him in the chair and allowed him to fondle her in public. However, it was forbidden inside the club. Unbeknownst to Mackie, he was closely watched.

At the end of her performance, Passion shifted around and sat on his lap without bothering to put her dress back on. Instead, she whispered into his ear, "That was nice. You wanna go somewhere private?"

She was in awe of him.

After Passion did her main stage performance, the girls working at Open Tease did a showcase walk, after which they did 2-for-1 lap dances. After that, Mackie left with Passion for a private dance in one of the private rooms inside the club.

Sincere cleverly followed them and frowned at the man, watching him disappear into one of the isolated rooms. He couldn't react right there but had to wait. He knew Mackie was there when they killed Maurice and knew he was one of Mob Allah's right-hand men. Nevertheless, seeing Mackie living the good life with money, women, and respect ignited his anger.

The night continued into the early morning, and the crowd at Open Tease began winding down. Mackie and three of his men exited the club in high spirits. They had giggling ladies with them, and though it was late, everyone wanted the party to continue somewhere else. Mackie and Passion had connected, and they planned on being together sexually. He had the temperament and the money.

The streets of Yonkers were quiet. It was nearing the hours when men and women were about to get up and dress for work, and sanitation workers would start collecting trash. But the gangsters continued to party. Then, finally, they approached a 4Runner parked nearby. Each man was distracted by pussy and laughter, and they were cohorts of Mob Allah and Zulu . . . So who would dare come after them?

Then it happened abruptly. A loud gunshot rang out, striking one of the men in the head. He went down, and the girls started to scream. Panic ensued, and chaos erupted with the girls running away. Mackie and the other two men pulled out their guns like they were in the Wild West and heatedly returned gunfire—but at whom? Suddenly, a second man went down with multiple shots. Mackie ducked for cover and crouched behind a car.

"What the fuck?" he cursed.

Gunfire continued to crackle, and gangsters fell to their knees in shock, clutching their bleeding chests with their guns clattering to the ground. Mackie quickly found himself alone, still crouched behind his 4Runner, pistol intensely gripped, and that feeling of power and entitlement quickly disappearing. He breathed heavily, knowing death was near. And it was. Unbeknownst to him, Sincere had crept behind him somehow, and when Mackie turned around, *Bang.* He was shot in the shoulder and stumbled to retreat from the threat.

"Nigga, you know who the fuck I am?" Mackie screamed deafeningly.

Sincere scowled at his victim with his emotions on high. He knew what this muthafucka did to his little brother, and he leveled the Glock 17 at Mackie's chest. His face only grew grimmer, and his grip tightened around the handle.

"I got money, nigga. However much you want, it's yours," Mackie uttered, begging for his life.

"Fuck you," Sincere exclaimed.

With a determined stare, he pulled the trigger with a booming bang. Sincere shot Mackie multiple times in the chest and head, emptying the clip. It was overkill. The gunshots were loud and echoed throughout the street, and the area was littered with bodies. Sincere stood there and stared at his handiwork for a moment. He was unfazed, and his eyes looked soulless. Killing Mackie would send a message to Mob Allah. He was coming for all of them.

He turned and disappeared from the scene, hearing police sirens blaring in the distance.

# Chapter Thirty-five

Mob Allah sat inside his extravagant penthouse palace at Trump Plaza holding a glass of scotch and looked detached. He'd heard the news about Mackie and was upset. He sat in a leather armchair shirtless, wearing cotton shorts. It was a sunny day, but there wasn't anything bright with Mob Allah. One of his top lieutenants was dead, along with three other men. He believed Rafe was behind the murders. Rafe had struck first before his men could kill him and Malik. Now, there was a deadly conflict between both sides, and it was inevitable to escalate. Mob Allah sat inside his home, seething and contemplating his next move on Rafe. It was a bad look, a war happening in Queens.

He downed his scotch and continued to sit and think. But then, suddenly, he burst into anger and rage. He leaped from the chair and heatedly pitched the glass into the wall, shattering it. Then he stood there cursing and ranting.

The front door opened, and Sonja walked into the large room looking sexy in a medium-length skirt suit with a conservative blouse and pumps. It was clear she was upset about something when she approached Mob Allah, who stood erect in anger. She irately slammed a newspaper down on the table and exclaimed, "What the fuck is *this?*"

The headline read: GANGLAND MURDERS AT YONKERS CLUB, FOUR DEAD.

Mob Allah glanced at the paper and replied, "I'm taking care of it."

"Taking care of it? How? Mackie's dead, and this is a bad look. It's bad for business, Mob Allah. The last thing we need is negative press toward you and Queens."

"You think I don't fuckin' know that?" he shouted.

Sonja wasn't intimidated by his outburst. She was fearless. She stepped closer to him and looked him squarely in his eyes to get her point across.

"If this links back to you or anything negative, the investors and everyone we're doing business with will be afraid to come close to you. Everything we've worked for will come to a stop and crumble. These people don't want to be involved in any bloodshed—and not read any headlines like this. This is a fucking problem, baby," she vehemently proclaimed.

Mob Allah stood there in silence. He understood.

"This can't escalate, baby. If it does, we're fucked," she warned him. "You *cannot* be connected to this. Insulate yourself from it all right now. I'm speaking as your lawyer *and* a friend."

"I already have," he replied.

"And I'm sorry about Mackie. He was loyal," she expressed.

"He was. And he won't be forgotten," Mob Allah mentioned.

"Just be smart with future actions," she said. "I have an afternoon deposition in an hour, so I need to go."

She gave him a loving kiss, pivoted, and left the premises leaving Mob Allah alone, brooding. The last thing he wanted was to look weak in the streets if they didn't retaliate. Mackie's reputation was equivalent to being a made-man in his eyes. He stepped out on the balcony with a sweeping view of the Hudson River and the New Jersey shoreline and lit a cigar. Then he exhaled and collected his thoughts. This incident was only a temporary setback. However, everything Rafe loved was about to be exterminated.

Rafe unhappily stared at his little brother's grave. It had been three months since Drip-Drip's death, and the feeling of hatred and rage continued to swirl inside of him. He felt he hadn't avenged his brother's murder. He'd killed a few people, but they were murdered because of heated temperaments and accusations. Someone had to pay for Drip-Drip's death, no matter who it was. However, Rafe felt that his brother's killer was still alive and out there, mocking him. And he still blamed Mob Allah and Zulu. From the bottom of his heart, he knew that they were behind everything that happened to his brother and his organization. Rafe believed he was a threat to both men because he wasn't scared of them and wasn't backing down.

"Mob Allah is a man, not a fuckin' god," he vehemently proclaimed to his crew. "That muthafucka gonna bleed like a gutted pig. I promise y'all niggas that."

While Rafe paid his respects at the Long Island cemetery, a half-dozen armed men stood watch nearby. They gave Rafe the distance needed to pay his respects but had his back against any rivalries. They were at war, and Rafe wasn't taking any chances. He was vulnerable at the cemetery.

"I love you, little bro," he uttered expressively. "Damn, I wish you hadn't been so fuckin' hardheaded. You never knew how to fuckin' listen. Always thought you knew it all. But the one thing I loved about you, you were fearless, little nigga. Most times, you acted with stupidity, but you had heart on these streets."

As Rafe was having a heart-to-heart conversation with his deceased brother, Malik arrived at the cemetery with his goons. He climbed out of the Lexus and walked briskly toward Rafe. They looked at each other, and Rafe knew Malik had something important to tell him.

Right away, Malik uttered, "Mackie's dead."

Rafe was shocked by the news but also pleased. "How?"

"He was killed the other night, he and three other men. They were gunned down in Yonkers," said Malik.

"It seems I'm not the only one beefing with Mob Allah. After that, the untouchable becomes touchable," Rafe laughed. "You know who did it?"

"No. But whoever it was, to get at Mackie and his men like that, they knew what the fuck they were doing. Of course, Mob Allah and Zulu are gonna think it was us."

"And I'm happy to have them believe that," Rafe replied. "Fuck 'em. I'm glad that nigga's dead. Bitch-ass nigga was probably responsible for Drip-Drip's death." Rafe turned to stare at the grave and exclaimed, "You hear that, little brother? It's on. What they built, watch me tear it all the fuck down in your honor."

Rafe took a deep breath. He then turned to Malik and uttered, "You know what time it is. Tell all our soldiers to tool up and get ready. Make some noise out there."

Malik nodded, turned, and marched away. He and his men were prepared to become the Grim Reapers. Meanwhile, Rafe continued to stand at his brother's grave, and he proclaimed wholeheartedly, "Never go to war unless you're willing to win."

War is war. The only good human being is a dead one. It's how the soldiers felt inside the Pathfinder as it traveled through Jamaica, Queens, during a late evening. The passengers in the front and back seat became locked and loaded with duo MAC-10s. They were clad in all black and determined to kill everything in sight. The driver, Zodiac, was calm and focused. Their orders from Zulu . . . They kill one of ours, we kill many of theirs.

The Pathfinder traveled toward Big Pockets Billiards, believing Rafe and his men would be there. What they had in mind for the place and any unfortunate occupants inside wasn't going to be pretty. The gunmen were nearing their site with dusk fast approaching in the city. The setting of the sun showed the end of the day's journey. It felt like everything was put on pause for a moment, with colors flying in the sky to paint the world. But these men didn't have time to appreciate anything picturesque. Heavy scowls were on their faces as they gripped the intimidating MAC-10s, ready to put in work for their organization.

The Pathfinder turned the corner to the block of the pool hall, and it slowed down. Each man masked up and was ready to implement destruction. The pool hall had a few occupants inside, including some of Rafe's men just shooting the breeze. The Pathfinder crept toward the pool hall. One of the gunmen emerged from the moonroof of the vehicle, and the other protruded from the back window with their weapons hot and ready. And the moment they became parallel to the location, they opened fire.

*Rat-a-tat-tat-tat-tat. Rat-a-tat-tat-tat-tat. Rat-a-tat-tat-tat-tat.*

Bullets started flying, windows shattered, and panic ensued. Immediately, everyone inside the pool hall went scrambling for cover and safety. Zodiac stopped the car because he didn't want just to do a drive-by. The gunman in the back seat leaped from the vehicle and continued spraying the pool hall with gunfire.

*Rat-a-tat-tat-tat-tat. Rat-a-tat-tat-tat-tat.*

Rafe's men were overwhelmed by heavy firepower. Their guns were drawn, but it felt like they were in World

War III. The gunfire came at them in rapid succession. People were screaming. Men yelled out, "What the hell?" Then quickly, the masked gunman retreated into the back seat of the Pathfinder, and Rafe's men came barreling from the pool hall with their guns and heatedly returned gunfire at the fleeing vehicle. But it was too late.

"These muthafuckas," someone shouted. "Get Malik on the phone now!"

Fortunately, no one was killed.

No mercy, no regret, only violence. Keys and Donny were edgy when they entered the project apartment in Baisley Park Houses to do a pickup. Both men were still disheartened by Mackie's brutal demise. But the loss of a prominent lieutenant didn't stop the show or any business in the streets. There was still money on the streets that needed to be collected. The shooting at the pool hall only escalated things between both crews, and men on both sides were out looking for blood.

Keys knocked on the apartment door, and a man carrying a sawed-off shotgun cautiously opened it, expecting them. Both men entered the apartment/stash house armed and on high alert. The place was a low-level stash house where Keys and Donny were collecting $30,000 from drug profits. Only two men occupied the apartment, and they both carried shotguns for security. The place was fortified with multiple locks and a camera. The inside looked like a regular, furnished, two-bedroom apartment. One of the men went into the main bedroom and returned to hand Keys a bag filled with cash.

"Y'all niggas be careful out there," said the man with the sawed-off shotgun.

Keys nodded. "We got this." He lifted his shirt to reveal a .45 in his waistband.

With the cash in hand, Keys and Donald left the apartment with two more runs/pickups to do before they went to the mattresses like they did in the Mafia. It wasn't safe to be on the streets. Zulu and his crew were hiding out in secret and secured Brooklyn locations. They had to vacate their homes and rent places in safer areas. No man was supposed to travel alone. Everyone was preparing for a lengthy war. And to protect themselves, they hired soldiers to sleep on the floors in shifts.

Keys and Donny took the elevator down to the lobby from the sixth floor. Being extra cautious, Keys removed his pistol and held it by his side during the duration of the trip—better safe than sorry. He looked at Donny, and slight nervousness registered on their faces. The ride to the lobby might as well have been a mile long, with it feeling like they were in enemy territory. Finally, the elevator touched the atrium, the bell sounded, and the door slid open. Keys stepped into the atrium first. But then, abruptly, a baseball bat viciously slammed into his chest, and he curled over into instant pain. Both men were immediately attacked by three men wielding metal baseball bats.

Donny got hit upside the head like *pi-yah*! And he went down like Frazier. Pain shot through him like fire. It exploded in his head with blinding whiteness. It made him dizzy. Both men were struck multiple times with baseball bats, and they started bleeding like stuck pigs.

"This is for Drip-Drip," one of the attackers shouted.

The pain was like needles dipped in alcohol that had been jammed through their skin. They had broken ribs, fractured skulls, and broken eye sockets. It was a level of violence so brutal that it was almost unfathomable.

Their attackers grabbed the bag of cash and left them both for dead.

# Chapter Thirty-six

A war was going on outside, and no man was safe. They could run, but they couldn't hide forever.

Sincere was a different breed in the streets. He didn't want to become a killer, but they forced his hand when they murdered his kin. Now, he was hell-bent on revenge, and there was no turning back from being knee-deep in shit. Finally, he started to see his truth. Killing had awakened something inside of him. He was good at it, and he couldn't walk away. His brutal murders were making the front-page news, and people linked them to a drug war in Queens.

The military had trained him to become this monster, not knowing he would be effective in a different kind of war. In boot camp, he'd lost a sense of his own worth as an individual. And being a soldier, a new recruit, he had undergone brutal and sometimes humiliating training experiences that wore down his sense of individuality. But on the other hand, it helped him chip away any of the resistance most people have to the notion of ending someone else's life.

The military conditioned Sincere to become effective, and that he became. Unfortunately, his drill sergeant was a mean sonofabitch. He was a pit bull in fatigues and personally attacked the recruits. Drill sergeants were the role models in the military. Their job was to demonstrate aggression while maintaining discipline and create soldiers capable of killing an enemy in combat.

Sincere sat in the park watching his son play with a few other kids. Tyriq was happy and full of life. Sincere watched the boy go from the sandbox to the jungle gym, the monkey bars, then to the slide, all within the blink of an eye. Tyriq was the Flash on the playground, and Sincere happened to smile. It was a peaceful moment for him. Watching children play blocked out the murders he'd committed. It was the moment when Sincere felt normal and had his guard down. But while watching his son play, he thought about his daughter, Akari, and he got sad. He missed her and her mother, Asuka, profoundly. Every night, he would stare at the one picture he had of Asuka and his daughter. She was 2 years old now. Sincere would reminisce about them. He was in love with Monica, but he was also in love with Asuka. There was something about Asuka that he couldn't let go of or forget.

*Sincerity is the foundation of trust. And trust is the foundation of a strong relationship,* Asuka believed. When they were together, they had no secrets from each other. Her hidden magnetism, mysterious culture, and pleasant appearance captivated him. Sincere thought about her smiling face, her mesmerizing melody of speech, and unsurpassed figure. He felt that nowhere else in the world would he find such a phenomenon. She spoke three languages. And he wanted to learn Japanese and improve his knowledge of the Japanese language by communicating with her. In their communication, it became a mutual sympathy and transformed into a strong relationship.

The first time they had sex, it was so sensual and mind-blowing that the experience left a significant mark on his mind. She had chosen him and trusted him completely. And being inside of her was a heavenly pleasure. She was warm and tight, and her vagina naturally wrapped snuggly around his dick. He couldn't stop seeing her. It was inevitable that she would become pregnant by him.

Sincere snapped out of his daydream when he heard his pager going off. It was Nasir trying to reach him. He stood up from the bench and called out to his son. It was time to go. He made sure his son couldn't see the gun in his waistband. It was the life he lived now, having to carry a weapon on him and watching over his shoulder.

Tyriq came running to his father with the brightest smile. Sincere matched his son's smile and asked, "Did you have fun?"

"Yes, Daddy."

He stared at his boy and saw the resemblance. He was foolish to think Monica would cheat on him with Mighty. He knew Monica loved him deeply like Asuka did in Japan. Now he had children with both women. He thought, one day, if he had to choose one, who would it be? They both were unique to him, and they both had their ways of loving him, and he loved them. But he was a man being torn inside out by revenge. And he wanted to keep his family away from the ugliness happening in Queens.

Sincere and Tyriq climbed into the Ford and left the park. It had been a wonderful father and son day where they'd gone to the movies, gotten some ice cream, and enjoyed the park. He wanted to spend as much quality time with Tyriq as possible. He'd missed four years of his life and had a lot of making up to do.

When they arrived home, he'd received another page from Nasir. He figured it was important. Monica came to the front door wearing a colorful, trendy summer dress, and she looked beautiful in it. She smiled, and he smiled.

"Did y'all have fun?" she asked them.

"We did," Sincere replied.

Tyriq nodded. "Yes, Mommy."

She smiled and then said to him, "Go inside and get washed up for dinner."

Tyriq ran into the house while Monica lingered by the door staring at Sincere's hesitation to come inside, knowing something was on his mind.

"What's wrong?" she asked him.

"I need to go take care of something," he replied lightly.

"Take care of what? I made us dinner, and tonight, I need to tell you something."

"I won't be gone long, Monica."

Monica stepped closer to him. The way she looked at him was as if he were an open book.

"Listen, I'm not stupid, and I'm no fool. I know who you are and what you're capable of doing, Sincere. I remember that look when we were young. You're not working, but you're able to support us. And I was never that woman to get into your business. The only thing I ever asked of you was to please not bring it here and into our home. Don't cheat on me and put us first. That's all I ask of you," she gently said to him.

"I won't. I promise."

"How long will you be gone?"

"Not long. I'm just meeting Nasir, that's it," he said.

Monica exhaled. "Okay. I'll keep things warm for you."

"You promise?" Sincere replied with a knowing smile, implying he knew what she meant by keeping it warm.

Monica displayed an innuendo grin and returned, "I promise."

When Nasir arrived at their meeting place in a brand-new Lexus ES 300, Sincere was displeased.

"What the fuck do you think you're doing?" Sincere griped, frowning at the vehicle. "You buy yourself a new car?"

"Business is good," Nasir replied. "Too good. Thanks to you, no doubt."

"And you think it was wise to buy yourself a brand-new Lexus?"

"Nigga, I'm a fuckin' drug dealer. It's what we do, right? Besides, Mob Allah and Rafe are too busy warring with each other right now to pay any attention to what I'm doing. I'm independent, and I underestimated you and your plan. You're a smart nigga, Sincere. I forgot how cunning you can be."

"And I forgot how hardheaded you can be, Nasir," he spat. "You need to be smart and keep a low profile," Sincere warned him.

"It's just a Lexus. And I was making money before you even came back. And I've been in these streets for a long time. So, don't talk to me like I'm some off-brand muthafucka, nigga. You took a break from this shit. I didn't," Nasir proclaimed.

Sincere sighed. "I know that. But Rafe and Mob Allah, they aren't stupid."

"And neither are we," Nasir countered. "I know how to watch my back out there. And like I said I would, I sold them keys off nice and slow. I cleaned up in Charlotte, Baltimore, and South Carolina. Developed quite a clientele in those cities."

"What now? You're looking for a re-up?"

"You're doin' this for revenge. But we can do this to make money," Nasir suggested. "Mob Allah and Rafe, you got them killing each other. And think about it. We can come in coolly, pick up the crumbs, and take over shit. With you, they won't even see us coming."

Sincere chuckled at the proposal. "What, you want us to become the new power, become drug kingpins?"

"It's our time, Sincere. We deserve it," Nasir uttered wholeheartedly. "Think about it. For years, we put in work out there on those streets. We made shit happen, and niggas overlooked us. So where are Dominque and Trey-Trey now? Gone. But we're still here."

"That was a long time ago," Sincere replied.

"Not for me, it wasn't."

The look in Nasir's eyes said it all to Sincere. His friend was willing to do anything now to seize the throne. The essence of wanting power and control was a powerful force that would drive men's thoughts and emotions.

Nasir went to his Lexus and opened the trunk. Sincere wasn't sure what he was up to, but he kept his guard up and his gun close. Nasir removed something from the trunk. It was a small backpack. He tossed the bag at Sincere's feet and said, "Open it."

Sincere was curious. He crouched to the backpack and unzipped it, and inside were bundles of cash.

"There is $50,000 in the bag," said Nasir. "Take it. It's yours. You started something, Sincere, and you need to finish it. As a matter of fact, we need to finish it together."

With that said, Nasir climbed into his Lexus and drove away. Sincere stood there holding the backpack of cash. He was conflicted with some intense emotions and mixed feelings. He did start this war, but he didn't want to die in it.

# Chapter Thirty-seven

Two men lay dead in the front seat of a Nissan Maxima. They had been viciously gunned down when a dark-colored sedan pulled up next to them while they stopped at the red light, and someone inside engaged in gunfire, shooting them. It was a bloodbath. Both men were shot multiple times in the head and body with an Uzi machine gun and pistol. They didn't see it coming.

The intersection of Sutphin Blvd. and Linden Blvd. had been shut down entirely. The police were all over the gruesome crime scene, and detectives asked questions they already knew the answers to. It was clear to everyone that the two men were fatalities in an escalating drug war. They seized two pistols from the car and an AK-47 from the back seat. The victims were linked to being soldiers of Mob Allah's organization.

"It's becoming fuckin' Fallujah in this damn borough," Lieutenant Malecki uttered. "We got a got-damn gang war and a serial killer happening simultaneously. So what are the fuckin' odds?"

The news got back to Zulu about the murders, and he threw a heated fit. Everything was going to shit. Earlier, Coffee had griped about business slowing down on the track. His bitches weren't making him any money. They were scared to work because of a serial killer targeting young prostitutes, and the cops hadn't arrested him yet. Also, the NYPD was now patrolling the urban communities, city parks, and the ho stroll heavily. The thick presence of law enforcement frightened away the customers. There were even rumors that undercover officers were posing as prostitutes to try to capture this killer.

"This muthafucka serial killer is bad for fuckin' business, Zulu," Coffee had griped. "I got hoes ready to revolt because of this nigga. Pussy on got-damn standby and shit, and tricks out there scared of being arrested because there's more fuckin' cops on the track than there is at One Police Plaza."

"I'm gonna take care of it," Zulu had promised him.

"When? Closed fuckin' legs ain't makin' us no money. What about Mob Allah? What's *he* doing about this?"

"I told you, I got this," Zulu shouted. "You don't fuckin' need to worry about him. Worry about me, muthafucka. I'm on it."

Coffee was taken aback by the reaction. He meekly replied, "Okay."

Zulu was upset because he was in the trenches with the soldiers trying to hunt down Rafe and end this war while Mob Allah was tucked away and hidden somewhere. Mob Allah continued to play his away games with his lawyer while no one was making any money in the streets. War did that. It brought everything to a standstill, and business declined. The bodies piling up on the street brought negative attention from the police.

Zulu felt Mob Allah had changed since he'd come home. At first, he was this ruthless muthafucka with a reputation that preceded him—and it still did. He made sure his name continued to ring out the way he handled the stash house robbery. Everyone involved was dead. But now, Mob Allah's inner circle seemed to change, along with his motives. It seemed like the new council in Mob Allah's life were his lawyer, Sonja, the corrupt property developer, Michael Kostroff, and Bobby Spyros. This angered Zulu because he felt these people, empty suits despite Bobby Spyros, didn't know their world, but they were becoming heavily involved with it.

The next day, Zulu met with Mob Allah at a construction site in Brooklyn. Zulu arrived with a few of his men, but they were instructed to remain outside while Zulu entered the construction site alone. Mob Allah was already there wearing a nice suit and a hard hat like he was Donald Trump instead of Nino Brown.

"What the fuck is this place?" Zulu asked him, looking around.

"This is the future for us, Zulu," Mob Allah replied.

"There isn't gonna be a future if we don't handle this nigga, Rafe."

"And where are we with that?" he asked.

"Can we talk here?" Zulu asked.

Mob Allah nodded. "Yeah. It's secure."

Zulu exhaled. "This muthafucka is like whack-a-mole. He pops up here and there. And he's careful. This cocksucker killed two of our men the other day. Truth, finding and killing this fool ain't gonna be easy."

Mob Allah groaned from the news. "He should've been dead yesterday. Every day this fool breathes, he costs us money and our reputation. I got Bobby Spyros on my fuckin' ass about this shit. And the last thing I need is to make him unhappy."

"What the fuck you think I'm doin' out there? Playing pitty-pat?" Zulu retorted. "We out there in the trenches taking heat and losses while you sit on the throne building Lego blocks with these fuckin' suits."

Mob Allah scowled at Zulu and uttered, "You have a problem with what I'm doing, Zulu? If so, let me know."

Zulu took a deep breath and placed his emotions on hold. Then he coolly replied with, "All I'm saying is this. We are at war right now, and now is *not* the time to be playing half a gangster. You're distracted with these people around you, forgetting who you are."

Mob Allah chuckled at his friend's remark. "You really believe that I'm playing half a gangster and forgot who I am? Muthafucka, I'm far from it. Let me remind you of something, Zulu. I am an undisputed gangster. To me, that means playing by my own rules. And you need more than guns to be a good gangster. You need ideas."

Sonja arrived with Michael Kostroff at the building site wearing a lace detail paint suit set and her hard hat as the men conversed. The moment Zulu spotted her with Michael, he frowned at them. She always seemed to be around, and he didn't like that.

"We'll talk later," said Zulu, curtailing their conversation. "I got other engagements to take care of."

Before he could leave, Mob Allah said to him, "I don't care how you do it but get it done. If we don't end this war, it will end us."

Zulu heard him and walked off, passing Sonja in doing so. They both exchanged looks without saying a single word to each other. It was evident that they didn't like each other. Before he made his final exit from the place, Zulu watched Mob Allah happily shake hands with Michael Kostroff like he was some executive suit in a board meeting. Zulu frowned and walked away.

"What did he want with you?" Sonja asked Allah.

"Business," Mob Allah replied, being concise with her.

"This is your business now. Look at how far you came in such a short time," she said.

"But I still need to handle that other thing out there too," he replied. "It's getting out of hand."

Sonja smiled. They didn't want to say too much in front of Michael, though he was distracted by a call on his cell phone.

"A successful man can lay a firm foundation with the bricks others have thrown at him," said Sonja.

Michael finished his phone call and turned his attention back to Sonja and Mob Allah. He had planned a fixed land deal, and Mob Allah wanted a piece of it.


Queenie climbed out of the Range Rover looking more masculine than feminine. She was a tough bitch with a man's haircut, and her body was covered with tattoos. She wore a black fedora hat with a stylish vest and Tims—and she was nothing nice to play with. Queenie was one of Mob Allah's vicious killers on standby. The only thing he needed to do was give the order no matter who it was . . . man, woman, or child. They were dead.

But tonight, she was on a different mission, becoming more of an investigator than a homicidal killer.

Queenie and two intimidating thugs entered the strip club Open Tease in Yonkers. Since the killings of four men a few weeks back, business at the place had been slow, and things were tense. But, now, things were picking up. It was a Saturday night, and it was growing crowded inside with strippers walking around enticing and teasing the men. And though Queenie loved tits and ass like every man in the room, she was there on business.

She was searching for information about the night Mackie was killed. Queenie came there with enough money to tip every stripper $500. But the cash wasn't for pleasure. It was to bribe certain people for info. First, it was the bouncers and then the owner of the place. Queenie moved around the club with authority, like she owned the establishment. She did what she wanted, however she wanted. Who was going to stop her?

"I need to talk to a few of your bitches in here," Queenie said to the club owner, Robbie, a frail-looking white boy who looked like he had no business running a strip club.

Robbie was easily intimidated by her. "Who?" he questioned.

"Who was working the night of the shooting?"

"There were a few ladies. It was a packed night."

"Who was with Mackie and his crew?"

"That would be Passion," Robbie answered.

"Is she here tonight?"

He nodded. "Yeah, she's in the dressing room, about to start her shift."

Queenie left his office. She marched toward the dressing room alone and stepped inside it, into a world of tempting, young bodies ready to entertain tonight's crowd with their sexuality. Queenie was impressed, but she had to remind herself it was business.

"I'm looking for Passion. Where is she?" Queenie called out, immediately catching the girls' attention.

At first, there was awkwardness and confusion. No one wanted to speak up. Finally, Queenie paid attention to the girls' faces. When she noticed a particular girl look to her left, she immediately knew who Passion was. She approached Passion and declared, "We need to talk about that night when a friend of mines was killed."

Passion nervously stared up at this well-dressed, attractive butch and replied, "I don't know anything."

"Let me be the judge of that," Queenie uttered. "And I know time is money, so I'll make it worth your time for whatever you tell me."

Queenie pulled out a bankroll so big that Passion was no longer nervous about her presence.

"What do you need to know?" she asked.


"First, what other girls were with you that night?" asked Queenie.

Passion and Starlight sat inside the owner's office, being interrogated by Queenie. Robbie attended to the main floor, giving them privacy to talk.

"The other two girls quit right after it happened," said Passion.

"They got scared," Starlight mentioned.

"Tell me everything about that night," said Queenie.

Passion told Queenie everything she needed to know, how she met Mackie and how good he was to her with his money.

"I was leaving with him that night to get a motel room to have sex," Passion confirmed. "He was going to pay me $400 for my time. And he said he wanted to celebrate with me."

When it got to the shoot-out, Passion said, "I didn't see anyone. It happened so quickly, I ran. I was scared."

"You didn't see any faces? Don't know how many there were?" Queenie asked her.

"No."

"It was one guy," Starlight chimed in.

Queenie shot Starlight a surprised look. "How do you know it was one guy?"

"Because I hid behind a car and saw it. It was one guy, and he was fast. They didn't stand a chance," Starlight continued. "And he was military."

"What makes you think that?" asked Queenie.

"I'm an army brat. My father and my two brothers were all in the military. And the way this guy moved, he knew what he was doing. He was fast, accurate, and he seemed fearless. He executed your friend like it was nothing. It was like he had some kind of personal vendetta against him."

Queenie took in the information with a deadpan stare. She was satisfied with what she heard. And as promised, she paid the girls for their information, placing $300 apiece into their hands. It was the start of a good night for them, but Queenie seemed troubled by what she heard.

# Chapter Thirty-eight

Christopher was the perfect gentleman tonight. He was dressed handsomely in a collared dress shirt, necktie, and dress shoes. He looked like a *GQ* model, and he charmed his lovely company with his golden smile and affable personality. He and his date, Jennifer, arrived at a City Range Steakhouse Grill restaurant in Midtown Manhattan. It was the home of juicy steaks, spirited drinks, and Aussie hospitality.

Jennifer was full of smiles and laughter from when he picked her up and when they entered the restaurant. Christopher was great company. He pulled out her chair for her to sit at the table, and then he sat across from her.

"You do look beautiful tonight," he complimented her.

She blushed and replied, "Thank you. And you're handsome yourself."

Jennifer was dressed conservatively in a long, modest dress and her hair was in a neat ballerina bun. It showed off her flawless facial features. Together, they looked like an attractive, average couple. Christopher liked the way she was dressed. She seemed pure and innocent and easygoing. They attended the same church, and Jennifer had been attracted to Christopher for a while now. It was about time he asked her out.

"I'm glad you asked me out," she brought up. "I'm having a wonderful time with you."

"Me too. It's good to see that we have a few things in common."

"We do. We both like the pastor's preaching," she joked.

He laughed. "Yes, we do. The man can preach now."

"And you're no slouch yourself, Deacon Mathews," Jennifer mentioned. "I've heard you a few times. You need to get behind that podium and spread some of that gospel."

He laughed. "No thanks. I'm a man that likes to be behind the scenes and preside over the liturgical services."

"You're an intelligent, kind, and loving man, Deacon. I'm surprised you're not married."

"The Lord hasn't provided me with the right woman yet."

"Well, hopefully, that will change in due time," she said with an unmistakable smile.

Their waitress approached the table to take their orders, and they both politely responded. They ordered some wine and water first, followed by a few appetizers.

"This is a nice place. Is this your first time coming here?" Jennifer asked him.

"It is. I heard about it from a congregation member. He recommended this place when I told him that I was taking you out."

"Well, I like it. And thank you for bringing me here. I haven't gone out on a date in a while now."

"A beautiful woman like yourself, single and lonely, how is that possible?"

"Oh, I'm single, but I'm *not* lonely," she corrected him.

"Pardon me."

"No. It's fine. I'm, let's just say, I can be picky when it comes to dating."

"Understandable," he replied.

Before long, they were enjoying the wine and appetizers while waiting for their entrée to arrive. Christopher was utterly opposite of his dark side tonight. His desire for the flesh had been put on pause . . . for the moment. He was a classic case of Dr. Jekyll and Mr. Hyde. To

Jennifer, he seemed to be the perfect man for her—a fantastic Christian. But unbeknownst to her, she was sitting across from the devil himself, laughing and flirting with a man who'd murdered nearly three dozen young prostitutes in different states in a decade.

Christopher enjoyed an eight-ounce grilled chicken breast served with BBQ sauce with a Caesar salad. And Jennifer dined on the seasoned salmon with a Caesar salad too. Their conversation intensified, along with their laughter. They started talking about politics, religion, and the exploits of African Americans. And Christopher seemed to be very well educated in all areas.

"I don't mean to sound like a spoilsport, but it seems that emotions of materialism overshadow the religious significance of both Christmas and Easter," he stated.

Jennifer was intrigued by his statement. She took a sip of wine and said, "Interesting that you believe that. I'm listening."

Christopher smiled. "It's affecting our children. I believe these same emotions about Christmas and Easter are passed on to our children by fabricating such fictitious individuals as Santa Clause and the Easter Bunny. It's about profit, and they're using religion to help them make money. Giant corporations want to lay the emotional foundation for another generation of preprogrammed consumers. These companies and society want to use religion to make a fortune at the expense of other people . . . especially Black people."

Jennifer nodded. He was interesting.

Christopher added, "The history of Christianity should be of particular note to Black people. It played a key role in the development of the slave trade. Many civilizations deemed Africans to be soulless individuals."

After dinner, the two went for a nice walk around the city. It was a warm, clear night. The traffic was buzzing, and the people were out and about. While they toured the city, they held hands and continued to converse. Jennifer's smile was bright like electricity, and she was having a wonderful night.

When the time came for them to depart, she hesitated at her front door and looked at Christopher with such admiration that it was clear to tell what she was thinking.

"Do you want to come up for some tea or coffee?" she asked him.

Christopher smiled. The offer was tempting, but he refused. "Maybe next time," he replied. "I have to be up early in the morning."

Jennifer smiled. "I understand."

She wanted to kiss him, but it took her by surprise when she simply received a hug from him. He continued to be a gentleman tonight, even though she expected some slight affection from him.

"I'll see you Sunday in church, okay?" he said.

"You will."

Christopher pivoted and departed from her, leaving Jennifer behind, a bit frustrated that their date didn't end with any kind of affection. She watched him climb into his 1997 Cadillac DeVille and drive away. Finally, she exhaled and went inside her home.

Meanwhile, Christopher took a minor detour while he was on his way home. He ended up cruising through one of the seedier parts of Brooklyn. It was after midnight, and the ho stroll seemed like a ghost town. The nasty creatures of the night seemed to have taken a night off in his eyes. Maybe they were scared.

The Wolf navigated his Cadillac through the area, but he wasn't on the hunt tonight. Instead, he wanted to observe things. Besides, he would never use his personal vehicle to commit a crime. It was too risky.

Seeing that no one was working the track, he decided to leave the area. The Wolf turned right onto a busier street, but a marked police car suddenly flagged him down. Its bright blue and red lights flashed behind him, indicating him to pull to the side of the road. He complied. The Wolf kept his cool and his car idling as he watched a single cop exit from his vehicle and approach the driver's side.

"Is there a problem, Officer?" asked the Wolf, mild-mannered.

"License, registration, and insurance card?" the cop asked him.

No problem. He had everything organized and up-to-date. So, there was no need for him to be worried. The cop inspected the information and then asked him, "Is there a reason you're in this part of town?"

"I was just coming home from a date with a lovely woman. I didn't know it was a crime to ride through this way."

"It's not. And the reason I pulled you over is because you have a brake light out on the left side," said the cop.

"Oh. Well, I didn't know. Thank you for informing me of this. I'll get it fixed first thing tomorrow."

"Please, do that. I'm just going to issue you a warning for now," the cop said.

"I appreciate it, Officer. Thank you."

It was a quick exchange, and the cop didn't see anything wrong with the driver. The Wolf was a well-spoken and nicely dressed individual who didn't exhibit any red flags that he was a serial killer.

"You have a nice night and get that brake light fixed."

"You too, Officer. And will do."

The cop marched back to his marked car and left in the opposite direction, making a U-turn while the Wolf lingered for a moment staring at the warning he was given. He then smirked and drove away.

# Chapter Thirty-nine

Family is where life begins, and love never ends. Family is the compass that guides us. They're the inspiration to reach great heights. And the comfort when someone occasionally falters. Sincere's family was his circle of strength and love, and it grew with every birth and union. And every crisis faced together made the circle stronger.

Monica was pregnant. It was great news, but Sincere felt ambivalent about the pregnancy. His world was in turmoil with murders and revenge. And though he'd taken a step back from the murders, he was still haunted by the violence. This wasn't supposed to be his life, warring with drug dealers and killing people.

Nevertheless, Sincere had plans when he returned home from the military. He thought about marriage, his kids, and a career in law enforcement. Sincere was looking forward to changing. But was that his destiny . . . his fate?

The funny thing about fate . . . If you don't follow, it will drag you where it wants to go. Sincere felt survivor's remorse. There was this deep, abiding guilt over having survived the streets, shootings, murders, and indictments where Maurice didn't get the chance to. But Sincere shouldn't be haunted by his little brother's fate. Maurice made his choice, and things didn't turn out in his favor. However, that wasn't good enough for Sincere. His mental condition was severe, and it felt like he was deteriorating. He was doing his best to live his life, heal, and move forward with family and happiness. But every night, when he put his head on the pillow to sleep, the emotions would surface, and the nightmares began. Sometimes, Sincere felt that he was all over the fucking place.

It was a beautiful Sunday evening. Denise was playing with Tyriq in the backyard. And Monica was cooking burgers, chicken, and shrimp at the grill. She was eight weeks pregnant and picture-perfect in a stylish tank top and jean shorts. It was Labor Day weekend, and Sincere was having a merry moment with everyone. It was a natural moment where his guard was down, and his destructive feelings had subsided. He stared at Monica. She smiled at him. She was happy and in love.

"Are you just going to sit there and watch me cook, or will you help me? *I'm* the one pregnant," she said jokingly.

"You're better at it than me," he replied. "You and Denise."

"But you can still learn. I probably won't be able to see my feet in a few months, and I'm going to need you to wait on me, hand and foot. So, this is your second chance at making it up to me."

Sincere smiled and stood up. He walked toward the grill, where Monica was still eyeing him teasingly. He stood behind her, wrapped his arms around her, and kissed the side of her neck.

"That can wait until tonight," she uttered gleefully, laughing. "Besides, I got to go pee."

She turned, handed him the spatula, and went into the house. Sincere sighed, knowing Monica was a good woman, and he was lucky to have her in his life. They would have another baby, and he had a second chance to do things right this time.

He flipped a few burgers and the chicken, and then he stood by the grill. He took in his surroundings, his family. Denise continued to play with her nephew in the backyard. They were now renting a three-bedroom house in Uniondale, Long Island. The suburbs had open front lawns and manicured grass, garages, and backyards with paved driveways. It was something he had to get used to.

Monica was an administrative assistant at a law firm in Queens. She'd been working there for three years and was great at her job. She made good money on paper and planned on going back to school to get her law degree soon. She was a strong, educated Black woman with dreams and goals and was fortunate to leave the hood. And the last thing Sincere wanted to do was get in her way with his issues.

For a moment, Sincere just stood there, thinking. What was next for him? What was his next move? He had everything he needed with his family, right? A beautiful woman, handsome son, loving sister . . . maybe a second chance at life. But what was his purpose in this life? Why couldn't he escape that feeling of anger and revenge? Why couldn't he let it go and just be happy? He came off as delighted and regular on the outside, but he felt it would bring others down if he allowed his inner struggles to appear. He didn't want anyone to see his pain. This was his fight and no one else's.

"Sincere, you're burning the burgers," Denise said, snapping him out of his daydream.

"Oh shit. Sorry," he uttered and quickly reacted, flipping over the burgers.

"Are you okay?" she asked him.

"Yeah. I'm fine."

Denise stared at her brother for a moment. There was something on her mind too.

"I want to see Mommy," Denise said out of the blue.

"What?"

"You heard me. I want to see her. I miss her. I haven't seen her all summer, and I'm worried about her, Sincere."

"I am too."

"So, take me to see her," she insisted with a steely glare.

"She's not in the best condition, Denise. She's sick."

"I don't care. It's like we abandoned her by moving out here on Long Island. And I did what you wanted by transferring schools. But I want to see our mother, Sincere. You owe me this," Denise proclaimed expressively.

Sincere sighed. It wasn't happening. He couldn't afford to put his little sister in any danger.

"Look, we'll talk about this later," he suggested.

"No. Fuck that. I want to talk about it *now,*" she cursed, frowning at her big brother.

"Do you *really* want to do this now, Denise? Right here? I told you that you can't see her because she's sick, and it's too dangerous. I'll let you know when the time is right. But until then, you need to chill out," he vehemently proclaimed, setting down his foot.

"Fuck you, Sincere. I fuckin' hate you for keeping me away from her," Denise hollered before heatedly storming away.

She stomped into the house right by Monica as she was coming back into the yard. She looked at Sincere and asked, "What's going on?"

He was at a loss for words.

That night, Monica tried to take Sincere away from his issues with Denise and his mother by having them soak together in the tub and enjoy a luxurious and romantic bubble bath. She felt it was a great way to shake off the stress by feeling the pleasures and relaxation of the warm and fragrant foam. She had arranged candles on a reflective surface to magnify the soft candlelight effect, with music to set the desired mood.

"If I'm having a girl, what do you think we should name her?" Monica asked.

Sincere didn't respond. He was someplace else in his mind.

"Sincere, I'm talking to you," Monica uttered.

"Huh?"

"I asked you what would be the perfect name for our daughter? Where are you?"

"I don't know, baby. You should name her if it's a girl," he responded calmly.

"Are you still upset with Denise? I mean, why won't you let her see Janet? She does miss her mother."

"It's complicated."

"What's complicated about it? I know you're going through something, but you won't let anyone in," Monica let known.

Sincere huffed. "Denise doesn't need to see Janet in that condition. I was there. It broke my fuckin' heart to see the way she looks. It would be too much for her."

"She's a big girl, Sincere. I think she can handle it. She already knows what her mother is. That still doesn't stop someone from loving them and being there for them," Monica countered.

He had his reasons, and he didn't want to tell the people he loved why. He was processing everything going on in his life at a fast speed. He would overanalyze the good and the bad, making everything impact him much deeper. Sincere felt like his brain was a sponge absorbing everything that came his way.

He sighed deeply and uttered, "I'll think about it."

With Janet's addiction and a lingering feeling of anger and revenge, Sincere felt he was dealing with a state of helplessness that would rock his world.

# Chapter Forty

War is cruel. There is no use trying to reform it. The crueler it is, the sooner it will be over. And Queenie believed every bit of that statement. She was becoming effective on the streets. Though she was a woman, she was feared. Mob Allah sent her on the hunt for a reason. Queenie was like a bloodhound. Once she got the scent of a rival, she would track that person down until they were disposed of. She was bred to hunt and kill. So, Queenie did some digging and snooping when Starlight mentioned a soldier had killed four of their men. And with the right money and influences, information quickly came their way like a bullet.

"His name is Sincere," a crackhead named Cherrie told Queenie.

"Sincere, huh? You know where he or his peoples stay at?" Queenie asked.

Cherrie nodded. "I do. I know his mother. We get high together. She said her son came home from the army a few months ago. His younger brother was killed soon after."

Queenie was connecting the dots. "What was the brother's name?"

"Maurice."

Queenie nodded. Her nose led her to the perpetrator she'd been looking for. And it made sense to her. Sincere was acting out of vengeance for the death of his brother. He was warring against Mob Allah, and he was bold enough to kill men on both sides and rob stash houses. It was a suicide mission.

If the man wanted to die, Queenie was about to grant him his wish.

"Does he have any other family?" she asked.

"A younger sister. She was in school at Jamaica High School. I know this 'cause she went to school with my son."

"What do you mean was in high school?"

"I haven't seen her around lately, or him . . ."

Satisfied with the information from Cherrie, Queenie pulled out a large wad of cash, and Cherrie's eyes lit up dazzlingly like the Christmas Tree in Rockefeller Center. She peeled off $200 and handed the crackhead a small fortune in her eyes.

"You earned it," said Queenie.

Cherrie happily accepted the bills and was thankful. "If you need me to tell you anything else, I'm ya girl. Thank you so much."

Cherrie turned and hurried away. It was no surprise to Queenie what the money would be spent on, but it wasn't her business. Cherrie's addiction made men like Mob Allah and Rafe wealthy titans in New York City. And she wasn't doing so bad herself.

Right away, Queenie removed her mobile phone to make an urgent call to Mob Allah. She knew he would want to hear what she'd learned.

The phone rang, and he answered. "You got something for me?"

"I do. You and Rafe, y'all been played," said Queenie.

"What the fuck are you talking about?" he griped.

"This war between Rafe is over a lie," Queenie said. "It's about revenge. And Rafe didn't kill Mackie that night. Some nigga with a death wish named Sincere is coming after you. You know the name?"

"No. I don't."

"Well, you know his little brother, Maurice."

Mob Allah remained silent for a brief moment. He didn't want to incriminate himself through the phone, knowing at any time, phones could be bugged and tapped by law enforcement. Moreover, he was a high-profile target who rarely ordered murders via mobile phone. But his emotions were getting the better of him.

"What do you want me to do?" she asked him.

"Everything this man loves . . . I want it gone. But I want him alive," Mob Allah commanded.

"No problem. I already know where his mama stays."

"Good."

"And what about Rafe?" she asked him.

"What about him?"

"Your beef with him is over a lie. You think we should reach out and let him know it wasn't you that came after him? This war started over a lie. Maybe it can be stopped by the truth."

"Fuck him. There wouldn't be a war unless lies were believed. So, war has to be nourished by lies, right?" With that, Mob Allah ended his call.

Queenie didn't argue with his decision. She had her orders.

Queenie and her three goons had their game faces on the following night. This was her element and her moment to implement death and chaos. She took a pull from the Newport while she sat in the passenger seat of the Range Rover. They were parked on 164th Street, staring at a row house which was a crack house. There was a lot of foot traffic in and out of the place. For a moment, Queenie watched the drug fiends while plotting her move inside.

"What, we killing everyone inside?" asked Marco.

"No. No need. We're just looking for that bitch, Janet," Queenie replied. "She tells us where her son is, and we make it easy on her. If not, y'all already know."

The men nodded approvingly.

Finally, they exited the vehicle and marched toward the location like Terminators. They all were fixed on one thing, with her goons carrying baseball bats.

The men followed Queenie inside the crack house, which was in a deplorable condition. It wasn't the same place Sincere came home to several months ago. It was now a place where time was lost. Users ended up staying much longer than they expected because they couldn't keep track of time without missing something. There was a lot of junk in and around the place and a bad smell. Users were too focused on smoking crack than cleaning and their hygiene. And there were the vultures, people who were there for no reason other than getting free crack if possible.

Queenie entered the place with a menacing gaze and behind her were her demonic-looking thugs entering the gates of hell. People were lying on the floor, some sleeping and some just zoning out. There were crackpipes and empty vials littered everywhere. A crackhead was asleep while a butane torch sat next to him with a flame burning away. The living room was furnished with a few pieces of furniture and a stained mattress sporting huge burn holes. And the place smelled like urine, shit, and burned plastic.

Queenie and her men had to step over several people lying around while searching for Janet with the help of a male crackhead because they had no idea what she looked like.

"She might be upstairs in the bedroom," the crackhead mentioned.

The four followed him up the stairs, where the smell and vulgarity continued. They moved through the foulness of the place unfazed and reached the master bedroom, where inside, Janet was spotted passed out, half on the floor, half on the mattress.

The crackhead pointed, confirming, "That's her right there."

Queenie placed fifty dollars into his hand, and he displayed a toothless grin, being extremely grateful. Then, the three men approached Janet with baseball bats, and they roused her awake by kicking her and the mattress.

"Wake ya ass up," one of the men shouted, kicking her in the side.

Janet opened her eyes to see them towering over her. She was high and dazed but managed to curse, "What the fuck y'all want? Huh? Get the fuck outta my house, muthafucka."

They found her amusing. "This bitch."

Queenie quickly took charge of the situation. She crouched near Janet to have a personal talk with her. Staring at Janet, Queenie uttered, "You know me?"

"No, I don't," Janet answered.

"We're looking for your son, Sincere. Do you know where he is?" Queenie coolly asked her. "We can make it worth your time."

Queenie tried to entice Janet by displaying her large wad of cash she carried, thinking this crackhead would take the bait.

"Just tell us where he is, and we'll take care of you. I promise," Queenie added.

"I don't know where he is. And even if I did, I wouldn't tell you shit," Janet exclaimed.

"C'mon bitch, don't be stubborn. You can't afford to be stubborn *and* stupid," Marco chimed in.

"Fuck you," Janet cursed at him.

"This bitch is stupid. She isn't talking," said Marco.

Queenie huffed, becoming impatient and knowing Marco was right. She glared at Janet and uttered with finality, "You sure about that? So, you don't have anything to say to us about your son?"

"I said fuck you," Janet angrily screamed back.

Queenie stood up, knowing her time had expired. The third goon stepped closer, aiming his gun at Janet, ready to blow her brains out, but Queenie stopped him.

"Don't waste a bullet on this bitch," she said. "Make her *feel* it."

The man smirked and nodded, knowing what she meant. Queenie looked around. They were alone. But for good measure, she closed the bedroom door. The moment it was shut, all three went to town on Janet with the baseball bats. Right away, she was struck in the back of the head with a powerful blow, and she went down. Then the other two men struck her repeatedly. They brutally swung away, striking her multiple times in the head, chest, back, and legs, creating visible gross deformity with blunt force trauma injuries.

Queenie stood there watching a woman being beaten to death. She smiled. What would be disturbing to others was entertaining to her. And within a minute, it was all over. Janet had been cruelly beaten to death. Her body lay bloody, broken, and contorted against the mattress.

Queenie stared at the body with apathy and uttered, "That should send him a message, right? Maybe this fool will kill himself when he hears about his moms."

The men laughed at her comment.

# Chapter Forty-one

Mob Allah was nervous, and he had the right to be worried. He was on his way to a meeting with Bobby Spyros in the city. He had an idea why Bobby wanted to meet with him. The war with Rafe created too much negative attention, and nobody was making any money. Bodies were piling up, and Queens was experiencing horrific scenes indistinguishable from cartel violence. The other day, firefighters discovered two bodies in a burning dumpster behind a local business after the firefighter extinguished the flames. The bodies were badly burned and dismembered. Some body parts were unaccounted for. The viciousness of the scene had Rafe and Malik written all over it.

But what was worse, it had come to Mob Allah's attention that a vengeful brother may have manipulated both organizations into fighting each other. Mob Allah was furious. He didn't predict this. And he immediately did his homework on Sincere. It was a clever play—a chess move he respected but hated. And Mob Allah knew to take this individual seriously. So, he sent Queenie on the hunt to find out everything about Sincere. It didn't take long to reveal he came up under brothers Dominique and Trey-Trey. He was a soldier who flew under the radar, and he'd escaped indictment when the hammer came down on the Gotti Boys. Also, he had a friend named Nasir.

"I'm placing a $10,000 bounty on his head," Mob Allah had declared. "And keep an eye out on the mortuary and funeral homes. His mother's dead, so he will have to pay his respects. The moment he does, kill him."

Mob Allah had put the hit out on Sincere and anything that was connected to him. He felt embarrassed, and he wanted to tear this nigga apart with his bare hands. The death of Sincere's mother was only the beginning, and he thought it would bring Sincere out of the hole he was hiding in.

The meeting with Bobby Spyros was set in Central Park, of all places. And Mob Allah felt it was odd that Bobby wanted to meet with him in such a public place. He arrived that evening, and the moment he climbed out of the Benz, one of Bobby's men was there to meet him.

"Follow me," the man said.

Mob Allah followed him into the park. It was a lovely evening. People were out and about . . . tourists, locals, cyclists, and dog walkers. It was a large and active park, and they didn't stand out. Mob Allah noticed Bobby sitting on a park bench on the trail, and he looked casual and relaxed.

"He's waiting for you," said the man.

Mob Allah coolly approached Bobby as he sat on the park bench, looking pensive. When he got close, Bobby stood up and said to him, "Let's walk."

And that they did.

Central Park served as a peaceful haven for New Yorkers. It was an escape from the city grind and a place to encounter nature up close.

"I love coming here," said Bobby. "It's one of my favorite places in the city. Ever been to Central Park?"

"Nah. I never cared for parks," Mob Allah replied.

"Sometimes, you need to take the time to appreciate the beautiful things around us. It helps to keep you healthy and focused. Beautiful park, yet there's a captivating story of how this became a world-class destination site. This was once all swampy land, rocky, and rugged terrain."

Mob Allah didn't come for a history lesson, but he knew not to rush Bobby. If there was a story to be told, there was a lesson behind it.

Bobby continued. "New York City's population was growing exponentially in the mid-nineteenth century. As a result, many immigrants came to Manhattan and lived in crowded, unhealthy conditions. But there was this place called Seneca Village. It was a community of predominantly African Americans, many of whom owned property. This place offered Black people the opportunity to live in an autonomous community far from the densely populated downtown."

It was an exciting story, and Bobby had Mob Allah listening. Finally, they reached the pond of Central Park and stopped walking. Bobby stared at the pond.

"But there was this vision for Central Park inspired by Birkenhead Park in England. It was the first publicly funded civic park in the world. And white folks in New York City now wanted their own park, something similar or bigger than Birkenhead Park. And where did they plan on building this park?" It was a rhetorical question.

Mob Allah knew.

"Seneca Village was prominent, but it wasn't touchable. So, the city acquired the land through eminent domain, allowing the government to take private land for public use with little compensation paid to the landowners," Bobby said.

He then turned to look at Mob Allah.

"You may think you have it all, power, wealth, and a great life. But the true powers that be will intervene and snatch it away from you in a heartbeat. Seneca Village was in the way of something bigger and more important," Bobby wholeheartedly proclaimed.

"What are you trying to say?"

"I gave you something, and you're fucking it up, Mob Allah, bringing too much attention with this war in your territory. And you may think you're important, but I'm fucking eminent domain. I increased your bank account tenfold by promoting you to distributer. More product but less risk."

"I'm handling things, Bobby. And you have my word, this war will be over really soon," Mob Allah promised him.

"I do not doubt your efforts to end things, Mob Allah. But you see, I have my own problems. And the last thing I need is for your shit to pile on my shit. I don't want to believe I made a mistake with you."

"You haven't, Bobby. How long have we known each other? Years, right? You know me," Mob Allah argued. "My word is my bond."

"It's always wise to put more distance between you and the streets. The more distance, the better. The distance is significant," said Bobby. "Therefore, until your issues are resolved, I'm putting some distance between us. I can't afford the liability."

"What the fuck are you saying, Bobby?"

"Do I need to spell it out to you?" he replied.

He didn't. Mob Allah knew precisely what he meant. It angered him, but he was in no position to argue or debate over Bobby's choice. What he said was final. Bobby spun around and walked away, leaving Mob Allah standing by the pond, fuming.

Mob Allah angrily marched back to the Benz, where his goon was waiting for him. He was so mad that he could take on the Hulk right now and win.

"Get me the fuck out of here, *now,*" he shouted at his goon.

As he headed back to his place in the city, Mob Allah placed a phone call to Queenie and Zulu. He uttered with irritation, "I'm upping the bounty on this cocksucker, Sincere. I want $25,000 on him *and* Rafe. And everyone's priority is to find both of these muthafuckas and eliminate them. If not, they're gonna have to deal with me."

War does not determine who is right, only who is left. And Rafe was determined to be the last man standing. To win this war and defeat Zulu and Mob Allah, he knew he needed two things: critical information against his foes and loyalty from everyone in his organization. Without them, there could be no family, and there could be no trust. He expected everyone in his crew to die for what they believed in, and there shouldn't be any excuses.

He, Malik, and two goons sat in a dark-colored Dodge Durango parked outside a six-story resident building in Park Hill, Staten Island. Everyone sat patiently in the Jeep during the downpour. Rain was hammering the Jeep like bullets, leaving any activity in the area paralyzed. Then, finally, the thunder crunched, and lightning briefly lit up like a bright red apple.

"Loyalty is hard to find nowadays, huh?" Rafe said to Malik.

"And trust is easy to lose," Malik replied.

"Fuckin' tell me about it," Rafe sighed. "Bad enough I'm at war with these muthafuckas, losing business. So now I gotta fuckin' worry about niggas in my crew. And I hate fuckin' Staten Island. The only good thing that came out of this fuckin' borough is Wu-Tang."

Malik chuckled. However, Rafe scowled and huffed. He looked ready to do something diabolical to someone. He looked angered in what many New Yorkers would call the forgotten borough—and during the downpour.

Finally, Rafe and Malik perked up. Some activity was happening. A gray Toyota Camry pulled up to the building, and Olay climbed out of it. Rafe frowned, seeing one of his men in Staten Island clandestinely meeting with someone.

"I had my suspicions but didn't want to believe it," Malik said. "He's playing both sides of the fence."

"This muthafucka," Rafe growled.

It angered Rafe to see Olay's betrayal. He played pool with Olay and thought Olay would be the last one to betray him. But Rafe saw he couldn't trust anybody. So, they watched Olay hurry into the building lobby under cover of rain.

"You know the apartment he's going into?" Rafe asked Malik.

Malik nodded. "Yeah. I do."

"Fuck it. Let's break up this nigga's party with our own surprise party."

Everyone exited the Durango and hurried toward the building lobby. Once inside, Rafe said to his goons, "Y'all niggas take the stairs, Malik and I will go up in the elevator. Olay doesn't leave this place alive."

They nodded.

Rafe and Malik took the elevator to the sixth and last floor. They exited onto the hallway, and Rafe followed behind Malik to the targeted apartment. His two goons, Spring and Dwight, joined them at the apartment door. Rafe couldn't wait to surprise Olay and kill him personally for his disloyalty.

They broke into the apartment with their guns drawn, and to everyone's surprise, Olay was found in bed with another man, Freddie. It was one of Mob Allah's goons. Olay was wide-eyed with shock and terror.

"What the fuck?" Rafe shouted in shock. "You a faggot, nigga?"

"Rafe, look . . . It ain't what you think," Olay uttered fearfully.

The statement angered Rafe, and he snapped, "It ain't what I think? You think I'm stupid, nigga?" Rafe charged Olay and snatched him from the bed while Malik and the others held Freddie hostage at gunpoint.

Rafe slapped Olay twice with an open left hand full across the face. It rocked him.

"You a faggot and disloyal with this bitch-ass nigga," Rafe screamed.

"Leave him alone," Freddie shouted.

"Shut the fuck up," Rafe shouted back at Freddie.

Malik immediately struck Freddie with the butt of his pistol, and blood filled Freddie's mouth. The pain was blinding. But there was blinding rage on Rafe's face. He didn't know what was worse, Olay's betrayal or him being gay. Either way, Olay was a dead man. Rafe stood over Olay, grimacing with his fists clenched. There would be no redemption, and Freddie would watch his boyfriend's demise. He proceeded to punch him repeatedly. His fists collided with his face and cheek, shattering his teeth. Olay was helpless, his demise growing closer as Rafe went on a rampage with his fists and legs—punching, stomping, and kicking. Finally, a loud crunching sounded, and Olay's nose spewed blood.

Everyone stood there and watched, including Freddie, as Rafe continued beating an opponent who couldn't fight back. Olay tried to crawl to his feet, but his body was in agony with blood draining from his mouth. He then lay there, his breath wheezing and his eyes closed. Rafe beat him until he was dead.

Freddie was distraught. Rafe looked at him next and bellowed, "You gonna tell me something about Zulu or Mob Allah, or I swear, what happened to Olay will feel like paradise compared to what I'm about to do to you."

"Fuck you," Freddie shouted defiantly.

They dragged Freddie into the bathroom, where they planned on brutally torturing him for information on their rivals.

Olay had decided to play on both sides of the fence, but eventually, his leg got caught trying to get over on the other side.

# Chapter Forty-two

Sincere was alone when he got the glum phone call from Nasir. The news came out of nowhere, and it hit him like a ton of bricks.

"They found your mother dead. She was beaten to death inside her home," Nasir informed him.

"What the fuck?" Sincere shouted. This couldn't be real. "What you mean, beaten to death? By whom? What the fuck happened?"

"I don't know, but it isn't pretty. They really fucked her up. Word on the streets is three men beat her to death with baseball bats. They're looking for *you*," said Nasir.

Sincere gripped the phone so tightly that it was about to break in half. His emotions and anger were boiling like a pot of water on a hot stove. And steam was about to escape from him. They'd killed his mother. They'd taken something away from him again.

Monica had taken Denise and Tyriq shopping at Green Acres Mall for school clothing and supplies. It had been a good day for Sincere . . . until it wasn't.

"I'm on my way to Queens right now," Sincere exclaimed.

"Chill, Sincere. If they came after your mother, they will be looking for you," said Nasir. "And if they know about you, they probably know about me too."

"Fuck that. I swear to God, Nasir, every last one of them is dead," he growled into the phone. "We need to meet—now."

"I'm already ahead of you. You know where to meet me," said Nasir.

"I'll be there in an hour."

Sincere hung up, but the anger and grief continued to flow through him like he was on fire. In a fit of rage, he heatedly pitched the phone into the wall, breaking it, then punched a gaping hole into another wall. His fury and anger flooded out of him all at once. He screamed and kicked over a lamp.

While Sincere was in a fit of rage mixed in with profound grief, the front door opened, and Monica arrived with the kids carrying shopping bags. Immediately, everyone saw that something was wrong. Sincere's eyes were coated with tears, and the living room was in shambles.

"Baby, what's wrong?" Monica asked, concerned. "What's going on? What happened? Why are you destroying our living room?"

Denise stared at her brother, and Sincere looked at her. Everyone knew it was bad news. But what? When Sincere continued to lock sorrowful eyes with his little sister, Denise immediately picked up on it. It registered to her.

"Is it our mother?" she asked him sadly, fearing the worst.

Sincere sighed heavily and replied. "I'm sorry, but she's dead."

Denise didn't want to believe it. At first, she thought she had misheard him, but she didn't. Then, she was suddenly overcome with profound grief.

"What happened? Did she overdose or something?" Denise wanted to know.

Sincere remained quiet. He didn't want to tell her the truth. Monica too was saddened by the news. She was cool with Janet. The only regret she had was Tyriq not knowing his grandmother.

"What happened to her, Sincere?" Denise screamed. "How did she die?"

Sincere huffed, reluctant to tell her the truth. It was grim, and his silence and reluctance angered Denise. She became hostile toward her brother. Finally, she stormed toward him with a slew of punches, and he stood there, taking it.

"This is all your fuckin' fault. You wouldn't let me see her. She's dead now, and I never got to see her. I didn't even get to say goodbye," Denise yelled out in heartache. "I hate you, Sincere! I fuckin' hate you."

Monica pulled Denise away from her brother and grabbed her in her arms to console her. She collapsed to the ground with Denise still in her arms. Then she stared up at Sincere, who stood there like a ghost.

"She wants answers, Sincere. Me too. What happened to Janet? Did she overdose?" Monica asked him, hoping he would answer her.

But Sincere was too angry and heartbroken to spill it. He was stubborn. Instead, he pivoted and marched out the door like he was on some kind of mission. His sister's sobbing continued, and he did nothing about it.

"Sincere, where are you going?" Monica called out to him. "Sincere!"

He ignored her and his sister. Instead, he climbed into his car and drove away, leaving everybody behind stunned and upset.

Nasir checked the clip to the Glock 17, and it was fully loaded. He urgently moved around his bedroom, packing the necessary items he would need while he was gone. He knew he was no longer safe at his place. He figured he was a marked man, and he wouldn't take any chances with his life. As he packed a few things, including guns and ammunition, he constantly looked out his window to see if there was any trouble coming his way. So far, things were quiet and clear.

His first move was to meet Sincere, talk this shit out, and then he would leave town for a moment and keep a low profile. He had enough money to set up somewhere else. And it was the plan—stay alert and cautious and perceive everything as a potential threat. However, he couldn't figure out how they knew it was Sincere. Did his friend fuck up somehow and leave behind some trail that connected back to him. These were questions Nasir knew he wouldn't get the answers to.

He packed light clothes, cash, and a sawed-off in a duffle bag, and he carried two pistols on him, including the Glock. Each gun was already cocked and ready to implement death. Once again, he peeked out the window to see if the coast was clear. It was. Nasir hurried from his home and urgently marched toward the Lexus parked on the street. He tossed everything into the trunk and closed it. But suddenly, a dark green Grand Cherokee turned the corner onto his street, and Nasir eyed the car distrustfully. Something inside his gut told him it wasn't a civilian vehicle.

He coolly removed the Glock 17 from his waistband and kept it close. And as he predicted, the Jeep came his way and stopped. The doors flew open, and several goons emerged from the car. Seeing Nasir about to leave, Zodiac shouted, "Nasir, where the fuck you going? We wanna talk to you."

*Fuck that.* Nasir reacted. "Fuck y'all." With a determined stare, he pulled the trigger with a reverberating bang.

*Bak bak bak . . . bak bak!*

The driver went down instantly while Zodiac and the others returned gunfire, and a shoot-out ensued on the block. Bullets whizzed by Nasir's head as he evaded death and leaped into the driver's seat of the Lexus. He rushed to start the car, with gunfire penetrating his vehicle. The engine roared to life, and Nasir wasted no time slamming his foot against the pedal and escaping.

Finally, he exhaled, seeing that he wasn't being chased, and shouted, "Fuck me!"

# Chapter Forty-three

Sincere walked back and forth by his car, trying to keep his cool. But it was nearly impossible as raw anger shot through him. The only thing he could think about was his mother's murder. How they'd killed her was troubling. She was a crackhead, but his mother didn't deserve to die like that. He knew the brutality of it was to send a message to him. They were coming for him next, and his agenda was to protect the rest of his family by any means necessary. It was personal when they'd killed Maurice. Now, he was ready to implement some apocalyptic and biblical shit to all his enemies and make it hell on earth.

His mind was spinning wildly like race car tires in NASCAR when Nasir finally arrived forty minutes late. He got out of the Lexus, looking disheveled.

"What the fuck happened?" asked Sincere.

Nasir was breathless with anger when he responded, "They came at me at my fuckin' house. These niggas shot at me. I barely escaped."

It was expected. Both men knew it was either take flight or fight.

"I'm going to slaughter these muthafuckas," Sincere growled.

"How?" Nasir uttered, upset. "Your window of cloak and dagger is gone. You don't have that element of surprise anymore, Sincere. They're looking for you and everyone connected to you. So why the fuck you think they came at me tonight?"

To Sincere, it didn't matter. Revenge was heavy on his heart.

"It wasn't your mother who they beat to death with baseball bats or your little brother they tortured before killing him," he countered.

"Listen, we've known each other for a long time, Sincere. So do like I'm doing. Take the money and leave town for a while. Get the fuck outta New York. Go start a new life somewhere, maybe out west," Nasir advised him.

"I'm not going anywhere," he rebuffed. "This is my fuckin' home, and I'm not running. *They* started this war, and *I'm* going to finish it."

Nasir sighed. "You're outnumbered, outgunned—"

"And I don't give a fuck," Sincere retorted.

Nasir saw the hellish look in his friend's eyes, and it was scary.

"Let's do this together," Sincere uttered. "Help me take these muthafuckas down."

"I can't do that, Sincere. I can't go there with you."

"And why not? You're supposed to be my friend, right? So, what happened to 'It's our time. Let's pick up the crumbs and take over shit?' Huh? When I kill 'em all, these streets will belong to you."

Sincere was thinking irrationally and acting out of emotions. Nasir replied, "Things are different. Now, they see us coming for them, and they'll be ready."

Sincere looked disappointed in his friend's decision. "So, this is it, huh? You leave town, and I stay and fight? Remember, you have family still here. What makes you not think they won't go after them too?"

Nasir huffed. "I know, but I already arranged things with them. My baby mom was smart to keep me out of our daughter's life. I see it now. Unfortunately, I can't go down that road with you. You're about revenge, and I'm about money. I'm sorry."

"Fuck it, I understand. You do what you need to do," said Sincere regretfully.

"And since I can't talk you out of it, take this," Nasir said, handing his friend a piece of paper with some information on it. "It's an address to one of Zulu's baby mamas. Don't ask how I came about it. But start there."

Sincere nodded and was appreciative of the information. Then the two friends traded mournful gazes. But Nasir stared at his friend like it would probably be the last time he would see him alive.

"You be safe out here, Sincere," he said.

"You too."

"Real niggas ain't scared of shit . . ." Nasir began.

". . . Real niggas take care of shit," Sincere finished.

The two gave each other dap and embraced in a brotherly hug. Then Nasir walked away, not looking back at his friend. He got into his Lexus and drove away, leaving Sincere behind, brooding over a few things. One thing Nasir said was true about him earlier. Revenge was his drug of choice.

It was suicidal to continue to go after Mob Allah's organization. Still, Sincere was determined to go through with it at any cost. He'd made a promise to his deceased little brother. And it was a promise he wasn't about to break.

While he stood there with airplanes soaring above, nearing the landing runway, he received a sudden 911 page from Monica. It worried him, and he flew into action. He leaped into his Plymouth and raced to the nearest pay phone.

He quickly called Monica, and she answered, "Sincere, she's gone!"

He was confused. "Who's gone?" he asked.

"Denise. She's not here. She left a note behind saying that she was going back home."

Sincere's heart sank into the pit of his stomach. He knew she was going back to Queens. No. He didn't want to panic, but he was panicking.

"How long's she been gone?" he asked.

"Maybe an hour."

"I'll find her," he said, hanging up.

Sincere's mind started to race, and he needed to think. She had no license and no car. He knew how his sister planned on traveling back to Queens. He hurried back to his car and sped to Hempstead like he was in a high-speed pursuit.

The Hempstead LIRR station and the Greyhound Bus station were right across the street from each other. It was one of the main transportation hubs in the area. It was late, so traffic and pedestrians were sparse. Still, it wasn't going to be easy searching for Denise. And Sincere went on a hunch that she would come to the LIRR station in Hempstead to travel back to Queens.

He parked erratically near the LIRR and sprang from his car in desperation to find Denise before she got on any train. Sincere hurried into the station, and his eyes danced in every direction. But he thought, *What if I missed her? What if she's already on a train or bus back to Queens?* There was no way he was going to lose his little sister too.

He continued to move through the station, frantically searching for Denise. And then, by a miracle, he finally spotted her. She was on the platform waiting for the next train to arrive. Sincere rushed over to her with mixed emotions, happy that he found her but angry that she would put her life in danger. When Denise noticed her brother coming her way, she immediately reacted.

"No, I'm not going back there," she shouted, becoming defensive. "I'm going home."

"You can't go back to Queens. I told you, it's not safe there," he argued.

"Why, Sincere? *What's* going on?" Denise shouted with her eyes swamped with tears. "What happened to Mama? Huh? Tell me?"

Sincere stared at his little sister, defeated and heart-broken. She deserved to know the truth. If not, he figured he would lose her too. Then reluctantly, he admitted to Denise, "She was murdered."

"How? Why would someone want to kill our mama?"

He sighed profoundly. "Listen, if you go back to Queens, they might kill you too."

It was terrifying news to hear from Sincere. She was taken aback and became scared. "What?"

"Just get in the car with me, and I'll tell you everything. I promise," he said.

Denise looked unwilling. She stood there, not sure what to do. But she didn't have a choice. She wanted to know what was going on. So, she relented and left with him. They exited the train station quietly, and Denise climbed into the passenger's seat with an apprehensive stare. Her life was becoming hell. Within a year, she'd lost her mother and Maurice, and she wondered if Sincere was to blame.

# Chapter Forty-four

A serial killer keeps going until one of four things happens: they're caught, die, kill themselves, or burn out. The Wolf didn't plan on killing himself, and he wasn't burnt out—not yet. His lust and hunger continued to grow stronger. And the gaps between kills were shrinking. When he started killing young prostitutes, mostly Black girls that were lost or fell through the cracks of society, a span of a month or so would pass. Now, he was killing a prostitute every two weeks.

No one cared about these girls. There was a term in the world of crime for these victims. They were called the "Less dead" people. They were the folks that serial killers often prey on. They were the poorest, most disenfranchised citizens, folks who can go missing, and no one even reports it. Sometimes, they end up as Jane or John Doe in the morgue, even if the police did have an ID for the victim. Due to their low socioeconomic status, their murders wouldn't arouse much sympathy from the public if they had a rap sheet or criminal background. And most likely, they weren't the most urgent cases for homicide detectives.

The Wolf knew that these young Black prostitutes would be seen as less alive, less valued before they died. And when these victims were murdered, they became less dead. So, the Wolf was targeting society's most vulnerable . . . young Black girls who'd lost their way. He stayed in the ghettos because he believed no one cared about the ghettos in America.

But now, with numerous young prostitutes found mutilated in public parks and the brutal killing of a young couple in the Bronx two weeks ago, society *was* starting to notice. And detectives in every borough were ramping things up to catch this killer.

The Wolf quickly showered, and then he stepped out of the tub to towel off. While doing so, the TV in the next room aired the evening news. And it was about him. So, he knotted the towel around his waist and walked into the bedroom to listen.

*"News of another dead girl has fueled fear in African American communities throughout the tristate area. Already reeling from the murder of Katrina Hanson of the Bronx, the death toll has reached eleven girls in five months,"* the anchorwoman announced.

The Wolf moved closer to the television and listened intently to the broadcast.

*"The authorities have informed that they will increase patrol in certain areas and the parks where the bodies are being dumped. Therefore, the police are encouraging the community to remain alert and vigilant. Anyone who notices anything suspicious or knows anything regarding these cases is immediately urged to contact the police."*

The Wolf grinned and turned off the television. The room became silent. He walked toward the full-length mirror in the bedroom and dropped the towel around his ankles. He stared at his reflection blankly. His physique was impressive, and his manhood was above average. For a moment, he stood there, staring vacantly at his nakedness and the scars that covered his torso. Then he fell to his knees and exhaled.

His bedroom was neat and decorated with religious artifacts and trinkets. Everything was carefully placed as if he had OCD. A crucifix hung over his bed, and a Bible sat on a nightstand near the bed. The Wolf remained on his knees and lowered his head in prayer. Excessive religious thoughts, aggressive urges, and sexual fears had him fucked up.

"Forgive me, Lord. It won't stop," he cried out. "Food for the stomach and the stomach for food, and God will destroy them both. The body, however, is not meant for sexual immorality. So flee the evil desires of youth and pursue righteousness, faith, love, and peace, along with those who call on the Lord out of a pure heart."

He wanted to reduce his lust and anxiety.

"How long? I've been suffering for years," he exclaimed.

His mother was a young prostitute who had sex with men and abused him. He grew up poor and had problems with discipline and achievement. From the time he was 10 years old, he began having fantasies about sex and women. He was the oldest brother of two who received the bulk of the abuse from their mother. In one incident, she made him strip naked in front of his younger brother and a client, then whipped Christopher with an electrical cord until he bled. There were times when he would peek into his mother's bedroom and witness numerous sexual acts take place and sometimes see her being beaten.

The Wolf, a.k.a. Christopher Mathews, got dressed that night. He threw on a crisp white shirt, black pants, and black shoes. He was well dressed and an attractive male with a confident personality. In the mirror, he looked like Deacon Mathews, a good man involved in the church. But tonight, he would become something demonic, a wolf on the hunt to appease his flesh and desires.

Killing people was normal for him. It's what made him feel better and gave him some emotional release. But the Wolf was a complex man. He both simultaneously desired and hated these young Black prostitutes. He wanted them because they reminded him of his mother.

And he hated them because they reminded him of his abusive mother. So, he would kill them after sex because he wanted to make society better by murdering them. He would cut out their eyes because he believed they were the window to the soul. And keeping them in his possession meant he'd captured their souls. He would cut out their tongues because of blasphemy, believing they'd spoken sacrilegiously about God and sacred things. And he would cut off their fingers because they'd enticed him with their wicked touch.

As the news publicized, the tristate area was on high alert for a serial killer preying on young prostitutes, which put the young hoes on edge. Police were going to be out in full force in the areas where prostitution was substantial, but it was bad business for the pimps and hoes. A heavy police presence scared away the customers. But this wasn't going to stop him. Instead, his aggressive urges made him go elsewhere, somewhere where they wouldn't be expecting him.

The Wolf cruised through the seedy area of Newark's North Ward. His was one of several cars cruising the neighborhood in the late hours of the night, soliciting sex. There were a handful of girls working the track. They smiled and waved at passing cars, looking to pick up a date. He was patient, knowing the right girl would come his way. And she did in the area of Broadway and Irving Street. Her meaty thighs in a short jean skirt quickly secured his attention. So, he approached her with his winning smile.

"Hey there, beautiful," he called out to her.

She turned to see a dark blue Chevrolet Malibu coming to the curb where she stood, and an unassuming but handsome Black male in glasses was trying to get her attention. So, she coolly approached the vehicle and asked, "Are you lookin' for a date tonight?"

"Yes. How much?"

"A hundred."

He smiled. "I can swing that. Get in."

Before climbing into the vehicle, she looked around. She was alone. Then she hopped into the passenger seat, and he drove away.

They'd found a secluded location, and soon, he was inside her mouth, enjoying the pleasures of oral sex. The Wolf moaned and groaned as a warm, pleasurable sensation ran through his body. It was like a cross between having sex and masturbating, but a feeling of domination—a fulfilling one. But he was vulnerable, with his tenderest part being inside her mouth. She was 100 percent in control for the moment. Then, she straddled him in the back seat of the car. He was entirely inside her, and he wrapped his arms around her, panting. The sex was good, too good.

"I will not look with approval on anything vile. I hate what faithless people do. I will have no part in it," he suddenly uttered.

She heard the awkward verse, but she continued to fuck him. "Come for me, daddy. That pussy feels good, right?"

He continued to moan and said, "Do not lust in your heart after her beauty or let her beauty captivate you with her eyes." After his words, he reached for her neck and squeezed her aggressively.

Things suddenly went from bliss to pandemonium. Knowing she was in sudden danger, she madly fought back while he tried to strangle her or snap her neck.

"Get the fuck off me, muthafucka!" the prostitute screamed.

He squeezed tighter with her demise growing closer. But this young girl wasn't going out without a fierce fight. She repeatedly punched him in the face. But he was a brute, and no amount of punches was going to help her. So, she desperately reached for something to give her the upper hand. Her life was fading. She reached for a knife she kept concealed in her shoe. With it in her grasp, she hurriedly plunged the blade into his side, and it rocked him surprisingly. He jerked. His fingers loosened a bit. She stabbed him again, and finally, she was free. Seeing her chance, she kneed him in his groin, and the Wolf bellowed from the pain. But he absorbed the trauma, swallowing the pain, blood seeping from his wounds.

The girl tried to make her escape from the back seat. She pushed open the door and tried to dive from the car at full force. But he grabbed her leg. However, his hands were slick with blood. She screamed, "Get the fuck off me," and she kicked him in the face. In doing so, she fell to the ground. The Wolf was determined not to let her escape. He chased after her and caught up to her. They collided and fell to the ground with their arms and legs entangled. His fist sank into her stomach, and she cringed from the pain.

She wrestled with him. He was injured and bleeding, but his strength was still immense. While on the ground, the girl smashed her elbow into the side of his skull . . . the soft spot high on the temple. And then she attacked his stab wound, exasperating the pain, which gave her the ability to free herself from him finally. Immediately, she kicked him in the face for good measure, and he fell on his back. Quickly, the young prostitute took off running and screaming.

He lay there, his breath wheezing and the pain blinding. Finally, he managed to pick himself up from the ground, holding his bleeding wound. He was angry and frustrated. It was the first time a victim had gotten away from him.

"Fuuuck," the Wolf screamed out.

He had to leave the scene, knowing his window to escape from the authorities was small. He did everything as planned, but he didn't expect her to be carrying a knife. It was a margin of error on his end.

The Wolf got into the Chevrolet and sped away from the scene, bleeding profusely. He needed medical attention immediately.

# Chapter Forty-five

Detectives Acosta and Emerson felt there was finally a breakthrough in finding this serial killer. Word had gotten back to them that there was a possible survivor in New Jersey. It was the best news they had heard all year. So, with permission from their captain, both men hurried to Newark to interview the surviving victim. This serial killer was expanding his kill zone, which terrified the authorities. This psycho had killed too many people, and he needed to be stopped.

The men arrived at University Hospital, and it was a spectacle. They weren't the only cops there looking to talk to the victim. She had been beaten badly and nearly lost her life. A uniformed cop was posted outside her door. And this young Black girl had become critical in helping to catch this serial killer. Everyone was hoping she could identify her attacker.

The detectives badged their way to the victim's room and were granted a quick moment to speak to her. The moment they set eyes on her, they knew she was lucky to be alive. Her street name was Lucious, but her real name was Sarah Thomas. Sadly, she didn't have any family to comfort her. Her pimp didn't feel comfortable visiting her at the hospital with so many police around. She was young, beautiful, and vulnerable . . . the perfect target for the killer.

Sarah's nurse shot both men a stern look and said to them, "Y'all have five minutes. She needs her rest."

They nodded, understanding.

Sarah looked tired and defeated. She was someone that society had forgotten about and fell through the cracks. Acosta spoke first, politely introducing himself. "I'm Detective Acosta, and this is my partner, Detective Emerson. And I promise you, with your help, we're going to find who did this to you."

She was a bit rattled but brave. Both detectives stood gingerly by her bed and started to ask her a few questions.

"Your attacker, can you describe him?" Acosta asked her.

Sarah sighed. She had to relive her nightmare again by answering his questions. But she was willing to do so. She'd heard about his earlier victims, young girls like her who had been brutally murdered and mutilated.

"He was Black . . . and he . . . He was well dressed, handsome, and clean-shaven," she began.

Detective Acosta started taking notes and recording her statement. Everything she said mattered no matter how minor it was. Sarah went on to describe how he invited her into his car. Next, she mentioned how he didn't come off as a threat to her initially. But then he started to get weird and recite Bible verses. Finally, she explained in detail how he attacked her.

"What kind of vehicle was he driving?"

"It . . . It was a dark blue Chevrolet Malibu," she said.

"Are you sure?"

"I make it my business to know every car I climb into," Sarah countered.

Detective Acosta took a mental note about the vehicle because one young girl reported her friend climbing into a white Civic in another report. In another account, the ill-fated girl was seen getting into a black Ford. He thought either the killer was stealing cars or had access to an assortment of vehicles.

"You're doing great," said Acosta.

They had a few more questions for her until their time was up. Finally, Detective Emerson asked her, "How did you get away?"

Sarah expressed her nightmare in grave detail, but what she said next made both men light up like daylight.

"I stabbed him. I think twice."

"Where did you stab him?"

"In his left side. It was how I could get away," she said quietly.

He was injured. It was unbelievable. Acosta and Emerson glanced at each other, their look saying the same thing. It was a break in trying to find him. The detectives asked Sarah a few more questions until the nurse returned to the room and interrupted them.

"She needs her rest," the nurse reiterated.

The detectives had all the information they needed. They both wished Sarah the best "God speed" and left the room with their minds spinning like a whirlwind.

"She stabbed him," said Emerson.

"First thing we need to do is send out an alert to every hospital in the area and see if a patient was treated matching that injury," Acosta said.

But he felt, most likely, this serial killer was too clever to check himself into the emergency room. It was a stretch, but it was worth checking out. However, the authorities had their most significant lead ever. They were going to dissect every piece of information given to them.

Detective Acosta questioned the killer's transportation. Whenever he killed, he had always used a different car. But none of the vehicles that witnesses saw the doomed girls climb into were reported stolen.

The detectives walked out of University Hospital and climbed back into their vehicle, ready to head back to the city. Acosta sat in the passenger seat tired and sighed heavily.

"Don't worry, partner. We're going to catch this psycho," said Emerson.

"That girl in there, she looked to be what, 18, 19 years old," Acosta uttered. "What kind of world is this?" It was a rhetorical question. "She has no family, no support or comfort. And this psycho sees that, and he takes advantage, knowing that. These young girls, they don't have a chance out here."

"We'll give them a chance by catching this asshole and locking him up for life," Emerson replied.

"And then what? There will be others like him, preying and hunting on these young girls."

Trying to catch this serial killer was draining both detectives. But for Detective Acosta, him being a Black man and seeing young, Black girls murdered and mutilated, it was extra troubling for him. The brutal murder of a mixed couple in the Bronx captured more headlines than these young, Black girls. Black girls in the streets were expendable. They were mostly seen as "Sex Machines" programmed to please in life or death. Murderers of prostitutes have occurred in virtually every state of the nation, with many of the cases unsolved and discouragingly cold. Anyone trying to satisfy their violent fantasies could hunt the city's streets for these young girls trying to survive and get by.

"We got a lot of work to do. But I got an idea. So, let's just go," Acosta said casually.

Detective Emerson started the car, and they headed back to Queens.

# Chapter Forty-six

In war, there is no prize for the runner-up. And Mob Allah didn't plan on being the runner-up. But he was taking heavy losses and setbacks, and one of them was Bobby Spyros separating himself from his organization. It was a staggering blow, but not one to make everything crumble. However, Mob Allah knew that if he didn't get his house in order, everything he worked hard for would collapse.

Sonja was upset with him but worried too. She had plans for him—for them. They worked hard to build relationships with specific prominent figures in New York City. Mob Allah was becoming a respected and authoritative figure in their world of business and investments. He trusted her, and it was paying off. She was becoming the woman behind his façade, and Mob Allah was ready to take the whole lot by storm, wanting the best of both worlds . . . the streets and respect where it mattered, the 1 percenters. Now, things were being torn apart by a drug war, horrendous murders, and opposition happening inside the organization. Zulu was displeased and upset with Mob Allah's direction. He argued that Mob Allah had changed since his release from prison and was missing the mark. He felt Mob Allah trusted Sonja more and her vision for him than the friend he'd grown up with. It was an issue causing bitter dissension inside his group. And the last thing Mob Allah wanted was a civil war inside his organization.

"He's becoming a problem for us," Sonja mentioned. "We don't need any more problems."

"And what are you implying?" Mob Allah questioned.

"He's steadily undermining your position and authority. And if they do it often, it isn't a mistake; it's their behavior. I know he's your friend, and y'all grew up together. But I don't trust him, and you shouldn't either. He doesn't see our vision for this organization. He's a thug. He's the past, and you're the future."

Mob Allah frowned, knowing what Sonja was saying to him. But what she was implying wasn't that easy to do. Zulu was more than his friend. He was his brother. But their friendship had become estranged. Mob Allah had his vision, and Zulu had his. With Sonja's help, Mob Allah saw absolute power by having alliances with politicians, developers, and financiers. And by becoming commercial and real estate developers, they would acquire true wealth and influence. But Zulu wanted the streets. He was a gangster, and that's what he wanted to remain.

"Zulu is a bridge that needs to be burned down," Sonja boldly stated.

They argued. But Sonja was standing her ground against Zulu. She was his attorney advising him to kill a man, his best friend, before he brought them all down.

"Are you ready and prepared to fight an internal war with him? He's coming for you and me, baby. I know it. I see how he looks at me. He despises me. I know his kind."

"You know his kind?" Mob Allah exclaimed. "What the fuck you mean by that?"

"He wants it all for himself; control things how he deems fit. And you and I are in his way."

But Mob Allah had another problem. His past had come back to haunt him. He received a call in the middle of the night. Sonja was lying in bed next to him when the unexpected call happened. He seemed surprised and disturbed by the caller.

"How the fuck did you get this number?" he griped.

"I need your help," the caller pleaded. "You owe me."

Mob Allah frowned, but he seemed obligated and tangled by something, a distanced thought.

"Who is it?" Sonja asked him.

He refused to answer her. Instead, he replied, "Where are you?"

"You know where. Where it all started for us."

"I'll be there in an hour," he said.

He ended the call and got up from the bed. Sonja stared at him curiously and asked him again, "Who was that on the phone?"

"None of your fuckin' business," he scolded out of the blue.

She was taken aback by his response. She knew it wasn't a woman because she distinctly heard a male's voice. Mob Allah ignored her and got dressed. He was upset about something, or maybe someone, but he wasn't telling her what it was. He then removed a 9 mm Beretta from the drawer, placed it into his waistband, and disappeared from the bedroom like a thief in the night.

Sonja was baffled. Where was he going? And who'd called him?

Mob Allah arrived at a modest, one-story, two-bedroom house in Springfield Gardens, Queens. It wasn't fancy but quaint with a small front yard. The house sat across the street from Springfield Park and two baseball fields. It looked unoccupied. Allah stared at the place for a moment, dressed in unassuming attire. He was alone, and he didn't want to be noticed. It was late, after two a.m., and the neighborhood was as quiet as a mouse moving on cotton.

He sighed and entered the place through the back door, knowing it would be unlocked. The moment he was inside the house, he carefully looked around. Every room in the house was empty, dark, and still, indicating no one lived there. But he knew the place like the back of his hand. It was where he grew up. The memories he had of the home weren't pleasant. Mob Allah was surprised that it was still standing. He figured the city would have torn it down or renovated it. He hoped never to see the house again. Nevertheless, here he was . . . home sweet home.

From the living room, he heard some movement in the basement. So, he removed his gun and went toward the sound. He descended into the concrete basement, where a light was on, signifying someone was definitely down there.

He soon heard, "It's me. There's nothing for you to worry about. I'm alone."

Mob Allah stared at him. His older brother was in bad shape. He had been stabbed and was bleeding. His brother, Christopher, the Wolf, tried to stitch his deep wounds but wasn't doing a good job. As a result, he was weak and dying.

"Long time no see, baby bro," the Wolf said.

"Why did you call me?"

"I need your help. I need a doctor. This bitch got me good . . . stabbed me deeply. It hurts."

"I didn't even know you were back in New York," said Mob Allah.

"I've been back four years now."

"Four years, huh?"

"And I heard you came home. Did eight years state time. It's good to see you again, baby brother."

"I'm not your baby brother anymore. So, don't fuckin' call me that," Mob Allah claimed.

Mob Allah didn't feel the same way. Their reunion together wasn't an affable one. He looked around. The basement was a place where his brother mutilated the bodies of young girls. The room was covered with plastic so that no blood was left in the area. And there were sixty-four-ounce glass round jars on shelves filled with souvenirs of his victims: their eyes, tongues, and fingers. It was his collection, and it was sickening.

"And you're back to your old ways, I see. How many girls this time?"

The Wolf chuckled and replied, "Why does it matter to you?"

Mob Allah was disgusted by his older brother's behavior, but he wasn't shocked.

"You have always been a sick muthafucka. But this . . . What the fuck?" Mob Allah griped, staring at his brother's collection. "I'm a businessman now . . . and you calling me for help. That's a problem for me. I don't know why I came. I can't be involved with this shit. And I don't know how you got my number."

"A businessman, huh?" the Wolf chuckled cruelly. "Are you judging *me,* baby bro? You think you're *better* than me? Nigga, you're a fuckin' gangster. Who are *you* fooling? You come from the same fucked-up Mama and genes as me. Your roots are here—where we went through hell because of her."

Mob Allah frowned. "This was a mistake," he uttered, ready to leave.

"You fuckin' owe me, Jeffery," the Wolf shouted. "*I* was the one who looked out for you when we were young. I took the brunt of the abuse from Mama. And you didn't see the things I saw her do—what she did to me. I swear that bitch hated me more than you."

Mob Allah stood there quietly, remembering what it was like growing up in that house, his subconscious memory resurfacing. Their mother was a twisted and sick woman. There were nights when she would pull Christopher into bed with her, and they both would lay naked, cuddling. Sex was a frequent thing inside their home. Men came and went. Their mother was more than just a prostitute. She was an abusive whore on drugs too. She would walk around naked in front of her young children. Christopher and Jeffery had been exposed to so much from sex, drugs, and violence that they were seasoned to the hardship by the time they became teenagers.

"You remember how we used to sit in the park for hours to get away from it," the Wolf uttered, reminding his brother. "You and I dreamed of becoming rich and powerful one day, thinking that would change things. Look at us now. You a drug kingpin trying to play businessman." The Wolf chuckled again.

Mob Allah didn't like his sense of humor. He wasn't playing at all.

"I've been away, but I always kept tabs on you," the Wolf continued. "I tried to use the church to forget how it was growing up. I tried to seek redemption. I became a deacon and a successful businessman like you. I own my own car lot now in Brooklyn. But no matter how hard I tried to escape it, no matter how much money I made, my past forever haunts me. It created me like it did you. It's impossible for me ever to get rid of all my sins. As much as I tried to escape it, I couldn't. The only way I can truly stop is through death."

The Wolf suddenly let out a violent cough, not looking too good at all. He was weak and hurting. Mob Allah stared at him, knowing this was probably the end of the road for him. His sins finally caught up to him.

"To be honest," said the Wolf, "I contacted you because I wanted to see you again. It's been a long time."

"So, you don't want a doctor then?"

The Wolf laughed. "Would you have gotten one for me anyway? This is literally my only way out . . . My only escape from the clutches of my sins. I'm a wolf in sheep's clothing. So, it's only right for me to die where it all started."

He coughed again

"I bought back this house when it was on the market . . . I don't know why. I guess it was only right."

"They should have torn down this place long ago," Mob Allah exclaimed.

"Why? You became who you are because of this place," the Wolf argued. "We all have a sinful nature . . . a part of us that always leads us to sin because of the very first sin by the first people that God created."

The brothers had a moment between them. Mob Allah looked more expressive toward his older brother. He was the only family in his life, and they were alike in many ways but also very different. Rooted in hell, killers and businessmen they both were.

"I'm not dying in prison," the Wolf said. "You know what to do. You're a gangster, right? And like I said, you owe me."

Mob Allah knew what his brother was hinting at. Christopher wanted to die and finally escape his sins. So, reluctantly, Mob Allah aimed the gun at his brother's head, and the two men locked eyes, knowing their fates. Eventually, they would both die by the gun: one sooner than later.

"I love you, baby bro," the Wolf proclaimed whole-heartedly.

"I love you too," Mob Allah returned . . . and then he fired.

*Boom! Boom!*

He knew it was best to put his brother out of his misery. He was dying slowly and painfully. The Wolf was no

more. Mob Allah stared at the body for a moment. After
that, he turned and walked away. Leaving the house,
he wondered, with a mother and past like theirs, did
they ever really have a chance in becoming productive
citizens?

# Chapter Forty-seven

Monica and Denise were stunned by what they heard. They didn't want to believe what Sincere was telling them. But it was true. They both knew it. It was a real-life horror story. Sincere felt that he had to be honest with them for them to survive. And he told them what he had become—a cold-blooded killer seeking revenge for his little brother's death.

"And what gives you the fuckin' right, Sincere? Huh?" Monica cursed, being angry and hurt at the same time. "When you committed these murders, all you did was think about your fuckin' self. Not us . . . not your fuckin' family."

Denise was crying. She glared at Sincere and said, "So, our mother is dead because they were looking for you?"

He didn't want to answer that question, but she was right. Janet was killed because of his action. Denise was disgusted. The look she gave her older brother said it all. *You're a monster*. Could he redeem himself from this? He didn't know.

"You're a damn monster, Sincere," Denise hollered. "Everything you touch turns into shit. I want you to stay the fuck out of my life. I hate you. I hate this place. I hate that I don't have anything anymore."

Denise turned and ran away from him like he was the boogeyman. But Monica stayed in the room looking at Sincere like she was sucking on lemons and onions at the same time. She felt Denise's agony and disappointment.

"Take the money and get a hotel room," he said.

There was $50,000 inside a black bag on the floor near Monica's feet. She looked reluctant to pick it up and do what he had instructed.

"And you believe it's that easy for us? You want us to uproot our lives because you fucked up and did something so stupid and idiotic?" she argued. "I'm three months pregnant with your child right now, and you're putting us through hell. We don't deserve this."

"I know. You're right. But I'm going to fix this, I promise you," he assured her.

"How? By going out there and killing some more? *That's* how you're going to fix this?" Monica fired back with a steely glare.

Unfortunately, she was right. It's what he planned on doing. And he couldn't answer her, but they both knew the truth.

"I can't believe this is happening right now," Monica griped. "I took you back because I loved you. And there were only two things I asked from you . . . to not cheat on me and to not bring any problems here into our home . . . our lives."

She was tearful. It was hard to look at him—this killer, knowing what he was capable of doing. She wanted him to stop, but Sincere was in too deep to turn back now.

"I'm sorry, Monica. That was my little brother, and they were going to get away with it," he explained.

"And you had to become judge, jury, *and* executioner. But at what cost?"

Sincere sighed heavily. He knew the cost. "It's not safe for me to be in your life right now. So just take the money and leave."

Monica was in full-blown tears. How could she leave behind the man she was in love with? The last thing she wanted was for their children to grow up without a father.

She was scared. It seemed inevitable that Sincere's fate would be finalized by either death or prison.

"I need to go," he said.

It wasn't an easy moment, and he had to make a hard decision. Sincere had to sacrifice a career in being a cop, his family, and his well-being for justice. Denise hated him at the moment, and Monica's heart had been broken by him once again. Maybe his sister was right. Everything he touched turned to shit.

He turned to leave, but Monica rushed behind him, pulling at him, begging him to stay with her—with his family.

"Don't go, Sincere. Please," she hollered. "Just stay here with us. We can leave together."

But he was adamant. If he stayed behind or moved on, he felt doomed. They had taken too much from him. He started something that he needed to finish, and they would never be safe with his rivals alive. So, Sincere looked at Monica indifferently and said to her, "Maybe y'all will be better off without me. Take the money . . . start a new life."

"No."

"Don't be stupid, Monica."

"*You're* being stupid," she cried out.

He pulled himself away from her and hurried from the house. She couldn't stop him. Upset, she fell to her knees in grief. But Sincere was determined and moving ahead with his plans for revenge.

He climbed into his old Plymouth and sat there for a moment, his heart fracturing with mixed emotions . . . from anger, sadness, to regret. He was self-loathing about his own actions and having a helpless, powerless desire to change the past . . . not being able to get back what was lost.

***

Sincere arrived at the address Nasir had given him. It belonged to Zulu's baby mama, Cynthia. Supposedly, she had two kids with Zulu, and he kept her a secret. He wondered how Nasir knew about her. Sincere had no idea. But Nasir had his ways, and now he wanted to use Zulu to get to Mob Allah.

Sincere sat across the street from a lovely brownstone in a posh area of Brooklyn with a gun on his lap and a stern look on his face. He was waiting patiently for this woman to arrive. And while he sat and waited, he thought, *How far am I willing to go?* This woman was a civilian. Maybe. But Sincere was desperate to track down his enemies. He knew the baby mama would have some kind of information that could benefit him, or maybe Zulu used this place to lie low and rest his head. The only thing he could think about was how they killed his mother and brother. And now, here he was, stalking the home of some woman he didn't even know. But they were hunting him, and he was pursuing them.

While he sat, images of Monica crying, begging him to stay, plagued his mind. His sister becoming upset and angry at him, blaming him for their mother's demise, haunted him. The thought of losing them was a crippling and unbearable feeling. It was one that Sincere wasn't going to tolerate. So, he sat on the quiet street with an arsenal inside the trunk of his car. He'd become The Punisher in real life, ready for anything that came his way.

He had become a monster, but he believed it wasn't his fault. Sincere once had hope and joy. He had a passion and love and a future that burned bright like a thousand suns. But unfortunately, his family had been trampled by the cruelest actions, and now, Sincere's sanity was on edge or had been broken. They say if you gaze long enough into the abyss . . . The abyss will gaze back into you. And it stared back at him with the most painful experiences. And if everyone else saw him as a monster, then there wasn't any point proving them otherwise.

His attention was on a swivel. Every passing car or pedestrian he eyed cautiously. His fingers were wrapped around the Glock 17, and he kept a .45 on the seat. He wore all black, and he was trained for combat and mastered the art of surveillance. It was only a matter of time.

An hour went by, and still, no activity occurred. The front entrance to the brownstone was stagnant. Nobody came or went. But Sincere wasn't going anywhere. If he had to wait outside the place all night, he was willing to do so. Maybe he would get lucky and see Zulu show up. The afternoon transitioned into the evening, and the evening transitioned into the night.

Finally, a Ford Expedition arrived at the brownstone. It sat idling on the street, and Sincere watched a beautiful young woman climb out of it with her two children. They were 7 and 3 years old. The woman was dressed nicely, adorning a few fine jewelry pieces, and she looked classy, not ghetto. Sincere assumed it was Cynthia. But she wasn't alone. She had a bodyguard escorting her toward the entrance, and he was armed. This didn't intimidate him. It was now or never.

As Cynthia, her kids, and her bodyguard ascended the concrete steps toward the front entrance, Sincere coolly exited the car. His first objective was to take out the bodyguard. It was going to be cruel but quick. And then he planned on taking Cynthia hostage and forcing her to get in contact with Zulu. He figured Zulu would come for her knowing his family was at risk. So, this was the monster he became—kidnapping women and children.

Sincere calmly crossed the two-way street, nearing his victims with the Glock in his hand but down by his side. It was cocked and locked, with a round already in the chamber. He was ready to implement chaos because he felt this was the only way. He was trained to become a soldier, and there was no better time to put his skills to use than now.

A box truck briefly restricted his view while he crossed the street. And when it went by, Sincere saw he wasn't the only person that had information on Zulu's baby mama. Immediately, a dark-colored Dodge Durango came to a screeching stop right in front of the brownstone, and doors flew open. Several armed men, including Rafe, came flying out of the Jeep.

"Where the fuck is Zulu at, bitch?" Rafe shouted.

Their presence instantly sent Cynthia and her body-guard into a panic, and the bodyguard acted. Cynthia and her kids hurried into the building as shots were fired. The bodyguard took out one man right away, but he was out-numbered and outgunned. Bullets tore through the door and then him, and he went down like timber. Sincere was astonished by what he was seeing. Rafe and his goons were reckless and violent. They didn't care about the kids. Everyone shot first, and he knew he couldn't allow Rafe to kill this woman and her children.

He stood there watching shit unfold for a moment, and then he decided to strike. While Rafe and Malik were marching up the stairs to storm their way into the building, Sincere opened fire like he was trained to do.

*Boom, boom, boom, boom, boom!*

The spray of bullets tore through Malik, and he went down first. Sincere had opened up with sharp, precise, rapid bursts, and they didn't see it coming. Seeing Malik shot dead, Rafe flew into a heated rage, and his attention quickly went from Cynthia to Sincere.

"Muthafucka," Rafe screamed. "You're dead."

Sincere wasn't rattled. He quickly took cover behind a car as windows shattered, spewing glass everywhere. Bullets gouged through car doors and trees, sending a car mirror and shattered pieces flying. And while they wildly shot at him, he remained focused and sharp. It was three against one. And when he felt it was clear, he promptly emerged from his location and returned gunfire, striking another man with accuracy while shifting for cover behind a tree.

All guns were blazing his way. The sound of gunfire echoed throughout the street like fireworks on the Fourth of July, sending the innocent running for cover. Sincere took another deep breath. It was now or never. Neither he nor Rafe was intimidated by each other, and they weren't going away. So, he readied himself for the inevitable—life or death. Rafe was standing in the middle of the street like in the movie *Scarface*.

"Fuck you, nigga. Fuck you," Rafe hollered madly. "You the one that killed my little brother, huh, muthafucka?"

Sincere ignored him.

"I'm gonna kill you, nigga. Whoever the fuck you are," Rafe continued to yell.

Rafe was in an absolute rage. He and his goon charged toward Sincere with their guns blazing, and for Sincere, it was war. Then, things started to become hazy as bullets whizzed by him. Sincere sprang from behind the tree and cut loose with the Glock and then the .45. Both men went down, but a bullet tore through Sincere's leg and stomach, and he dropped. He had no idea if Rafe was dead or alive. Pain in his abdomen and thigh coursed through his body, and blood seeped from the wounds. He tried to move quickly to his car. He heard the police sirens, and he wanted to get away as fast as possible.

Sincere drove two blocks until he lost consciousness and crashed into a parked car.

# Chapter Forty-eight

Sincere awakened to the pungent and stark smell of hospital bleach invading his nostrils. He scrunched his eyes at the bright light spooning through his closed eyelids. He felt powerless and heavy and a bit disoriented from his injuries. The room was silent apart from his breathing and the beeping sounds of machines nearby. It was an indication that he was still alive. But he could barely move because he was handcuffed to the bed. For a moment, Sincere had no idea where he was or why he was restrained. But he had been arrested. He had been in a coma for a week.

A uniformed cop was posted outside his hospital room. The frightening part was he had no idea where his family was. And his reign of revenge had finally come to an end.

When Monica heard the news about Sincere, she was devastated. She hurried to the hospital to see him, but she wasn't allowed inside when she got to his room. The police officer guarding the room told her she had to leave. Sincere was under arrest, and he was being charged with murder. She cried and begged, but he was adamant. He had his orders. And once again, her heart was broken. She left the hospital crying, knowing that Sincere wasn't going to be around for the birth of their daughter. He'd put retaliation before his own family.

Meanwhile, unbeknownst to Sincere, Rafe was still alive, but he was in critical condition in the same hospital.

***

Zulu sat in the passenger seat inside the Benz in silence, fretting over past events. The shooting that happened at his baby mama's place had him outraged. Fortunately, his baby mama and his kids weren't hurt or killed. But the audacity that they tried to attack his family . . . He wanted blood. But from whom? Rafe was in critical condition, and Malik was dead. However, there was Sincere. Zulu wondered about him. If Sincere wasn't there for whatever reasons, his family would have been killed. But why was he there in the first place? Zulu wanted to know.

This war had become costly, and it had become personal. If Sincere were to be released, would he continue to come after them for the death of his little brother? Zulu felt he needed to do something about it. Unbeknownst to Mob Allah, he had pulled some strings to visit Sincere while in the hospital under police protection.

A well-dressed man in a suit emerged from the lobby of New York Community Hospital and stared at the Benz Zulu was seated in. Then, he casually nodded his head in Zulu's direction.

"I'll be right back," Zulu said to Zodiac and climbed out of the Benz, following the man into the hospital.

The stranger remained a few steps ahead of Zulu. They moved through the building, past the staff, and onto the sixth floor. When they arrived at Sincere's room, the suited man told Zulu, "You got five minutes with him."

Zulu nodded.

The suited stranger uttered to the cop, "He's okay," and Zulu was allowed inside to see Sincere.

He entered the room to see that Sincere was asleep. He closed the door behind him to give them some privacy. This was a killer they needed in their organization. What he was able to do was unbelievable. But then again, Zulu couldn't help but feel resentment toward this man. He was responsible for everything that transpired over the past few months.

Zulu stood over Sincere, and it would have been easy to snuff out his life right now. The man was helpless. But he gave his word. And besides, Zulu had other motives.

"Nigga, wake the fuck up," Zulu announced himself. "We need to talk."

Sincere opened his eyes to see his worst nightmare standing directly over him. Immediately, he became angry and lunged toward Zulu, but the handcuffs had him restricted to the bed. Sincere's nostrils flared outward, and his jaw became tense and jutted forward slightly. It was evident to Zulu that this man still had some fight in him, and if given a chance, he would have attacked him.

"Relax. I'm not here to harm you," Zulu said calmly. "If I wanted you dead, you wouldn't have seen it coming."

It was hard for Sincere to believe him.

"Then why are you here?" asked Sincere vehemently.

"We need to talk."

"We have nothing to talk about."

"I feel we do," Zulu disagreed.

Sincere was reluctant to converse with him, but he didn't have a choice.

"I want an honest answer from you," said Zulu. "Why were you at my baby mama's place?"

Sincere stared at him coldly and uttered, "To kill you."

"And were you going to kill my family?"

"I don't kill kids. I'm not a monster like you," Sincere angrily proclaimed.

Zulu laughed. "I begged to differ. You *are* a monster . . . worse than anything I've ever seen. What you did out there, *that's* who you are . . . a killer. And you're good at it. Too bad it was wasted on revenge."

Sincere frowned, knowing the man was right. Seeking revenge had taken him somewhere so dark. He was a progressing black hole where not even light could get through.

"Look, this needs to end right now," Zulu continued. "I came here to talk about the future. There's been too much death on both sides. Your little brother, he fucked up. But the way he was tortured and killed was on Mob Allah. Me, I would have just put a bullet in the nigga's head and be done with it. But Mob Allah had to send a message out there. So that's why he did your brother that way."

Sincere scrunched his fists so tightly that he almost drew blood. Zulu was honest.

"What do you want from me?" Sincere asked.

"When I leave this room, we're done—no more revenge. And I promise you and your family that you won't have to worry about Mob Allah anymore. I want to get back to business and make money. I want the streets," Zulu replied.

Sincere sighed heavily. It was a hard choice to make, making a deal with the lesser evil.

"I'm a man of my word," Zulu uttered. "Are you?"

Sincere nodded. "Yeah."

Grudgingly, the two men came to an understanding and a truce. Zulu slightly smiled at Sincere and said, "Get well soon."

He turned and left the room, leaving Sincere staring at the door with uncertainty.

Zulu departed New York Community Hospital feeling somewhat conflicted but accomplished. He planned on keeping his promise. Mob Allah had to go. It was difficult for Zulu to betray his friend of nearly twenty years when they became friends back in 1983, but he felt Mob Allah had lost his way. He cared more about doing business with Sonja and her kind than the streets. During this war, he and his crew were in the trenches while Mob Allah sat safe and comfortable with his attorney and her cohorts.

Zulu climbed into the Benz and instantly told Zodiac, "Make the phone call. It needs to be strategic and quick. We fuck this up, and we're all dead men ourselves."

Zodiac nodded.

Secretly, Zulu and Zodiac had been plotting an uprising/takeover. They had support from many people, including Bobby Spyros. It was time for a change.

# Chapter Forty-nine

A search warrant had been secured for several locations. Detective Acosta dug deep into the murders of the prostitutes. He wasn't giving up, and he had gotten a judge to sign the warrants in under an hour. Everyone wanted to find this serial killer, and he made his crucial mistake in New Jersey. First, a victim had survived, and she gave the sketch artist a detailed description of her attacker. Second, the killer had traveled into New Jersey, which meant coming into Jersey via tunnels. It was a long shot, but Detective Acosta meticulously tried to trace the killer's vehicle footsteps of a dark blue Chevrolet Malibu. He and his partner contacted the MTA Bridges and Tunnels to examine surveillance videos. Unfortunately, hundreds of thousands of cars travel back and forth each day. Fortunately for them, they requested to look at footage at a particular hour of the night when there was no heavy traffic.

"We're looking for a dark blue Chevrolet Malibu," Detective Acosta told the MTA supervisor. "And our window, let's say, is between one a.m. to four a.m."

It was a long shot, but it was well worth trying. They started to examine hours and hours of footage of cars coming and going via the Holland and Lincoln Tunnels. And though the footage was in the wee hours of the morning, there were still heavy loads of cars back and forth. It was painstaking work. It was New York City, known to be a city that never sleeps. However, both men were determined to investigate this case to the end.

And then they caught a break. They spotted the car arriving in New Jersey via Holland around two a.m., and they captured the plate. Then, the exact vehicle was seen leaving New Jersey after 3:30 a.m. But this time, the driver had to stop and pay the toll to enter back into the city. Again, it was the same car with the same matching plates.

"Bingo," Detective Acosta hollered. "We got him."

They knew in their gut that this was their guy—their serial killer. This was the monster who'd murdered nearly a dozen girls that they knew of. Acosta continued to dig and dig, and when they ran the plate numbers, they came back registered as dealer plates. Finally, they connected the car and the plates to a used dealership in Bay Ridge, Brooklyn. They were connecting the dots. Wasting no time, they traveled to the independent dealership in Bay Ridge. It was a reputable place selling really nice cars.

Detectives Acosta and Emerson entered the dealership with a sketch of their suspect the following afternoon. It was busy, and one of the staff mistakenly thought that they were there looking to buy a new car.

"How can I help you fellows?" asked a cheery salesman.

Detective Acosta showed him the sketch and asked, "Do you know this person?"

Right away, the man smiled and replied, "Yes. That's Christopher. He's the owner. Good guy."

Both men nearly jumped for joy, but they maintained their composure.

"And do you know where we can find Christopher?" Detective Emerson asked.

"He's not here at the moment."

"Where is he?" Acosta asked.

The salesman shrugged. "I have no idea. He didn't come in today."

"Why not?" asked Emerson.

"Don't know. Christopher is always punctual and reliable."

The detectives continued to ask the employee questions. Finally, they found out that his full name was Christopher Mathews, and he was a deacon at First Baptist Church in Flatbush, Brooklyn. It was stunning news to both men—this monster and killer of young, Black girls was involved with the church. They didn't have any concrete evidence yet, but they knew they were on the right trail. Detective Acosta deduced that Christopher used the cars on his lot to cover his tracks. First, he used different vehicles to pick up and murder the girls . . . then eventually sold the vehicles, limiting his chances of being linked to the murders.

The detectives traveled to the church in Flatbush and talked to the pastor, Malcolm Wright, and his wife. So far, they didn't share the actual reason why they were looking for their deacon, Christopher. The only thing Acosta said to them was, "It's important that we find him."

The pastor and his wife were concerned. But they cooperated with the detectives and told them everything they knew about their beloved deacon, including where he lived. The detectives were getting closer to finding him and linking him to the murders. So, Detective Acosta reached out to a judge he knew to get a search warrant for the car lot, the church, and their suspect's home.

When the authorities entered the two-bedroom apartment in Park Slope, Brooklyn, it was spacious, neat, and nothing seemed odd. Of course, their suspect wasn't home, but that didn't stop law enforcement from searching every square inch of the place. However, Detective Acosta feared that Christopher Mathew perhaps knew they were looking for him and left town. The last thing they wanted was for this serial killer to leave the state and kill somewhere else. But they had his picture and his identity.

No criminal evidence turned up at the apartment, but the dealership was a different story. The Crime Scene Unit found blood in two of the cars. The warrants included a detailed description of the places, the person to be searched, and whatever was seized. Now, it was time to tear Christopher's life apart, and Detectives Acosta and Emerson were adamant about finding him. They continued to follow the breadcrumbs. They were going to analyze the blood found inside the cars, question everyone he was close to, dissect his past, his businesses, and banking information. Nothing was sacred, not even the members of his church. The warrant authorized police officers to search for specific objects or materials at definite locations.

"We're going to find him," Detective Acosta assured everyone.

# Chapter Fifty

The tragedy of war is that it uses man's best to do man's worst. Queenie had done some horrible things at the behest of Mob Allah. So, to unwind, she and her girlfriend were partying at a gay Manhattan nightclub called Catches. The establishment catered to an exclusively and predominately lesbian, gay, bisexual, and transgender clientele.

Queenie was having the time of her life. With money, she was balling with champagne, some party favors, and pussy. She sat hugged against her boo, Shannon, in the VIP area of the club as they both downed champagne, played touchy-feely with each other, and danced to the music.

Brazenly, Queenie passionately kissed Shannon while she had her hand underneath her skirt, fingering her pussy at the same time, giving Shannon's clitoris some attention. Shannon cooed from the slight penetration. She felt light. For her, it felt like energy had rushed through her body and tingled her spine. The two women were becoming hot and bothered. Between the cocaine and alcohol, it had them horny like two teenagers.

"You wanna get out of here?" Queenie suggested.

"Of course," Shannon happily agreed.

Queenie left a hefty tip for their hostess, and the two ladies started to depart from the nightlife. They walked toward their car with their arms around each other, laughing, kissing, and flirting. Neither of them could wait to get home to fuck, suck, and finger each other. And while they walked, crossing the street, distracted by each other, a masked gunman stealthily came up behind Queenie, raising his gun to the back of her head . . . and he fired.

*Bak . . . Bak!*

The barrage of bullets plunged Queenie forward from her girlfriend's arms, and she fell face down against the concrete. With finality, the gunman fired another round into her head, then fled. Shannon screamed in horror. Queenie lay against the asphalt, her body contorted in death and her blood pooling thickly at Shannon's feet.

It was a warm evening in October. Sonja D'Agostino left the Queens County Criminal Courthouse after the arraignment for one of her clients, Jo-Jo. He had been indicted on multiple drug charges, and she was determined to get him released. But unfortunately, the judge denied her client bail because of his previous convictions.

Sonja exited the courthouse while talking to her paralegal from her mobile phone. She wanted the case files from the prosecutor, and she was ready to look for holes in the district attorney's case. She was assigning her paralegal to look for case reports that would support their defense and search for violations of her client's rights.

Sonja D'Agostino had her hands full.

"Listen, Lisa, I need those files by tomorrow," she said.

"I'm on it."

Sonja marched down the courthouse steps amid people trying to enter the building. When she touched the sidewalk, still talking on her mobile phone, a dark-colored SUV came speeding her way with the back windows rolled down. A masked gunman was slightly leaning out of the back window with his arm outstretched, and he had Sonja dead in his sight. And the moment she saw the threat, it was too late.

*Bang! Bang . . . Bang bang bang!*

All five shots struck Sonja in her chest, and she immediately collapsed, her mobile phone spilling from her hand. The gunshots sent everyone into a panic. Crowds went fleeing in different directions. Then, finally, the SUV sped off, leaving behind a dead defense attorney splattered across the courthouse steps.

Zulu and Zodiac arrived at an area of Far Rockaway that seemed to be no-man's-land. The site was littered with abandoned houses, sprawling vacant lots, and rats. Ironically, the area had been chosen for redevelopment in a few years. It was a project Mob Allah had hoped to be involved with. The sun had already ducked down behind the horizon. When Zulu and Zodiac climbed out of the car, a familiar cool breeze and a scent like salt came from the ocean.

It was the middle of the night, and no one was around for blocks.

Both men shared a knowing glance, realizing it had to be done. Silently, they moved to the trunk of the car. Zulu opened it and stared at Mob Allah inside of the trunk. He was gagged, beaten, and tied up. Zulu looked down at his fallen friend and said, "This ain't personal, Mob Allah. This is business."

Mob Allah shot a heated and murderous stare at him. If looks could kill, Zulu would have been slaughtered. But the shoe was on the other foot, and now Mob Allah was on the other side of fate.

"I told you to leave that white bitch alone, but you wouldn't listen," Zulu uttered. "Eventually, it would be either you or me, right?"

Zulu removed a gun from his waistband, and Mob Allah squirmed in his restraints. There was a bit of hesitation from Zulu. After all, this was his best friend for years. But sadly, this was the game, and things changed.

Zulu aimed the gun at Mob Allah's head and fired twice, killing his friend. He and Zodiac stared at the body for a moment, then closed the trunk. A second vehicle came to pick them up from the scene, and they left the area . . . leaving Mob Allah's body to rot inside the car.

It was a breezy fall day when police and the ESU team surrounded the modest house in Springfield Gardens, Queens. They were there to execute a high-risk arrest of Christopher Mathews, a.k.a. the Wolf. The Queens street had become an extravaganza of law enforcement vehicles and looky-loos. Christopher hadn't been at the car lot, church, or his apartment in weeks. And there had been a manhunt for his location. Finally, Detectives Acosta and Emerson could track down the house where he'd grown up. He had been hiding in plain sight for too long. Now, they anxiously awaited entry into the place, knowing he had to be hiding inside the house where he was raised.

ESU invaded the premises hard and fast with a battering ram, smashing open the front door and charging into the house tactically.

"Police, police. We have an arrest warrant," they shouted.

Men in tactical gear swarmed every inch of the house, quickly moving from room to room, finding each one empty. It was clear of any danger. And finally, the detectives were called into the residence. They were immediately hit with a strong, pungent smell that attacked them with no mercy when they entered the house. It was a smell they were familiar with . . . death.

"We found something," someone shouted from below.

Almost immediately, both men went down into the basement. There, they came upon a gruesome scene that made a few stomachs churn, along with a decaying body.

"Fuck me," Emerson uttered with disbelief.

He stared at nearly two dozen sixty-four-ounce round glass jars on the shelves filled with pieces of their female victims. It was so sickening that a few men had to leave the basement immediately. The location looked like a scene out of a horror movie. No one ever saw anything like this before.

Detective Acosta approached the body, knowing this was their man.

"Fuckin' coward took the easy way out," said Emerson.

"He may have been dead what, a couple of weeks?" Acosta suggested.

Detective Acosta crouched near the body to get a closer look at the man he had been chasing for months. It definitely was their guy. However, what struck him as odd were the two bullet holes in his head. It indicated that their serial killer didn't take his own life. But, unfortunately, he couldn't arrest the bastard for his crimes.

"Someone did y'all a favor killing this animal," one of the tactical members uttered indifferently.

*Yeah, but who?* Detective Acosta wondered. *Who else knew Christopher's sadistic secret before he was found out?* It was a mystery Detective Acosta figured he would never find out.

# Epilogue

*December 1999*

Sincere had been jailed at Rikers Island until he was transferred to an upstate correctional facility. Word had gotten around about his crimes, and he was respected, feared, and hated, all at the same time. Rumors had spread about him being the boogeyman. He'd taken down Rafe, Malik, and Drip-Drip. And some speculated Mob Allah too. But while some praised him for his actions, others wanted to see him dead. And there were some consequences behind his actions. He had been involved in a few "incidents" while on Rikers Island. He broke one inmate's jaw and nearly beat another man to death. Sincere had proven to everyone that he could handle himself.

His reputation preceded him.

But he was a lonely man. Monica didn't want anything to do with him. She was disappointed and angry at him. Sincere only thought about himself, leaving her behind to raise two kids on her own. However, Denise had a change of heart toward her big brother. Unbeknownst to Monica, she decided to visit him at Rikers. Denise entered the visiting room nervously. She was 16 years old now, but she needed a fake ID to see her brother because she was still a minor. Surprisingly, it worked. A correction officer guided her to a table to have a seat at.

When Sincere stepped foot into the visitor's room and saw his baby sister, he beamed. He was excited to see her again. The two hugged each other and took a seat to reconnect. And the first thing that came out of Sincere's mouth was, "I'm sorry about everything, Denise."

Denise sighed. She had forgiven her brother. "It's okay. I know it's been rough for you."

"I promise you, the moment I get out of here, I'll put you and my family first," he declared.

She smiled. "I know you will."

Unfortunately, he'd taken a plea deal and received a fifteen-year sentence for the murders he'd committed. Who knew, though . . . Would his family still be around when he was released? It was something he didn't want to think about.

Sincere stared at his sister with remorse and sadness. Then he asked, "How's Monica doing?"

"She's still upset."

"I understand. I fucked up. I let revenge consume me, and she's right; I only thought about myself."

"I'm here for you, Sincere. And I'll always be here," she promised.

He smiled.


### January 2000

Nasir arrived back in Jamaica, Queens. He'd heard about the demise of Mob Allah, Malik, and a few others. And Rafe was locked up, along with Sincere. There had been a violent changing of the guards. Nasir felt now was the perfect time for it to be *his* time to rise, even if he had to go through Zulu. Who would now become the king of New York?

*To be continued . . .*